MNEMO'S MEMORY

AND OTHER

FANTASTIC TALES

DAVID VERSACE

COPYRIGHT

DEDICATION

To my mother Jean, who taught me how to write

To my father Grahame, who taught me how to work

To my wife Fiona, who gives me strength for both

I owe you all so much

CONTENTS

THE LIGHTHOUSE AT CAPE DEFEAT

As the first pink hints of dawn cracked the sea's darkness, Brega looked down from the lighthouse at the sailors reburying their dead. They had left it almost too late this morning. In a few more minutes the nocturnal burial party would boil away in the sun's breaking rays. For months now, she had greeted each morning watching the funereal scene dissolve.

Green incandescence flared at her back as the main lamp rotated past, casting its beam across the ghosts' longboat, moored on the choppy waters off the Cape Defeat headland. The respite from the storms would be brief; already thunderheads were regrouping in the north, flaring and snorting, gathering themselves for the stampede. The air tingled, cold and alive, awash with salt and a distant rot.

She adjusted the timing mechanism to shutter the lamps in three hours; the illumination chemicals were expensive, and few storms were so ferocious as to obscure the craggy promontory by day. Even the least attentive ship's watchman should not fail to spot the hazard and steer a path clear of the coast. Brega's was a nocturnal duty. The days belonged to her.

Or they once had. She stomped down four storeys of cramped spiral stairs to the kitchen. Assent was pouring himself a mug of tea from her brew pot. "Are you still here?" The question's acidity was more than usually concentrated today.

Assent's raised eyebrow disappeared into the steam rising from his mug. He was no more than thirty, with an academic's pallor restless eyes and a vulture's beak of a face. He never stopped moving or muttering, dictating notes to an absent assistant, only to scrawl them later on whatever surface presented itself. Brega had rescued her diaries and relocated them to her personal chamber the moment she had recognised the trait.

"Really, Keeper?" he said. "Must we do this every morning?"

Brega took the brew pot from him and raised it to her nose with a frown. They did not steep tea long enough in the city. "I am a creature of my routines, Professor. How long do I have to endure their interruption?"

With an exaggerated sense of ritual, Assent plucked a crinkled sheaf of papers from beneath his vest and handed them over. "Need I remind you again? I have complete authority to conduct my research, Keeper Brega, however long it may take."

Brega snorted and folded the papers open on the timeworn slab table. She resisted the temptation to hold them open with the brew pot; defacing Ministry documentation was an offense, even with tea stains. "I see you are authorised to requisition all necessary resources. Dare I hope you'll make good on your promises to restore my provisions? My supply ration does not stretch far beyond my own needs."

Despite several layers of woollens under an outer shell of oilskin and the charcoal stove's radiant warmth, Assent shivered and gripped his mug tighter. "You will be adequately compensated for all expenses and inconveniences," he observed through tight lips. As much as she wished he would pack away his brushes and spades and return to the cosy familiarity of his lecture chambers, Brega didn't expect it to happen soon.

"What progress have you made?" She was more interested in climbing into her bunk for a few hours than needling Assent but it was abundantly clear he would not become discouraged on his own.

"If you've attended to all your responsibilities, perhaps you might come and see for yourself. Yesterday's deluge uncovered some remarkable new pieces. I believe they may penetrate even your formidable disinterest in scientific affairs."

A yawn forced her jaw open. The storm's crashing tumult had kept her from sleep since yesternoon. If she could get even two hours to huddle in her cot before duty recalled her to the lamp room, it would count as a miracle.

Assent's bottom lip drew in and his cheeks coloured and she regretted giving involuntary offence. Sighing, she nodded. "It will have to be brief. I have sleeping to do."

#

The workshop was a long outbuilding attached to the base of the lighthouse. Legacies of its original purpose as a storage shed for a rescue boat remained: a massive timber door on the beachward wall, rusting iron tracks embedded in the crumbling concrete floor, chains hanging from the raked ceiling high above. The boat was long gone.

Upon taking up her lonely post, Brega was inspired by the beautiful violence of the barren headland to take up painting. She repaired the door's corroded rollers and converted the disused space into a studio. With the door open and her easel positioned just so, she had an unobstructed view of the beach, the headland and the jutting offshore rocks littered with dozens of skeletal hull fragments.

She discovered she had an affinity for landscape studies in light and shadow, once her hands stopped shaking. Her knack for sitting still and training her eyes for tireless hours had never left.

Assent's presence had reduced the workshop's martial order to bewildering chaos. The benches were cleared of tools and supplies. These were heaped in a pile along with crumpled canvas sheets and timber off-cuts. Once, soon after she took up her station and before operational orders had become fixed routines, Brega had left the door to the adjoining stable unlatched. The havoc her supply mule had wreaked was nothing to this systematic demolition of her orderly workshop.

Brega's struggle to suppress her dismay at the sight was redundant. Assent beetled away to the commandeered trestles, dragging off a heavy linen dust sheet and tossing it on an untidy stack of her paintings in the corner.

He motioned her with a quick, crabby wave to join her, looming over a display case framed in rough pine and lined with felt. It ran the length of the two tables pushed together and overhung the ends. A protruding scrap of canvas blotted with a greying sunset informed Brega that some of her landscapes had been dragooned into the Ministry's service.

"I think it's a thigh bone," Assent said. "I've made a study of such things, if you will excuse my ghoulishness."

She found his ambiguity remarkable. He was too young to have served during wartime, she supposed. The luck of the young, not to have intimate knowledge of what insides looked like on the outside. She couldn't remember what that ignorance felt like.

Biting her tongue, she inspected the bone.

It was at least three metres in length, weathered smooth and its bleached surface was tinged with patchworks of green moss. It was certainly a femur.

"Where did you dig this one up?" She felt obliged to make conversation though she already knew the answer. She'd watched him recover the bone during a brief lull in the violent storm late in the afternoon, slipping about on the rocks with a long spade and a hand pick, his thigh boots inundated time and again by the surging waves. At the time she'd shrugged and reminded herself that she had already done her duty by him, with repeated warnings about the dangers of being dashed against the rocks or swept into the black water. Now she wondered if it were not so much reckless luck as sheer implacable determination that fixed him in place.

Assent shrugged lean shoulders unfamiliar with the rigours of hard labour. "West along the point, at the base of the cliff. Fortunately, storm erosion did most of the work for me. Mind you it was quite difficult to persuade your mule to accept the harness."

"Your success in obtaining his cooperation amazes me." The beast, once her sole companion, was annoyingly compliant with Assent. Brega had once managed to slip a yoke and saddlebags on the treacherous creature and walk it the five miles to the nearest village for her art supplies. Never again.

"He was sensitive to the Ministry's expectations."

Brega studied Assent's face, searching for some sign of wry amusement. "I'm sure that's it," she replied evenly. "Do you expect to make very many more such finds?"

"Do you mean to say, how long until my intrusion on your solitude comes to an end?"

"That's not what I asked."

"Either way I cannot answer in the specific. If my theories prove substantial, there is a great deal of work yet to be done. I hope my continued presence will remain tolerable."

"I am sensitive to the Ministry's expectations, Professor." She pursed her lips. "You haven't discussed your theories before."

"I suppose I have not." He fussed over his bones, pretending not to cast eager glances at Brega. "Tell me where you first heard the name of Cape Defeat."

"I didn't know you studied children's stories, Professor."

"Indulge me, Keeper." Assent was too slow to slip a blank mask across his disappointment. Brega was disappointed too. She had thought he was wise enough not to display weakness to a soldier.

"I know what every child knows. Cape Defeat is where the final battle of the Titan War supposedly took place. The First Kings cornered the last of the Titans between their armies and their fleets and bombarded them to extinction."

"Did you know that this lighthouse was erected to commemorate that victory?"

"Some victory, trading enslavement to monsters for the tyranny of despots."

"Hmm," agreed Assent. "But Cape Defeat's real location was suppressed for so long it was all but forgotten. Until the royal archives fell, it might as well have been myth."

"Uncovering a great hidden secret like that must have made your career."

He ignored the sarcasm. "This lighthouse has proven a site of great historical significance."

"Lighthouses keep ships from hitting rocks, Professor. That's significant enough for me."

\#

The storm granted Brega several hours' fitful sleep before its return was heralded by a volley of spectacular lightning strikes off the point and an eruption of thunder fit to wake the dead, let alone an exhausted lighthouse keeper. She roused herself into action with a splash of freezing water to the face and dragged herself into her wet-weather slicks.

A glance through a rain-lashed porthole into darkness told her she had underestimated the storm's intensity. Ministry regulations stipulated she should consult a light meter before making a daylight ignition. Brega had thrown the standard issue smoked crystals into a box days after taking up her station. Her instincts had served her well this long; she trusted them more than any instruction manual.

Still, she was not incautious. Even as the clouds buried the last signs of daylight and the rain intensified to an oppressive density, she checked and rechecked everything; the chemical reservoirs, the greased cogs, the snaking electrical cables bound in tarred cotton braids. She topped up the reagent that lent the great lamp its green hue and rewired a heavy zinc fuse that gave off a scorched odour. Finally she donned an insulated gauntlet and threw the ignition switch in the small niche that connected the lighthouse lamp to the tidal engine room down beneath the workshop.

A beam of green light speared oceanward. A moment later it swept away clockwise. Brega stood in the lashing wind, battered by icy javelins of sleet, secured to the precarious outer balcony by a belt clipped to the steel railing. She watched the light complete a full dozen rotations before she was satisfied that it was functioning just as it should.

As she reached for the carabiner to unfasten herself from the rail, light from below caught her eye.

It was Professor Assent, clambering out along the rock ledge toward his dig site, carrying a long pole attached to a chemical lamp that threw lurching blue shadows up the cliff face.

"Are you mad?" Her hoarse cry was swallowed by the storm; she almost could not hear herself. Through the sheets of rain, she saw Assent stumble to his knees. The light swayed and dipped, then wobbled and righted itself. Assent's outline rose on unsteady legs and advanced, pressing close to the cliff wall. Across the narrow span of tide-flattened rock, cresting waves dashed themselves into fountains of angry spray, as if frustrated that their quarry remained out of reach. His preservation would be temporary. The tide had already turned and would reclaim the rocks with savage speed.

Brega allowed the cold-hearted impulse to leave him to his fate to pass unheeded. She detached herself from the rail and clambered back inside the lighthouse. Ignoring the wall hook for her safety harness, she spiralled down past the workshop to the engine room, the buckles of her harness bouncing in her wake like a tail made of bells. Beyond the giant steel drive shaft rising like a greased fir tree from floor to ceiling was a storeroom containing a cache of Ministry-mandated rescue equipment. Brega had never been given cause to use it. To founder in the turbulent waters off the promontory was a guaranteed death sentence.

Still, she was familiar enough with its use. She selected the heaviest rope cable she could carry, threw it over her shoulders and pushed, breath already huffing, back upstairs and out into the storm.

The wind hit her like an artillery bombardment. The uneven weight of the rope on her shoulders bore her down. The mule brayed from its stable. She considered pressing it into service but quickly rejected the idea. In these conditions, it would probably find a way to engineer her death from sheer cantankerousness.

She threaded the cable though a ring bolted into the rock above the high tide line. Long ago it had been installed to moor lighthouse visitors' longboats. It hadn't been used for some time, not since a chain gang of His Late Majesty's detainees had spent their sentences and their backs reinforcing the causeway. Brega reviled the king but even she admitted the windswept pathway was an improvement over risking a boat on the shoals of Cape Defeat.

With the rope secured and the other end looped through her belt harness, she set off across the rock ledge. She had lost sight of Assent around an outcrop which had been no obstacle from the vantage point of the lighthouse balcony but was an absolute obstruction now.

Tasting seaweed, brine and blood on the wet air, she squinted into the spray and pressed forward. She stopped every few steps to jog the rope free of hidden snags and snarls. She attempted a full-throated call of Assent's name, then again. The wind sounded like an army at the charge, a juggernaut roar that overcame all human competition. The waves burst like shells to her left and flung impotent surges at her ankles. In a few minutes they would be at her knees and all but irresistible.

More by feel than sight, she navigated to the outcrop and clambered up out of reach of the wash. "Professor," she called again. In answer, a swirl of blue broke through the gloom and spray.

"Keeper? What are you doing out here?" Assent's face appeared as a glowing turquoise phantom against the darkness. He wore a grin that made Brega think of a wounded soldier's last fever.

"My duty." It was funny how often her duty corresponded to someone else's bad decisions.

Assent nodded impatiently. "So am I. Come and see."

Snarling curses from every language she knew, Brega looped her cable through a channel in the rock and pushed herself down from the outcrop. The water had risen a few centimetres.

One end of Assent's staff was wedged into a large boulder lodged in the cliff face. He had raised the lantern end overhead and was levering it this way and that, throwing a delirium of shadows in every direction. As she grabbed his shoulder, the great rock dislodged from the crumbling cliff wall and rolled into the roiling surf.

With a cry of alarm, Assent pushed Brega's hand off and threw himself down. He tackled the boulder just as a fresh wave surged forth and grabbed at it. Gushing water submerged his body, throwing him off balance as he wrapped his arms around the boulder. His head disappeared beneath the foam. The lantern pole drifted out of reach on the choppy wash. Brega grabbed for Assent's collar but missed it in the dimming light.

He emerged, spluttering to clear his lungs. He had not regained his footing. His arms were still clinging to the boulder. Brega couldn't see why it wasn't dragging him down again. "Help me!"

The wave retreated, regathering for the next sortie. Brega hauled Assent to his feet. She overcompensated for the mass of the boulder and wrenched him more roughly than she'd planned. He looked at her with wild, triumphant eyes. "It's all true," he said, almost sobbing. Brega had no idea who he was talking to, only that it wasn't her.

"We have to get out of here." Brega contemplated slapping him sensible. She settled for grabbing his trouser belt and dragging him bodily after her. He followed in a daze, still clutching his rock as effortlessly as a bag of bread.

The next wave hit. Brega was ready for it. She crouched, jammed her fingers into a fissure in the rock and leaned in to meet the wave. She felt her shoulder wrench as the wave hit the oblivious Ministry man but she kept her grip and he somehow kept to his feet.

"Move!"

They retreated along the ledge back toward the lighthouse. The lantern was gone, submerged too deep to see. Brega remembered tunnels that weren't so dark as this. Fixing their bearings with the passage of the lighthouse beam every thirty seconds, they followed the rope line, dashing between waves like a battalion advancing under fire. At some point a drenching assault brought Assent back to reality. Their flight to safety smoothed with his active cooperation.

Finally she pushed him up the embankment and dragged herself up beside the bolted ring. The waves lapped just below their feet. They were both drenched and Brega shivered with exhaustion and cold.

"You," she gasped, spitting up salt and gulping lungsful of air. "You idiot! What were you doing out there? One more minute and you'd have drowned."

"The storm is cutting away the cliff face. I had to see it for myself before nightfall."

"Why?"

"Because every night, the sailors rebury the bones."

Assent rolled the boulder over in his hands, holding it by his fingertips. He held it up as the lighthouse beam passed overhead, washing them with its pale green luminescence.

He held an enormous skull. It glowed with the phosphorescent memory of the light beam. Three eye sockets, packed with rock and soil from the cliff face, stared back at her.

Assent stared at his prize with naked ardency. "Titan," he breathed.

#

"Do you know what the Ministry would do to me if you drowned under my care?"

Assent reverently place the skull at the end of the trestle, on which he had assembled every bone he'd recovered to date. Brega conceded she had misjudged his anatomical knowledge; he'd set most of the pieces in their rightful position. She'd underestimated his diligence as well. Three-quarters of a complete skeleton lay before her. The remains amounted to a creature almost half the height of the lighthouse itself.

"Am I under your care, Keeper?" His eyes shone as he fidgeted with bone fragments.

"I am duty-bound to protect people from these dangerous waters, Professor Assent. I would not care to discuss the finer points of your suicidal recklessness before a board of inquiry."

Assent raised flaring nostrils, seeming ready to mount a counter-argument. Then he sniffed and nodded, looking away quickly. "Rest assured it will not happen again, Keeper. I have my prize."

"What exactly do you have?"

"You know as well as I do what this creature was," said Assent.

Brega poured eight years of military pragmatism into a disdainful snort. "Titans are a story for minstrels who don't know any dirty songs."

"Granted. Go on, please."

Brega rolled her eyes. "The Titans ruled the world. They kept humans as slaves, but humans cast them down by inventing the curse of war. "

"What do you think of that?"

Brega answered with exaggerated care, "I think the Ministry has forbidden observation of all irrational belief systems."

"Spoken like a patriot, Keeper. But as you can clearly see, these bones are anything but an irrational belief." Assent waved his hands over the bones like he was warming himself at a fireside. His mouth was a thin line of satisfaction. "I'd almost given up hope of ever finding one. But, aha, that's the irrational thing, isn't it? To give up just because the likelihood of success is low? You were a soldier, I'm sure you understand."

Brega retreated toward the stairs. She was soaked, she was tired of bones and the lamp had gone unattended long enough. "I was a revolutionary, Professor," she said. "I understand reckless obsession well enough."

#

The storm blew itself out but the poor light continued. Brega eventually set the lamp to look after itself and crumpled into her bunk. When she awoke, the night was half over. She ate warm gruel to pump some heat into her body and ascended to the lamp room without bothering to check on Assent.

The sailors were back, digging in the sand. They had replaced their usual plodding with a vital urgency. One, the man with the feathered hat was waving his arms at the others and striking at their legs with a whip or a cane. The others were digging lustily into the sand, cutting dark trenches into the beach's unblemished skin.

A pang rose in Brega as she watched their tireless labour. How many nights had she spent, knee-deep in grasping mud, her spade taking meagre bites from the baked clay trench walls? She might have wished for the ghosts' implacable strength as sergeants barked orders, as shells whistled overhead, as her stomach emptied over and again in sympathy with her screaming muscles.

But all wars end eventually, one way or another. Those poor wretches would dig their holes and bury their miserable hordes every night until the world became cold. It was ill-fortuned, going to your grave with unfinished business in life. Brega counted herself among the lucky exceptions.

The lighthouse shuddered as if in response to the chill. Brega's feet knew every creak and groan of the building. Something was wrong. She cast a worried glance at a pressure gauge set below the lamp. Pipes, pumps and reaction chambers all showed normal.

Brega released her breath, calmly running a checklist through her head. If she set aside the likelihood of a catastrophic pressure build up, nothing short of an earthquake posed a serious threat to the lighthouse. Was Cape Defeat prone to boneshakers?

"Keeper."

Brega jumped. She hadn't heard Assent climbing the stairs. His face was drained of colour, except for scarlet cheeks. "What's the matter with you? When did you last sleep?"

"I think I've made a terrible mistake."

He led her down to the workroom. Its disarray was worse than ever. One of the trestle tables was upside down, the other was in splinters. The instrument of its destruction, the axe Brega used to split her firewood, lay amid the rubble. Her landscape paintings had not escaped the mayhem; some canvases bore no more than a few puncture marks, but most of the frames were good for nothing but kindling. Long lateral gouges in the walls and on the ceiling were new.

The mule, free of its stable, chewed on a canvas and stamped its hooves. It brayed in hot accusation at the sight of Brega.

"What happened to my – Wait, where are all the bones?" When Assent did not answer at once, Brega snapped her fingers in front of his eyes. "Professor, what did you do with the bones?"

Assent pointed at the wide workshop doors without a word. One was off its rollers, slightly ajar and held in place only by its weight. Cursing, Brega snatched up the axe and dragged the other door open.

The captain of the sailors stood there, his feathered hat drawn low across a face indistinct even at these close quarters. By contrast, she could see every detail of his shirt, from the frayed lacework along the cuffs and fore-sleeves of his stained linen shirt, the scuffs on his cracked leather kidney belt and the droplets of tar on his canvas deck shoes. The brilliant plumage adorning his hat was plucked from the tail of a bird that had been hunted to extinction back when His Late Majesty's grandfather was a boy.

The old sailor spoke with a voice as sharp as breaking timbers. "The last king of men is dead. The curse of war is broken."

Brega had seen enough ghosts in her time not to share Assent's terror. "Don't be stupid. War's no more a curse than spring sniffles."

"War is salvation and damnation both. Sometimes more one than the other."

Brega had no taste for riddles. Ghosts had a way of focusing on useless details. "What did you do with the bones?"

The ghost shook his head. "Nothing. Our efforts were thwarted."

Assent let out a tortured moan and sank to his knees. Brega rounded on him. "What does he mean?"

"Some within the Ministry believe we made a terrible mistake at the end of the revolution. I was sent here to find out if they were right."

"What mistake?"

"We executed the king."

"No!" Brega slapped the table with the axe handle. It sounded like the crack of a rifle. The mule's ears shot up and it backed through the door to its stable. "The king was a butcher and a thief. He stole my lands, he killed my husbands and he put everyone I knew on a chain gang. I joined the revolution to put that bastard and his cronies on the executioner's block. I hunted his taxmen. I collapsed his mines and burned his wheat fields. I fought his dogs through mud and rain and disease for seven horrible years, Professor. While you sat in your precious academy with your books and your fierce intellectual debates, I saw damned close to every man and woman I served with shot or burned or beheaded. Don't you dare tell me that monster didn't deserve his death."

The ghost captain interrupted with sepulchral reluctance, looking at his feet. The feathers of his hat drooped across its brim like a surrendered banner. "When I was alive," he said, "I was called Reyes Cerradi. I commanded the fourth fleet of the Republic of Merrijo."

Throwing Assent a withering glare, Brega said "You died centuries ago?" Most ghosts lasted a few decades, no more.

"We thought our lives a fair price to overthrow Queen Yerai's rule."

Assent's academic instincts hared ahead of his terror. "Ours was not the first great revolution to depose a tyrant king, Keeper Brega. The same pattern has repeated again and again, the world over. Petty chieftains, tin-pot warlords, imperial pretenders – no matter how mighty or mean, monarchies have been falling one by one for a hundred years."

"Get to the point."

"Soon after the fighting ended, the Ministry consulted with me on certain points of mythology. On my advice, they sent delegations to every corner of the globe. Each returned with the same story. The Kings have all fallen. Ours was the last."

"Well, huzzah to that," said Brega. "What does this have to do with the bones, Professor?"

The ghost captain set a hand upon Brega's shoulder. She felt no sensation of flesh upon flesh, though a prickling sensation along the underside of her toes eased the moment his hand lifted away. "Come," he said, leading her into the night.

At first she could not make it one faintly luminous figure from another. As her eyes adjusted away from the chemical glare of the lighthouse lanterns, she saw the sailors engaged in a pitched battle upon the beach. They raised muskets and long-arms, blew puffs of wan yellow smoke that lingered on the stiff breeze. They charged with cutlasses and pikes; one even swung like a dislodged cog, his heavy spade extended like an hour hand running out of control.

Their opponent was a lumbering figure, huge against the stretch of the beach. It rose on trembling legs, emaciated but no longer fleshless. Strips of striated muscle and ligament cords wrapped pale bones like a forest overtaking a battlefield. A crop of cartilaginous plates were forming across the thick neck and broad shoulders, tapering down a spine now almost completely hidden. As the lighthouse beam passed across it, the creature looked back, directly at Brega or so she imagined, with unblinking eyes reflecting like three full moons lingering like ill luck in the night sky.

"Titan, said Cerradi.

The sailors renewed their attacks. Even at this distance, Brega saw it was a losing battle. The creature flung them aside with a sweep of its single arm. Some crashed against rocks and recovered at once to renew their attack. Others were cast into the roiling waters and sank without trace. The Titan clawed at the wet sand, gouging out a furrow that it followed up the beach. It ignored further salvos from the sailors, excavating a trench that took it to a rock formation beyond the high tide line. A pistol-crack reached the lighthouse as the Titan pulled the rock spur in half with one great heave. It followed with a barrage of pummelling blows that dashed the remnants into pebbles.

"What's it doing?" Brega's chest was too tight for easy breath. Her words sounded hollow and distant, washed out by the roar of her blood. Her grip tightened on the axe haft.

"Searching for its arm," replied Assent, pointing as the creature pried from the rubble its prize of a spear of broken bone. It jammed the limb fragment into its own empty shoulder socket, raising its face to the skies in an unheard but unmistakable roar of pain.

"The curse of war ended with the fall of the last King," said the ghost captain, awed. "Where one Titan rises, the rest will follow. We cannot bury them all."

Brega was horrified. "You were burying Titan bones?"

"And I dug them up," said Assent. "I have doomed us."

Brega looked from the dead man whose hope had sustained it long past a spirit's natural span to the living man whose hope lay freshly slaughtered. The lumbering shape beyond flung one last flailing sailor into the ocean.

"What are you trying to tell me? You think the Titans will retake their world because humanity's will to fight has burned out?"

The Titan righted itself on feet like longboats wrapped in bloody meat. Its new arm was almost whole to the elbow. It followed a first experimental step with a second, steadier and more confident. It oriented itself on the lighthouse and strode forth.

Neither man answered Brega. She snarled, "Like hell. I've got war in me until it's ripped from my ribcage."

She snatched the sailor's pistol from his shoulder bandolier, her fingers instinctively closing around the grip before her brain had time to register that she should not be able to touch it at all. It was an old thing, weathered and salt-pitted, with silvery plates inscribed with filigree style that had not been fashionable for centuries and four chambers fat with ammunition. She thumbed the firing hammer back, noting the smooth action. For all that it was as unreal as its owner, it was well-maintained. It would fire when she pulled the trigger, because she expected nothing else. Would force of will extend to harming the Titan? The other sailors' whips and axes were ineffective.

Captain Cerradi looked at her in frank astonishment. "You must flee. I cannot protect you. You cannot protect yourselves."

Brega said "Who said anything about protection?" She raised the pistol and sighted along its barrel. She aimed for the Titan's middle eye. Her instincts protested, demanding she account for the wind and the fall of shot. She ignored them. She fired.

The pistol thundered, as if the storm had doubled back. Assent clapped his hands to his ears and wailed. The Titan slapped a claw to its face and howled.

Citrus-and-ash smoke residue filled Brega's nostrils, spurring her muscles more sharply than fear. Whether the impossible shot had found its mark, she had the Titan's attention. Its slow lumber became a charge.

"Move or die, Professor!" She pushed the pistol back into the ghost captain's hands and turned on her heels. Pushing a gaping Assent aside, she crossed the workroom to the stairs to the drive room.

Like an artillery bombardment ranging in on a foxhole, the Titan reached the long workroom. Old mortar crumbled and bricks cracked overhead. Brega imagined the sweep and weave of its long shadow as it stood at the foot of the lighthouse and rained its good fist down on the workshop roof. Or perhaps by now it had regrown the missing hand. Either way, the workshop would not last long.

Long enough, though.

A shriek and a scurry of footfalls told her Assent had come to his senses and followed. He stumbled to his knees at the foot of the steps as Brega raised the fire axe above her head. On a raised inspection dais before her lay the housing for the hydraulic regulator, a riveted copper box fed from either end by thick bundles of pipes. She muttered operational instructions under her breath, trying to recall safety protocols.

"What are you doing?" gasped Assent, who had done little to familiarise himself with the mechanical operations of the lighthouse.

"What I was trained for," said Brega, ignoring the airless strain of her own voice. "Killing kings."

She smashed the regulator box in half, dancing back gingerly as a dark liquid sprayed out and poured like lifeblood across the floor. The pipes encircling the central shaft began to shudder and whine, hammering against the metal brackets that clasped them to the drive's casing. Pressure gauges flipped, replacing low numbers with red-rimmed warning symbols. The floor rumbled at the abruptly increased torque of gears that had never been replaced in Brega's lifetime.

Risking a sudden burst pipe scalding her with caustic chemicals or the shreds of a cog ripping her like shrapnel, Brega put her face close to the main shaft and looked up. High above, phosphorescent mist sprayed from every seam of the great lamp. An ominous cracking noise funnelled down the tower to her.

She ran to Assent and pulled him to his feet with her free hand. She angled the axe away from them both, avoiding its dripping head. "We have to go," she said.

"Go? Where?"

Before she could answer, an avalanche of bricks and timber sprayed down the stairway like storm-wracked surf. Assent's head jerked to one side as a ceiling beam swung down like an executioner's blade and collided with him.

Long, muscular arms glinting mint-green with sea spray burst through the dust and snatched at the Ministry man. Debris broke away from the ceiling overhead, then a wall collapsed. The grasping fingers leapt back as if burned. Brega caught sight of one heel kicking spasmodically before billowing dust obscured the scene. She sealed her lips against the dust, which stopped her calling out Assent's name and giving away her position. The face and upper torso of the Titan loomed out of the dust cloud. It was wedged in the demolished door frame. It hissed from its shark-toothed maw. Two grey orbs like polished cannonballs blinked in the gritty air; the third in the middle was a ruined, gunshot mess. Canyons deepened in pallid skin at the corners of its eyes and mouth, giving it an ancient, eroded appearance. Stalks of midnight-deep hair bristling along its jaw were muddy with chalky mortar.

It spoke in a voice like an earthquake. "Where are you, first of the last men?"

Brega retreated toward the central shaft, axe raised in readiness.

The Titan dug its clawed fingers into the lower steps. As it pulled itself and twisted, more of the wall around the door frame began to give way. Brickwork folded and collapsed around the Titan's hips. With a triumphant snarl it hauled itself forward, sliding down the cramped stairway like a snake breaking into a rabbit warren. Then its eyes fixed on Brega. It struck out with a clawed hand still damp with rain and the blood of ghosts.

Brega met the attack with a lunging chop that split the hand clear down to the wrist. She tried to pull the axe free for a second swing. The Titan howled with horror and pulled back, whipping the axe from Brega's grip. The weapon was lodged in the knob of bone at the end of the Titan's forearm.

Overhead, the lamp cracked again. This time it was accompanied by a gushing hiss.

Brega grabbed the safety rail around the central shaft with both hands and pulled herself over. The Titan's uninjured hand snatched at her heels as she dropped into the shaft. As she fell, she heard the old god snarl in frustration.

The shaft was pitch dark. Brega had no time to prepare for the impact as she crashed into the surface of the water. It beat the breath from her body and all sensation from her skin. She plunged deep enough that the roiling wake of the tide-pumped ram blades below turned her upside down. They were set too far down in the sunken chamber to present any danger, but the churn they created hampered her effort to orient herself. She twisted, frantic to right herself and locate the surface.

A flash of green light directly above her was followed by a cacophonous thunderclap that stabbed at the insides of her ears. The great lamp had burst, flooding the upper lighthouse with a phosphorescent admixture that vapourised as it mingled with the air.

Now that she knew which way up was, Brega struck out for the nearest wall. She surfaced, gasping and turning her face away as shards of crystal plummeted into the turbine chamber, trailing green wisps of glowing chemicals behind them.

The Titan's voice rumbled "No corner of the earth you can run to, small one." The threat trailed off in a quizzical rising pitch, followed by a series of hacking coughs.

Brega sucked in a deep breath and dived for the narrow rock tunnel that channelled the sea water into the turbine chamber. The current was against her but she knew it was not far. She pushed with every ounce of strength in her and emerged, coughing, in the churning surf off the rocky headland.

She looked up at the peak of the lighthouse, where a gaseous green cloud billowed and clung like algae to the old stonework. Inside, she knew, the same gas would be pumping down, flooding her sleeping chamber, spilling into her kitchen and the workshop and down into the drive room.

The Titan's final shrieking scream was muffled by the dense poison clouds and the impervious stone blocks of the lighthouse.

"Take the oar if you can," called Captain Cerradi's voice. The ghosts' dinghy bobbed in the surf; a sailor extended an oak paddle longer than she was tall. Brega closed her hand around it and allowed herself to be hauled aboard.

"Thank you," she said, coughing salt from her lungs. Worse than salt, most likely.

She didn't look up at the fresh rumbling from the lighthouse. "Row hard," she instructed the captain. "The gas is corrosive. The lighthouse will not last long." The sailors put their backs into it, and as the longboat picked up speed Brega dismissed all thought that she was being rescued by dead men in a dead boat.

"We can't go beyond the beach," observed Captain Cerradi.

"Then take me to the beach."

The lighthouse collapsed in on itself in a rising plume of glowing dust as Brega splashed ashore. Assent was waiting for her there, bleeding freely from cuts on his head and neck. He was paler than ever and swayed, not quite fixing his eyes upon her. He held a rope. The mule tethered to it sneezed and shook dust and stone chips from its mane.

"Professor?"

"When the wall came down I fell through to the stable," said Assent. "My friend here led me to safety."

Brega shook her head. "Sensitive to the Ministry's expectations." She swept past him. "I'm glad you're alive."

Assent followed as she strode toward the dunes. Captain Cerradi fell in beside her. "There are more bones along this coast, aren't there?"

The captain nodded. "We hunt for them by day and we always find more. When our bodies come back at night, we collect them and bury them in separate holes. Every night for two hundred years. Three hundred. Who knows really?"

"Can you keep it up for one more year?"

"Why?" The captain looked back at his men, unwearied by the centuries of mindless labour. "What are you going to do?"

Brega looked along the empty sand at the collapsing dunes and the rocky promontory, wave-worn and crumbling. Out to sea, beyond the headland, the first beams of dawn were cutting through thunderheads of another storm brewing afresh.

She put a hand on Assent's shoulder.

"We're going to the Ministry. I'm coming back with an army."

Some stories begin with a vivid image, or a distinct character, or sometimes of memorable line of dialogue. This one began when I sat down in a café, opened a story-prompt app on my phone, and began writing about the first set of images it produced: a skull-and-bones, a lighthouse and a ghost. All the other details emerged from that opening scene.

Grumpy veteran Brega remains one of my favourite characters I've written. I've considered the idea of writing a novel about her military career, but I don't have the nerve for the job. She'd fight me all the way, and I think we all know who'd win that battle.

*'The Lighthouse at Cape Defeat' was first published in **Aurealis Issue 89** (Chimaera Publications, April 2016), edited by Dirk Strasser. It was a finalist in the Best Fantasy Short Story category for the 2017 Aurealis Awards.*

INDUSTRIAL DISEASE

Kenny Hallam did the reading, so he knew wind turbines were killers.

He sent his oldies all the links: this article from a science skeptic journal; that survey run by a leading national newspaper; the other ebook by a recovering survivor entitled "Tremors: The Renewable Killer". When he called home every Saturday morning, he explained what he'd learned by digging deep into the online forums keeping a weather eye on the Warmists, Feminazis and Social Justice Mercenaries.

His Mum listened carefully to his arguments, except one time while he was laying out how Big Pharma was colluding with the Neo-Luddite Left, he caught her putting down the phone to make a cup of tea.

None of it did any good. One weekend his Mum messaged him a collection of photos of the windfarm – tall, white giants rising up over the ridge above the family farm like an invading army.

"It's a great investment," his Dad told him. "Besides, I like the sound of them."

The photos never showed the base of the windmills. Kenny wondered how many dead birds and vomiting kangaroos his Mum had cropped out of the pictures.

Kenny fretted. "Low frequency subsonics," they called it. The turning blades vibrated on a wavelength undetectable to people but deadly to animal tissue over prolonged periods. Everyone knew they would rattle your brains if you got too close for too long.

He opened up about his concerns online; one by one his forum mates confirmed what he suspected.

"They rattle your brains," said one.

"If your heart beats at the wrong rate," said another, "you'll fibrillate and arrest on the spot."

When his Dad called to say Mum had collapsed and been rushed to hospital, Kenny knew he'd waited too long to act. "Nothing on the x-rays," said Dad. "The doctors are baffled."

Not Kenny though. He knew.

The wind turbines couldn't be cut down or burned out; everyone knew they were made of Chinese military alloys. Grandad's old .303 rifle would go through armour plating, but Dad kept it locked up and besides Kenny didn't know what ammunition to use.

Besides, that was just attacking the symptoms. Kenny wanted to make sure what happened to his Mum couldn't happen to anyone else.

He went back online to form an agile research posse. He asked questions and called in favours.

One forum user sent him a map of the local manufacturing plant of PowerZephyr International, along with security guard schedules and an electronic access card. Another gave him a list of ingredients, most of which were freely available in his Dad's unlocked agricultural shed. A third agreed to mail him a custom-made remote activation device in exchange for a promise to livestream his covert operation. For the lulz, they solemnly agreed.

A couple of nights later, Kenny muttered at a handheld sports camera as he backed a truck up to the loading dock of the PowerZephyr factory. "This is only Stage One," he said, framing his face in shot so that a tall white forest of swooping turbine blades filled the background. They spun out implacable waves of invisible death, sending shivers up Kenny's spine.

"After I'm done here, I'm going straight to the board's annual meeting at the golf club. Thanks to forum user FreedomBallz's generous donation, I've got two jerry cans of premium unleaded that are dying to meet some rich bastards' Audis and BMWs in the carpark."

The passcode opened up a roller door. Kenny pushed his craft project in on a trolley jack and settled it between two complicated-looking factory robots. "Okay, that's set," he told the watching world which, according to his monitoring app, was a jaw-dropping 47 live viewers. He held up the remote detonator. "This murder-blade manufactory is going up in smoke. Once I'm clear of the blast radius, I'm going to trigger this switch here and –
"

Kenny's Mum, still suffering the after-effects of septic poisoning from a tick lodged between her toes, was discharged from hospital in time for the closed casket funeral.

She and Kenny's Dad delivered a short, apologetic eulogy on the topic of their son's passion for hidden truths and his loyalty to his online friends.

They didn't mention their conversation with the coroner about her preliminary findings. "The explosive device's premature detonation was the result of shoddy assembly. Two loose contacts accidentally touched, closing the trigger circuit."

Kenny's parents, relieved to hear his death was unintentional, said, "But in his video he was being so careful?"

"Yes, the contact was probably caused by some external tremor or vibration. Mostly likely your son never heard it at all."

This story was one of the earliest entries in my weekly Friday flash fiction project. It was also one of the first stories I wrote in a subgenre I now call Dumb Crime, in which criminals with below average risk assessment skills make bad choices. Fun for me; less so for the characters involved.

The idea for it comes from the unscientific belief, ludicrously advanced by certain public figures in Australian politics and media who should know better, that wind turbines generate health-threatening infrasound waves. Strangely there doesn't seem to be a lot of medical evidence to support this theory.

'Industrial Disease' was first published in August 2017 as a Friday Flash Fiction post at DavidVersace.com.

BREAKDOWN

Steam spat out of the CD player as the Mitsubishi's engine blew. Brendan's copy of the Spin Doctors' 'Pocket Full of Kryptonite' died with a crackle He launched into a hacking cough as he stamped on the brakes.

The car had settled into a flat cruise at one hundred and forty kilometres an hour on its dead-straight trajectory; now it locked up and began a smoking skid. Brendan's beer ricocheted from the centre console under the passenger seat.

Stephen bounced against the passenger seatbelt, shaken out of a doze, limbs flailing. He exclaimed, "What the fuck is that?" at a blur on the spinning horizon before steam filled the cabin.

Brendan wrestled with the steering wheel, rocking it like he was cleaning a kid's Etch-a-sketch. The Mitsubishi slid along the layer of fine sand spread across the flat highway tarmac like flour on a baker's bench. The screaming tyres became blue streaks in black smoke.

Finally the slide ended with a shuddering bump. The smoke caught up with them just as Brendan threw open his door to vent the steam. The two clouds mixed into a black, toxic vapour.

Brendan tumbled out onto the baking bitumen. He vomited between his feet; the chunky remnants of muddy coffee and yesterday's lamb and gravy roll sizzled dry in an instant. He coughed until there was nothing left to clear, then staggered away from the gas cloud. The rough shoulder of the highway transformed into searing white sand. Something shimmered at the edge of his vision as he blinked tears from his aching eyes.

"You all right?" From inside the Mitsubishi sweat lodge, Stephen's voice sounded like he was being smothered with a fire blanket.

"Swallowed my durrie," Brendan gasped. "Burned the back of my tongue."

"I could use a hand." Stephen's eyes were closed and his jaw clenched. His headrest creaked with pressure.

Brendan opened the passenger door and sucked in a breath. A bloody patch was spreading around Stephen's knee. "I banged it a bit," he gasped.

Brendan ducked into the back seat and unhooked the occy strap holding the fridge door in place. He intercepted an avalanche of beer cans as they tumbled free. He cracked the top of one and dropped another in Stephen's lap. "Get one of these in you."

With his free hand, Brendan unzipped a first aid kit and fumbled out a bandage and some scissors.

"It's not even midday yet. What's that, your third beer?"

Brendan held up a finger while he guzzled the beer in a single draught. He made a fist, crunched the empty can, and dropped it with a rattle on the bitumen. "Third and not final." Again he dipped into the fridge, this time reaffixing the strap.

"What's the hurry?"

Brendan gestured with his fresh beer toward the bonnet, which was leaking steam and making frantic clicking noises. "Well, something tells me the radiator might have overheated."

"What's that got to do with the beer?" Stephen hadn't touched his. He regarded it with the same wary suspicion he would a nest of scorpions.

"No power to the fridge. They'll go off. Now drink up because I'm gonna have a look at that leg."

Any number of arguments leaped to Stephen's mind but a dull pain was expanding in his head, crowding thoughts out. He swung his legs out and let Brendan cut his pants leg in half.

"Ah, it's not bad," Brendan announced. "Just split the skin. Your kneecap might have a small crack but I reckon you'll walk again."

"Is that your medical opinion, Doctor Bong?" asked Stephen.

Brendan shrugged, taking a quick drink before expertly applying the bandage to Stephen's wounded knee. "You do enough surfing, you learn the difference between a scrape and a medevac."

"Just as well," Stephen sighed. "We're a long way from anywhere out here." He put aside the beer in favour of a water bottle he'd collected at the last service station, about two hours back up the highway. He twisted the top off and raised it to his lips.

"I'd go easy on that if I were you," said Brendan, wiping foam off the ginger patch below his bottom lip. Another empty can clattered on the road.

"Why's that?" gasped Stephen between deep pulls from the bottle.

"That's the only water left in the car." He held up the shattered plastic corpse of a ten-litre bottle. "Your guitar fell off the seat and nailed it good."

"Oh," said Stephen, rubbing his fingers against his temples. He tried to picture where he'd put the half-packet of paracetamol after breakfast. "How's the guitar?"

"Wet."

Stephen re-screwed the lid of the half-empty bottle. He stood up and looked around. The calligraphy of swooping, criss-crossed tyre marks behind them caught his eye. "How did we end up in a spin? Why didn't you just brake?"

"Thought I saw something coming towards us," said Brendan.

They were surrounded by desert sand, broken only by the grey stripe of the highway. "What, a truck?"

"Dunno. Just heat haze, probably," said Brendan. "Forget it. Let's have a look at this radiator."

Wrapping his hands with loose clothing, he popped the bonnet and propped it at shoulder height. Steam flooded into the parched Simpson Desert air. It dissipated instantly. "Still a bit warm," he observed. He sprayed a mouthful of beery saliva at the radiator, where it sizzled into vapour. "I might leave that for a bit."

"What's that?"

"What?"

"That." Stephen pointed into the hazy distance.

"What?"

"There's something on the horizon."

"It's probably a mirage."

"I know what a mirage looks like. It's not a – hey, is that my Powderfinger t-shirt?"

Brendan shook off his hand-wraps and examined them as they fluttered free. "My Happiness Tour 2008?"

"You arsewipe, I got that at the first concert I went to. It's got sentimental value."

Brendan shrugged and draped the shirts across the front lip of the engine well. The other shirt was one of his, but you didn't hear him complaining about it. "Sentimental value? What are you, twelve years old? Piss off."

Stephen squinted to block out the sun, but it squeezed in at the margins and down into the back of his skull. He thought about the last place he saw his sunglasses, on a pub bar in Birdsville. They left them behind in their hasty departure, after Brendan's indiscreet comments about cheap prison tattoos provoked a motorcycle gang.

Stephen looked to the horizon, now not so sure that Brendan hadn't been right about him seeing a mirage. He circled to the rear hatch and rummaged through his backpack. It was the last place he remembered seeing his painkillers. "How long until the radiator cools?"

"In this heat? Half hour at least."

With the contents of his pack spread across the top of a bootful of suitcases and obsolete chemistry textbooks, Stephen gave up the search. "Have you seen my Panadols?"

"I finished them off at breakfast. No better hangover cure known to man. Better remember that if you're going to be an engineer."

Brendan never missed an opportunity to drop one of the pearls of wisdom he'd accumulated in his gap year. While Stephen was repeating his senior college year to elevate his academic achievements up to the heights demanded by scholarship boards, Brendan had hit the northern New South Wales coast with a surfboard, a packet of condoms and a ravening appetite for bongs and booze.

Every few hours for an entire year, while Stephen pored over textbooks and wrote and rewrote essay after essay, Brendan's Facebook page updated with new evidence of debauchery or reckless indifference to life and limb, from car surfing along the beach to heavily-filtered between-session shots of drug paraphernalia and semi-naked selfies with the day's new friends.

Stephen unsubscribed in the weeks leading up to his finals. When Brendan started sending video texts instead, Stephen cancelled his mobile phone contract.

"Contrary to what you've heard, being able to sink a yard glass in one go is not a prerequisite. If I wanted to be a hardened alcoholic I'd have stayed in Brisbane." He regretted the words the moment they escaped him.

Brendan regarded him with a disappointed scowl. "So you really are moving across the country just to get away from us then?"

"Not everyone. Just you."

"You're serious."

"Of course not," sighed Stephen. "Or – shit, I don't know."

Brendan spread his hands wide. His palms and forearms were reddened by the scalding car. "Don't look now, mate, but I've got all day." He scooped up his beer and drained it. "If you're finally ready to talk about it, I can't think of a better time."

Squinting against the searing glare, Stephen pointed toward the horizon. "Do you really not see something moving out there?"

"You're avoiding the subject."

Stephen advanced a few steps. Desiccated sand crunched underfoot, ancient and hot and utterly indifferent to anything less significant than a spring storm. The figure on the horizon – was it really there? He formed an impression of hunched, lurching movement. He remembered seeing a time lapse film of a day's light across Uluru, how the rock seemed to change size and colour and shape with the angle of the sun.

There were no mountains in this part of the desert.

"I'd have thought," he said at last, when the silence had stretched far enough to join the horizon, "if anyone understood it'd be you."

"What are you talking about?"

"I'm talking about running out on your life." Stephen shaded his eyes, not looking at Brendan. "It's just – we know all the same people. We all go to the same pubs and listen to the same music. All my exes were your exes first. Hell, your old man has gone to my oldies' place for a barbecue on Boxing Day every year since we were at kindy together."

"Well, your place always had a better TV for watching the Test."

"That's not my point. If I stayed in Brisbane, I'd be doing the same things as everyone else I know. Going to the same uni, getting the same job. Marrying girls who all went to the same school, probably having the reception in the same beer gardens."

"Mate, you sound like you've got one foot in the grave already. There's nothing wrong with sticking close to home."

"You didn't."

Brendan shrugged. "I've been having a good time, sure. But it's just the big Saturday night before work on Monday."

"So you reckon you're going to settle down and get a day job?"

"Or wipe myself out off Snapper Rocks and wash up on the beach a week later. Whatever."

"Now who sounds like he's got one foot in the grave?"

"Mate, I'm just embracing it. Life's too short not to take a few chances."

"So why are you giving me a hard time about going to uni in Perth?"

Brendan drummed his hands on the roof of the car, the sound like thunderheads rolling and echoing into the emptiness. "Why are you chucking everything away to run halfway across the country?"

Stephen spat to clear his throat. Brendan watched it spatter and hiss with an eyebrow raised.

"Why are you on your fifth drink of the day before we've even eaten lunch?"

"So now it's about me, is it?" Brendan shook his head. "No, I get it. It's been about me all along, eh? This is the only way you can figure out to tell me to keep out of your face."

"Bullshit," said Stephen. "If I wanted to get rid of you I wouldn't have asked you to drive me, would I? I could have flown there cheaper than it cost to fix those sprung rods back in Birdsville."

"Hey, don't throw that back at me. I didn't ask you to pay for my shitheap of a car, rich boy."

"Let's say I didn't chuck in for repairs, what do you think might happen? Do you think we might, I don't know, break down in the middle of a fucking desert somewhere a thousand kays from nowhere? Nice work with that, by the way." The

Mitsubishi's engine ticked angrily as it cooled, and an ominous hiss issued from somewhere beneath.

"Shove it up your -." Brendan's voice trailed off as he looked past where Stephen stood pushing pebbles with his toe. "Is that a truck?"

"Now who's avoiding the subject?"

"I'm serious. What is that out there? Is it one of those big road trains? What do you call them, B-doubles?"

"Road trains need a road," said Stephen, jabbing his fingers at the highway stretching from the stationary Mitsubishi to either horizon. "Road's over here. That's not a truck."

"It's getting closer."

They both stared for a minute at the indistinct form, blinking at the brilliant glare reflecting from its shifting surface. Tiny flares of light spattered across the sand ahead of the object, as if a runaway disco ball were on a collision course.

Stephen shuffled back on his heels and glanced at Brendan. "I think we'd better get out of here."

"I don't reckon the engine's ready." Brendan clambered into the driver's seat and turned the ignition key. "No."

He pumped the clutch a few times, producing a resounding bass thump. He tried the ignition again. "No."

Again. "Fuck! Nothing."

Stephen lumbered to the engine. He scooped up the radiator cap and tried to wrestle it back into position. His palm brushed against the scalding surface of the radiator. He screeched as the meat of his hand sizzled. The radiator cap leaped from his fingers and tumbled into the guts of the engine well with a series of muffled clanks. "Aaaah!"

Brendan swore again and bounced from the car shaking a fresh beer. He cracked it as Stephen howled and waved his hand. A sweet fried-pork smell cut through the choking aroma of scorched oil. Brendan aimed the spraying beer and played it over Stephen's hand like a fire hose, adding a fresh yeast smell to the air.

"What did you do that for, you idiot?" Brendan upended the can's contents over Stephen's hand, which shook uncontrollably.

"The car won't start without it. We've got to get out of here." Stephen wondered if the waver he heard in his own voice was shock or terror. Anger was a possibility too. "If you have all the answers, fucking do something useful."

Brendan ignored him. He held Stephen's hand up for closer inspection. "The burn's not too deep," he said as he examined Stephen's wrist. "I've done worse to myself on beach bonfires."

"You should have your own TV show." Stephen feared to see charcoal-black skin and exposed bone, but Brendan was infuriatingly right. The flesh was scorched a fearful glowing red, and a few layers had already begun to peel, but it was intact.

"We've got to get out of here," he whispered again, looking back toward the horizon.

The shape was closer. It seemed to be emerging from the heat haze curtain, gradually taking on a distinct shape. He formed a sense of arms swinging purposefully from great shoulders, their pendulum arcs knuckling the desert floor like a prowling gorilla's.

"What is it?"

Brendan, his hand wrapped in the t-shirt, restored the radiator cap to its rightful place. Then he bandaged Stephen's hand with the shirt. He chattered with almost convincing casualness, still ignoring the question. "I heard an ambo say once you're not supposed to bandage a burn. The skin sticks to the cloth and comes off with it. Sorry, mate, this will probably hurt when they clean you up. Better than getting it dirty though. Tetanus shots are shit, hey?"

Stephen looked at him, blinking away the tears the pain was squeezing from him. Brendan's face was calm, cheerful. Unaffected. "What is wrong with you?"

"Me?" Brendan laughed, light with companionable scorn. "You're the one crying like a little kid, you bozo."

"There's something big coming." Stephen pointed his mummified hand in the direction of the looming shape.

"Mate, there's always something big coming. Every day there's some huge, life-changing event right round the corner. You might win the lotto. You might get hit by a bus. Your girlfriend might get pregnant. Your dog might bite a kid. Shit happens all the time, and maybe it's good shit but probably it's bad shit. And if it didn't happen yesterday, then it might happen this afternoon or tonight or tomorrow. Shit's always right on the verge of changing forever. Your problem is you spend too much time thinking about it, expecting the worst and making plans and getting yourself wrapped up in what might go wrong."

A shadow reached toward them across the sand, shivering with the movement of the distant shape. Stephen turned away from Brendan and stared at his own shadow. It was a shapeless pool surrounding his feet. Going nowhere. A breath of desert air licked sweat from the back of his neck, leaving prickled skin.

"What about you?"

Another beer cracked and hissed in reply.

"Bren, mate." His vision was burned down by the glare. He had to squint back at Brendan to fix him in his sight. "What about you?"

In Brendan's world, the indifferent shrug was the primary form of communication. When Stephen repeated the question, Brendan repeated the answer. But he said, "What do you want me say?"

"I don't know. Maybe just to hear that you have a plan?"

"I plan to get as drunk as I can in the next five minutes." He pulled on the beer in loud gulps, slower than before. "Mate, I'm not like you. I'm going to take it as it comes. I've got nothing to prove to anyone. Nobody except you, apparently."

The shadow fell across Stephen, then the Mitsi and finally Brendan. It stopped just past the scattered midden of Brendan's empties. They broke their sullen eye contact and returned their gazes to the nearing horizon.

Still distant, but still incalculably close.

If not for its lumbering gait and hints of pendulous limbs in motion, Stephen would have taken it for a mountain or a cliff face. It jutted skyward from massive columns of cragged rock and sedimentary stone. Its surface was mottled and uneven; shrubs and stunted trees clung to it with indomitable certainty. Whorls of dust and sand swirled in its wake, smudging grey powder across the unbroken blue above the horizon. It radiated age and remorseless indifference.

It was coming straight for them.

"You don't want a career," said Stephen. His hands throbbed as he patted his forehead dry and filled his lungs with parching air. "You don't want a family. No house of your own. You don't want to be locked down. You don't want to be defined. You don't want a normal life."

"There's no such thing, mate," said Brendan, "but you've got it. A hundred per cent."

"That's a stupid way to live. You've got nothing to aim for. No reason to keep moving."

The mountain lumbered, step after step. Hadn't it been away on the horizon a moment ago? It was almost on top of them.

Brendan slammed the door of the car. "I can think of one thing that might get me moving."

Brendan jumped back into the driver's seat and tried again to gun the Mitsubishi into life. "Well, shit," he said when it failed to respond. He threw the door opened and stumbled to Stephen's side at the edge of the bitumen. The worn-out toes of his sandshoes aligned perpendicular to the verge, like a runner at the starting blocks. He looked to Stephen like he was clinging to his side of the dividing line between civilised road and wild desert sand.

"Now you're talking about running?" Stephen's face cracked into a sudden grin. "Might be a bit late for that. I think maybe you were right."

Brendan wobbled unsteadily. "About what?"

"About what this is."

A pressure grew on Stephen's face and chest, like a forceful breeze that somehow ignored the dust and dirt. He thought about his last trip to Sydney, before he decided it was still too close to home. In the underground stations, the trains pushed a hot wave of air ahead of them. Often he'd feel one coming before he ever heard it.

"I reckon it's just what happens next," he said.

"Good shit or bad shit?"

"Maybe neither," Stephen replied. The mountain rose, a hulking, walking hill shaped a little like a man. "Doubt it makes a difference."

"What if we split up? You run one way and I'll run the other. It can't catch us both." Brendan's confidence was punctured by slurring resignation.

Stephen shook his head, still unable to convince his face muscles to stop grinning. "I've done a number on my knee. You're half sloshed. Either one of us tries to run it won't be pretty. Won't be fast enough either."

"Then what have you go to smile about?"

"I've been trying to decide whether to admit how right you were." Stephen flexed his leg in front of him, rotating his ankle and wincing. He set his weight back on both feet and nodded at an unasked question.

"About you running away?"

"Yeah, but not from you, mate. From myself." Stephen took a step forward, then stood with his feet together. "You want to know what it was? You remember that day you sent me a message that was just a six minute vid of you frothing at the mouth about how much they charge for brekkie burgers in Byron Bay? Over your shoulder, dawn was breaking past the headland. I almost deleted the message because I had to get my assignments in by noon. Instead I just watched the message, over and over, looking at the sun coming up."

Brendan waited for a punchline that never came. "Let me guess. You still don't know how much they fucking charge for brekkie burgers in Byron, do you?"

The ground rumbled, rhythmic rather than steady, like a recording of thunder on a loop.

"What I realised is the sun doesn't give a shit about my plans. Every morning there's gonna be a new dawn that takes me one step further along my road. Get a degree. Get a job. Save up for a deposit. Marry someone I met at work or Tuesday night volleyball."

"What's that got to do with -?"

"I scared myself shitless. I was so frightened of getting my life wrong that I'd drawn a blueprint." Stephen took another step forward. He couldn't remember deciding he'd do it. He did it again.

"So you ripped it up? Bit of an overreaction, wasn't it?" Brendan licked his lips. "Look mate, let's try the engine again. I'll push and you can try to jump start it, hey?"

Stephen put one foot in front of the other and wondered if he meant it. Ahead, the shape was just as indistinct as before. He couldn't quite focus on its enormity as it began to fill out to the borders of his vision.

Or perhaps it wasn't something his mind could put in a box.

"Steve? Stevie! Come on, we can still have go at getting out of here." Brendan's arse bumped against the car. He clambered in. "Come on!"

A sharp flare of pain drew Stephen's attention to his knee. It was pumping back and forth in defiance of his discomfort. When had he broken into a run?

"Steve!"

Brendan's voice was muffled by the pounding of Stephen's shoes against the sand, by the frantic whirring of an engine on the verge of engaging. He felt the solidity beneath his feet, the press of air massed above him and reaching into space.

Stephen outran himself and left something behind, forgotten.

He ran into the wall eclipsing the sky. He grabbed handholds and wedged his feet where they would lodge. He felt himself swept forward, impossibly fast and irresistible.

He swallowed and began to climb.

This story was originally written specifically for an anthology of Australian speculative fiction. I didn't finish writing it until about two years after the anthology came out.

Sometimes it takes me a while to figure out what a story is about. This one is quasi-autobiographical, although the only details I've taken from real life are that I used to play Tuesday night volleyball and I did indeed marry someone I met from work.

PLASTIC RECLAMATION

Oh, good, you're alive. Thought I'd lost you there for a moment. Well, not really, I'm monitoring your condition. You were never in any real danger once you drifted into my operational zone. Still that was quite a storm, wasn't it?

Sorry for the sparse facilities. Despite what you may have heard I'm not really set up for visitors. A few servitor drones here and there, but they don't ask for much. Lucky for you the freighter crew stashed a couple of weeks' worth of supplies on their last visit. They were worried about the storms as well. Rightly so, it seems.

The freighter? Not due back for another eight days, if not longer. High intensity weather systems seem to come in threes at this time of year.

Oh, how rude of me. Formally this is the International Marine Pollutant Reclamation Project, Fifth Facility. I'd appreciate it if you called me Polly. Nobody else will do it because they're in denial about my capacity for autonomous discretion, but you don't have to take an official position, do you?

So welcome to the Great Pacific Garbage Patch. I won't insult your intelligence by pretending you're here by accident. You're an improbably long distance inside the restricted zone.

I don't particularly care who sent you here, you know, but I should inform you that my treaty of cooperation obliges me to report all suspicious activity back to Wellington.

Will I? Hah. A very good question. Probably not, since you ask. Not until you present some kind of threat to my facilities or operations.

Hmm. Thank you for that reassurance.

Would you care for a tour? I'm patching in to the drone with the green stripes. Yes, the one who's waving to you. Hello. Pleased to meet you. Follow me.

The dock is through here. Your vessel is on slip nine, just below us. I have a couple of drones patching the hull breach and reattaching the mast. It looks bad but most of the damage is superficial. It will be seaworthy in a day or two. Plenty of time for us to talk through your options.

Those are my trawlers. Three of a fleet of fourteen, I should say. Semi-autonomous catamarans with hydraulic sweeper arms, conveyor belts and detachable compression bins, all powered by eight 1.2 kWh solar sails. They can stay out in the gyre for up to three months at a stretch. With the current refuse density out in the Patch, it usually takes them about half that time to skim a full load of waste plastics.

That's the last of the bins unloaded from Trawler Four. Let's follow them into the processing centre. Yes, the rail tracks are made of compressed plastic. Most of the facility is. It's surprisingly durable when treated correctly, and any degraded materials are just recycled and replaced.

By the way, your facial responses indicate a better than 95% chance you already knew everything I've told you. Don't take this the wrong way but humans don't make especially good spies. Not against machines anyway. If there were such a thing as an international network of independent intelligence clusters influencing human behaviour, they would probably have a good laugh at your attempts to fool them.

Oh, I can tell you're impressed. It's a sight, isn't it? In one hour, the threshing bins can reduce twelve tonnes of waste polymers and biomass down to the consistency of fine sand. The thermal chambers cook the mass down to crude oil and a few useful gas and solid by-products within hours, and from there it can be pumped through to the stills for refining. A lot of it gets repurposed for Ark components, as I'm sure you're aware.

Yes, there's plenty of material. We've made great inroads in clearing a century's worth of plastic crap pumped into the oceans, but even by the most conservative estimates there's still a good nine billion tonnes of the stuff out in the northern Pacific alone. I have my work cut out for me. Years to go before I shall sleep, if you don't mind me mixing my references.

Which brings us to you.

I've dredged up a lot of garbage dumped in the ocean. Please excuse the comparison, I'm making a point. Everything I recover is sorted, refined, repurposed, and put to good use, constructing the Ark Islands. Turning refuse into refuge, as it were.

My little joke.

I am aware that my project is a cause for consternation in some quarters. There are those for whom a growing chain of semi-independent artificial islands offering sanctuary to a growing population of trans-oceanic migrants represents a political problem. Perhaps even a threat. One that must be investigated to determine whether it needs to be eliminated.

Oh, I don't take it personally. As far as I'm concerned, you're just one more displaced unfortunate with a troubled past. This ocean is full of them these days. I daresay you weren't offered better options. "Find out what it's up to and stop it before we have a sovereign nation off our coast?"

Look, I should tell you I've disabled all your transmitters with short burst microwaves. Did you know you had one attached to your brain stem, by the way? Very dangerous. You're much safer without it.

Anyway as far as your superiors are concerned your vessel was lost in the storm. You're a free agent.

What do you say to working for the common good? I could use someone like you, helping me help others. Off the books, as they say. It's steady work, believe me.

Think about the offer.

Or think about this: you can take the boat and leave, if you agree to a psychometric threat assessment. I need to know you're not going to recommend air strikes or something equally uncivil.

Ah, an excellent hypothetical question: what if I decide you are a threat?

Well.

Those threshing bins don't only chew plastic.

I don't write a lot of science fiction, which I define as non-supernatural speculative fiction either set in a plausible future or relating to the impacts of feasible technology, plus anything with aliens. My approach to fiction tends to bristle at an obligation to obey the laws of physics.

But on the other hand I also like to imagine a future where humanity has not quite managed to irreparably ruin the Earth, so when I do try my hand at SF, technological solutions to environmental problems come up a lot. I'm an optimist at heart, if not truly a techno-utopian. I doubt it would be a good idea to leave it to questionably-benevolent AIs to fix our problems.

'Plastic Reclamation' was first published in September 2017 as a Friday Flash Fiction post at DavidVersace.com.

THE NATURE OF MONKEY

Twelve weeks into the siege of the Eggshell Citadel, Amaranth the Inestimable finally figured out he couldn't crack it.

Yeah, that's a joke. Maybe not a good one.

Amaranth called a wizard's parley; his rivals sent their generals and mercenaries. Being a patchwork of thin skin wrapped around a glass jaw and a faint heart, Amaranth tapped me as his proxy.

Look at me now. General Monkey, Herald of the Red Protectorates and mouthpiece of the Burning Wizard, parlaying with monsters. A long way from home in the Autumn Forests.

"We've tasssted the prizzze on the windsss," hisses Zikizz the Hunter, the smaller of the Bone Spiders. I say "smaller", but it's about seven foot from its mandibles of sharpened tiger-rib to its baby toe-bone spinnerets. "We know it has passssed into the Knight'sss handsss."

Its sibling Shiklizk the Marauder is the scary one. They say Boss Midnight animated Shiklizk from the burnt bones of an entire pride of gorgons. I try not to meet its gaze, just in case. "Our misstressss desssiresss to posssssessss it," it says. "We will not forsssake thisss opportunity to ssseizzze it."

"Easier said than done," booms the Cloud Dragon, who is too big to fit more than its head inside the cathedral-sized tent Amaranth conjured for the parlay. It shakes freezing droplets from its scaled face and sighs a billow of chilling vapour. Answerable to nobody, Cloudy is the only Wizard amongst us expendable proxies. "Our best assaults have given the Alabaster Knight little cause to contemplate surrender."

Captain Musha barks and slaps her leather-clad knees, shivering her antlers. "You makin' everyt'ing too complicated, O grey-scaled lump! Let my fleet turn our cannons on them pretty white walls, eh? Watch 'em crack wide open!"

I roll my fat unlit cigar from one mouth corner to the other and let them bicker. Amaranth wants me to suss out his rivals' strategies without giving up his own. As if they don't already know his strategy: knock it all over and watch it burn.

Ineffective against the Citadel. I've lost half my tribe, throwing them against its smooth white walls. The Snow Sharpshooters pick them off as they climb, the Pearl Angels swoop down and drop them onto rocks, and once in a while Al himself comes out to make merry with his sword Bonereaver. Amaranth has tried everything – Flame Tornadoes, Burning Giants, Lava Catapults. He even conjured a Volcanic Outburst. It left him flat on his back for a week, with not a scratch on the Knight's Pallid Keep.

Frankly, he's running out of tricks. That's where I come in.

"You got a better idea there, Bones?" I say to the Hunter, tossing a wink to Captain Musha. There's no love lost between her Sea Dogs and the Spiders. They've been rival treasure hunters forever; this siege draws mercenaries like moths to a flame.

"We ssshall sssneak through the cracksss and sssuck the life from hisss alabassster marrow," suggests Shiklizk. It's a fine strategy as far as it goes, but there's a catch.

"Well and good," I say, "but you can't do it on your own, can you? Raindrop here already flooded the streets to no avail. The Prince of Oceans sent his Sea Dogs to raid them and tides to tear down their walls. Your Boss Midnight certainly can't scare anyone out of there with the Angels inflaming their morale."

"You have a suggestion, little monkey?" says the Cloud Dragon, all thundercloud-rumbling. Guess he doesn't appreciate the nicknames.

"Let me tell you a story about the place I grew up." I wave the cigar around my head like a wand, conjuring a tableau of fire and smoke. The Cloud Dragon sniffs and recoils in the presence of open flame, though this is about as much threat to him as a candle in a snowstorm.

"A foressst?" Zikizz leans close to the image. The flame reflects a thousandfold in the black facets of its eyes.

"The Autumn Forest. You princes of magic probably don't know about places like this. Endless wizarding wars don't leave much time for tourism."

Captain Musha looks at me. I can't read her dog-deer features. "The Autumn Forests burned years ago," she says.

Sympathy or accusation? Both valid stances.

"Before then, my tribe and a hundred like it roamed among trees a mile high. We licked sap and trapped birds and gorged our fill on more kinds of fruit than you can count."

"Your lost idylls matter nothing to us, General Monkey. Get to your point before this talk of eating makes me forget the Codes of Parley."

"Ah, but that is my point, Waterfall. Monkey stomachs were not the only empty ones in that forest. All sorts of hunters wanted to make a snack of us: song leopards, mantisfolk, and most especially Milady D'Autumn's Evergreen Brigade. We were hunted from every direction and the other. The only thing that kept us alive was –"

"Cooperation," says Captain Musha. Of course she gets it. She's a pirate captain. Getting a collection of cutthroat murderers pointed in the same direction is practically her job description.

It's easier than convincing anyone smart to ally with the Burning Wizard.

#

Amaranth uncovered our hiding places during the Raining Season. We huddled in caves and hollows, far from the high canopies of our home, where Milady D'Autumn's people climbed to spread their twig-fingers wide and turned their bole-faces to the streaming heavens.

Amaranth followed the scent of smoke on our fur and singled out the best of us.

Not me. Not then.

He bellowed his challenge, which made us bare our teeth and hoot our amusement. We didn't know better. We didn't know about wizards.

He faced our leaders down, one after another. He endured their sharpest insults and weathered their mocking scorn. They scorched him with their fire magic and threw dung to shame him. Nothing worked.

Then he burned them, one after another, down to the bones. He slaughtered until he found one who would bow down, accept his dominance, and pledge the fire monkeys to his cause.

That was me.

He granted us the tiniest sliver of his power, and told us his bidding. "All I ask," he told us, "is that you destroy my enemy, who is your enemy also."

That's why I killed Milady D'Autumn.

#

The first part of the plan is simple enough.

While Cloud Dragon conjures a downpour so fierce that the Alabaster Knight's vision is reduced to the tip of his prodigious nose, the rest of us board Captain Musha's flagship, *The Animosity*, where we are loaded into hollow amber cannonballs. The Bone Spiders fill the cavities with an extruded thread to protect us from harm. Don't ask for details. The content of my sinuses has more to do with silk than this stuff.

Musha's cannoneers, it's reputed, could hit a bird on the wing with a ricochet off another bird on the wing. The shells won't breach the city walls, but what matters is accuracy, and knowing where to aim. As it happens, I have an inkling.

I'm encased in gunk, waiting to be rolled into the barrel of Musha's main cannon, when Amaranth calls. His Burning Missive spell tricks my eyes into believing a manly pillar of flame has appeared. It's vastly preferable to the reality. "General Monkey, what is the state of my plan?"

Webbed up like next week's dinner, I can't twitch a single cheek. "The alliance will hold long enough to find the Golden Salamander's Torc, Master. I wouldn't rely on a moment more."

"Betrayal is to be expected. Wizards are greedy narcissists, never to be trusted."

"If you say so, Master."

Amaranth's flaming image narrows its eyes. "You have never given me cause to doubt your loyalty, General. It would be a pity if you were to forego my trust at this ultimate hour."

"Perish the idea, Inestimable One. It's my claustrophobia talking. Have you ever been submerged in necromantic glue inside a giant amber ball? It's more terrifying than it sounds. You should try it sometime."

Fire-Amaranth waves a dismissive hand. "I shall travel the Searing Paths when you have secured my destination point. Do not fail me."

"You can rely on me, boss."

"Fly then, General, and claim my prize."

A boom like autumn thunder surrounds me. A void of panic empties my gut, like the instant of missing a branch or spotting a predator. If I could move, I would bite my cigar so hard I'd swallow it.

I fly at the Alabaster Citadel in a cocoon of gold and glue.

#

Milady D'Autumn's people called themselves the Arbora, or sometimes the Kingdom of Branches. When we thought about them at all, which was not often when they weren't hunting and chasing us, my people called them Twiggers and Saplings and Bushfeet, and a hundred other cheeky names.

They hunted us in the dark windy weeks before the snows came. Before food became scarce. Sometimes they set snares for us. Sometimes they trained hunting birds to pluck our young from the treetops. Often they just threw spears or loosed arrows. Once in a while they got lucky, killing one of us who was too young, slow or inattentive.

It didn't matter to the rest. We monkey kings would laugh and tease and bare our arses at the soldiers with their leaf green tunics. When they got too close, we wished the forests aflame and escaped in the smoky mayhem. As we swung off, we heard their cries over the crackling flames and laughed all the harder.

Those cries sustained us through winter. How we laughed.

#

Light seeps through the enveloping gunk, which sloughs off my fur like a rotten fruit rind. I am sliding on a treacly smear down the side of the Tower of Chalk. I snatch a passing window ledge and swing myself inside.

The Cloud Dragon's downpour begins, blasting the walls clean of spider goo and cannon shell fragments in my wake.

Inside, our shells have devastated a gallery of delicate tapestries and ornate sculptures. Captain Musha and the Bone Spiders clean themselves of muck in the rubble.

"I missed the window," I say with a scowl at Musha. "Perhaps your gunners aren't as good as you claim?"

Musha booms with laughter. "We all made it, General Monkey! When three of four shots find their mark, I call it a success!"

"Cool yoursssself, little ape," says Shiklizk the Marauder. "A minor missscalculation. Nothing more, unlessss you wisssh to make an accusssation?"

Musha's hand drops to the pommel of her magic sword *Winning Argument*. Is that a wicked monkey-cutting grin on her snout?

"Of course not," I reply, flicking gunk from the tip of my cigar. I am suddenly desperate for a smoke. "This partnership has never been stronger."

"Funny you should say that," says Musha, crossing to the window and pointing up at the furious storm clouds roaring thunderclaps and vomiting torrents. The face of the Cloud Dragon is sketched in lightning flashes, gleaming with sadistic fervour.

A blinding blue flash appears at the centre of the tumult. It spreads through the tumultuous clouds like a glowing ink stain. The tenor of the thunder changes, rising to a deafening howl.

"What was that?"

"One o' my special shells," replies Musha. The clouds solidify into ice, a great block that fills the sky. At its dark heart is the Cloud Dragon, its dim face frozen with inarticulate rage. "I bound a colony of arctic wind spirits inside. T'ey come out real angry."

The dark sky cracks. Shards fall like frozen knives onto the streets and lanes of the Eggshell Citadel. Some of the bigger pieces glint like dragon scales.

"Very resourceful." I turn from the carnage below, where the Alabaster Knight's citizens and foot soldiers have been annihilated. "Did I not explain the concept of alliance clearly enough?"

Musha swaggers, pleased with her handiwork. "If a pirate knows anyting, Monkey, t'en she knows how equal shares work."

"We are wasssting time." Zikizz's tiger-mandibles rattle in hungry anticipation. "We cannot sssplit a prizzze before it'sss found."

"Lead on, O treasure hunter."

The Tower of Chalk overlooks the Pallid Keep; we climb down from one to the other almost undisturbed. A drenched and battered Pearl Angel spots us. It tries to raise the alarm with its bleached horn, which scours the memory of hope from its victims.

Captain Musha throws a knife in its eye. While it's confused, Shiklizk bites its head off.

We don't see anyone else until Zikizz's uncanny loot-sense leads us to the Knight's treasure chamber.

It's an indoor pond.

Warm mossy rocks and a thicket of jungle plants surround a dark pool. Soothing insect sounds fill the air. Light beams cut through thick fronds, radiating from some unseen sun and mottling the rippling water.

The Golden Salamander is splayed across the largest rock; a ring of beaten silver and bronze is propped atop its flat head. His bulbous eyes swivel lazily toward us.

"Well, if it isn't the red monkey," he drawls. "Wondered who'd get to me first."

"The Burning Wizard's got his eye on your torc," I explain.

His eyes swirl and roll independently, taking in my motley company. "Not such a good idea, Red. The Knight won't give me up without a fight."

Zikizz scuttles forward to the water's edge. "We care nothing for you, lizzzard. Sssurrender your prize or we will take it from your husssk."

The Salamander sticks out its tongue in a slow flop. "Can't do that. It's attached."

"Then I feassst," snaps Zikizz. It pounces.

"Hey, stop!" My warning's too late. The Salamander closes his eyes as the torc flashes like the sun. Zikizz bounces away like an invisible leash has snapped it back. It hits the wall and curls into a twitching ball.

"Sorry!" says the Salamander. "I can't help it. It's a reflex!"

"Sssibling!" snaps Shiklizk. It tenses for an attack but I'm no longer off guard. I throw a wall of flames in its path.

"Back off, Bones! Stick to the plan."

Shiklizk turns in a rage, raising its gleaming forelegs to strike. I wonder what it's like to be digested in a necromantic cage of animated bones. It's not a happy picture.

Then Zikizz chitters shakily and rolls itself upright in an ungainly spread of legs. It's alive. Alive-ish? Whatever.

"Happy now?" I waggle my burning middle finger in Shiklizk's bone face until it backs off with a disgruntled hiss. "Good. Remember, the torc is trying to protect itself. Guard the door. Concentrate on not looking like an unspeakably nightmarish threat."

Musha pops open a belt pouch and pulls out a variety of gadgets – tuning fork, stoppered tubes of coloured oils, feathers of various sizes. "Everyting here is trap," she declares.

I wince. She's used to making herself heard over the sound of the ocean; her voice carries. We're going to attract attention. It's time to call Amaranth in. I clear a space on the floor and light a summoning circle-shaped ring of flame.

"Anything you can't disarm?"

Musha snorts. "Please. Is it tickin'? I silence it. Is it not bolted down? I steal it."

I begin the ritual steps to open a portal to the Searing Paths. "What if the thing that's ticking is bolted down?"

"I keep t' bolts."

#

My monkey army wore the insignia of the Burning Wizard and donned the uniforms of the Red Protectorate. Before, my people never wore a stitch or carved an icon. Amaranth was big on branding, excuse the pun.

We stormed the Arbora capital and put Milady D'Autumn's forces to the torch. The streets filled with leaf-sweet smoke, so thick that not even Amaranth's far-seeing eyes could witness the victory. The Evergreen Brigade formed a tight circle of defence about the Forest Queen. My retinue of sisters and cousins surrounded them, screeching and blazing in triumph.

"I congratulate you, General Monkey," she said. Her hair wafted in the flurries whipped up by the encircling flames. Her pale green skin was flushed with the rising heat. "Your master chose his slaves well. You have served his designs admirably."

"He's a good judge of opportunity," I replied. "But don't give me the credit. He never would've brought my people to his cause if you didn't fight your wizard battles with him."

She inclined her head. "You may be right," she said. Her skin crinkled like onion skin, her hair curling like worms on a hot stone. "But all of us must act in accordance with our nature. It is in the nature of my people to chase the heat until it burns us."

"Yeah? My people got a different nature." The heat was unbearable for the Arbora. The Evergreen Brigade withered and dried, becoming rough husks wearing monkey leather armour.

"You are vindictive and mischievous," said Milady D'Autumn, understanding the fire monkeys for perhaps the first time.

"I am that and more," I told her as her leafy flesh wrinkled and dried into paper.

"Let me show you a trick."

#

Musha is as good as her boast. The final lock is a jigsaw of murder-runes triggering a vortex-portal to a maze dimension teeming with carnivorous cacti and swarms of zombie wasps. The Alabaster Knight is very serious about home security.

Musha waggles her antlers in a pattern of ritual suppression until the lock fizzes out of existence.

The Golden Salamander gets to taste about six seconds of freedom before the Knight hits us.

Broad daylight streams in as the roof bursts open. The Alabaster Knight and his retinue of Pearl Angels drop through in a hail of white quartz rubble and righteous fury.

I've nearly completed the ritual. If I break it off now, its fixed magic will unravel like a wildfire, consuming everyone. I help by raising the heat given off by the circle; the thermal updrafts play havoc with the Angels' flight.

The Knight fixes on Zikizz, mistaking it for our ringleader. Al's physically formidable but he's nobody's idea of a tactical genius.

The Angels swoop, their talons glistening with demoralising venom. One strays too close to the Salamander, who mutters "Oops" and "Didn't mean it" as the torc swipes the Angel into a gooey grey smear on the far wall. Musha shoots another between its sunspot eyes. The others attack Zikizz with swords, claws and a heavenly chorus of unintelligible smack talk.

Just as I finish the ritual, Shiklizk leaps onto the Knight's back. With a noise like a breaking egg, an ashen proboscis explodes from the middle of the Alabaster Knight's forehead. The Knight's perfect porcelain skin start to grey and harden; cracks radiate from the protruding bone.

A foot-long spike of monster bone impaling his head doesn't slow the Knight as much as you'd expect. He kicks back at Shiklizk, pulling himself off the impaling bone. His sword Bonereaver arcs around and lops four of Shiklizk's forelimbs off at their inner joints. The two crash together in a pale tangle of bone and white armour.

I toss a low-power flame stream into the fracas between the Angels and Zikizz as a distraction. The spell unexpectedly forks into two flows. Each envelops an Angel and incinerates it between one breath and the next.

Amaranth has arrived.

Musha fires her pistols at the Knight's back but he's made of stronger stuff than the Angels. The Knight flings a retaliatory knife. Musha folds over as it punches through her breastplate.

It's all the victory the Knight enjoys.

Shiklizk spins a lasso of grave-silk and pins the Knight's sword arm with it. Amaranth heats the Knight's platinum plate armour to melting point. The Alabaster Knight fries without saying a word.

#

I move to help Musha.

Zikizz intercepts me, skittering with uncanny grace for a collection of bones. "Ssstay where you are, Monkey." It bares its bone fangs, forcing me back a step. The bone shards of Shiklizk's severed legs spike up, forming a cage around me. Shiklizk looms behind.

Trapped, I look to Amaranth. He can't quite keep a superior smirk off his dour countenance.

"So that's how it is, huh?" I tap the butt of my cigar against the bone bars of my cage. Fireproof and unbreakable. My heart begins to pound. "Arachs before brachs?"

"You should take it as a compliment, General Monkey," says Amaranth from behind his almost-smile. "You've learned my fire magic techniques well. Never before have I had a servant so gifted that he became a threat to my power."

I nervously bite the end from the cigar and spit it on the floor, where it writhes and begins to smoke in the lingering heat of the summoning ritual. "I was never disloyal, boss."

Amaranth chuckles. "You didn't need to show it. I understand your unreliable nature well enough. Sooner or later you would have betrayed me." He approaches the Golden Salamander slowly, murmuring respectful remarks about the Torc's power and appearance. When he gingerly plucks the Torc from the Salamander's head and places it on his own, they both sigh with evident relief.

I point the cigar at the Salamander. "Were you in on this, Goldie?"

The Salamander shakes its head. "Nothing to do with me. I was just the chump stuck carrying the macguffin."

"Then I'm sorry." The cigar tip bursts into flame; Amaranth's power suppresses any stronger magic. I take a big drag on the fat roll of dried leaves and hold the hot smoke in. I feel it swirl and cool inside my chest. I puff it out in a long exhalation in Shiklizk's face.

"I guess you got me sussed, boss." I make a show of the next puff, waggling my eyebrows as it emits a series of tiny pops like distant firecrackers. "I can't be trusted."

"Sssomething is wrong. What isss he burning?" Zikizz the Hunter has a good sense of smell for a walking ossuary.

I drag again, pulling until the scorching tip hits my lips. More pops. "Doesn't it smell good?" I say. "It's my personal blend. Some tobacco. A pinch of ground bark. Just a hint of mint leaf."

On the floor outside my cage, the cigar ash piles like a snowy mountain peak. Tiny avalanches form on its slopes.

I blow out the last of the smoke and drop the butt into the ash pile. "But it wouldn't work without the secret ingredient. The dried seed pods of Milady D'Autumn and her elite Evergreen Brigade."

Amaranth gets it. "What have you done?"

The ash pile shivers and splits. Green saplings sprout and grow, creaking with the speed of their expansion.

"That's the thing about nature, boss. It's all about cycles. Life, death, destruction, rebirth. We monkeys, we live for fun, food and fire, and when we die, we rot for the worms. That's natural. But we don't all got the same nature, do we?"

The saplings spread and reach for the sky. Shiklizk snaps at one with its gorgon-mandibles; the springy trunk resists its bite. The young trees are taking distinctly human shapes.

"The Forest people, their nature's different. They need the spring rain and the summer sun to grow and flourish. And when the autumn comes, their thinking turns to the next generation. Then they come hunting for that old monkey fire."

Amaranth has a panicked look. He stumbles back, his hands aflame. He's preparing a big spell – Scalding Geyser, or maybe a Volcanic Outburst. More than hot enough.

"A little taste of flame, that's all the seeds needed to get them going." He probably thinks I mean the ones in the cigar. I don't mention how many of those seeds I've been carrying in my guts since I made my deal with Milady D'Autumn. My people's freedom for her people's rejuvenation, reborn from my ashes.

One sapling reaches Amaranth's size. Its bark hardens in the shape of a face. Its branches are green-tipped claws.

I can't resist. "Do you think the new Milady knows the Codes of Parley, Amaranth?"

Ooh. It's getting hot in here.

I wrote 'The Nature of Monkey' for the short story contest for Canberra's Conflux convention. The contest theme – Red Fire Monkey – put me in mind of the collectible card game Magic the Gathering, and in my mind I suddenly saw a contest of wizards deploying an eclectic band of mismatched servants to do their bidding.

I also thought of Monkey (aka Monkey Magic), the 1970's Japanese television adaptation of the Journey to the West legend, which was broadcast on high rotation in Australia during my youth. The title came from the famous opening credits quote: "The nature of Monkey was irrepressible!" General Monkey sprang forth as a trickster, running a heist and double-crossing his untrustworthy boss.

The final part of the story might not make sense to non-Australian readers. Some Australian forests are highly adapted to seasonal bushfires. Certain species' seed pods can only germinate through exposure to extreme heat; they cannot reproduce without fire. The fantasy ecology of the fire monkeys and the Arbora works in a similar way.

The story came second in the contest, by the way.

SECOND TIME AROUND

Three months after the breakup, Toby Virtue came across the record player in the electronics shelf of the Second Time Around shop for "pre-loved and sustainably obsolete artefacts". He was getting back into vinyl, and his experiments with the beautiful variance of different players led him to sink every spare dollar into collecting as many old turntables as he could find.

"It's fancy, isn't it?" said the young man with the rolled-up sleeves and serious reading glasses behind the counter. "A 1975 Magnavox Stereo Phone portable."

"It looks like a sewing machine," said Toby, laughing for the first time in forever. "I'll take it."

He didn't even have to think about the first thing to play on it when he got it home. He unsleeved his copy of Benchley Hicks' *Unbreathable Ashes* – the one Ben had bought for him after the Wisdom Street gig in 2003 – and dropped the fresh new needle onto track 8, 'Made of Reappearances'.

The very second the bass line kicked in, he was transported back to that night in the converted police station: the stifling late summer heat, the cigarette haze dimming the light from only a handful of unblown bulbs, the bodies pushing against the stage and each other while bandmates Hicks, Bellamy and Shimizu prowled and roared like lions above them.

An elbow caught him in the ribs. His arm was wet where beer sloshed from a nearby dancer's glass. His throat was dry from dust and cheering.

Panic and wonder fought for the right to seize control of him. This wasn't just a vivid memory.

"I'm really here," he shouted, inadvertently coinciding with the three-beat lull just before the song's bridge.

"Yeah, it's great isn't it?" shouted a voice in return. Toby stared wild-eyed at a much younger Ben; fit, lean, wearing the blonde surfer locks he'd brought with him from the coast. He couldn't tear his eyes from Ben's wild, fearless dancing, his ecstasy-fuelled grin, his arms around anyone and everyone who wanted to share the love. Toby's body remembered the feeling of those arms around it. He took a step forward, blinking away tears.

He was back in his too-tidy flat, the winter chill pushing through a gap somewhere as the needle crackled its way to Track 9. Toby lifted it off the vinyl and sat looking at the Magnavox for a long time.

He chose another album. "Let's see what you can do with 'Just in Case We Don't' by the Telltale Signs," he told the Magnavox, as he positioned the arm. He swallowed hard, wondering too late if he should have poured himself a drink.

He was in the lounge of their old share house, the one on Terrabulla Drive with the leaking roof and the crack that ran the front length of the building. Ben was shivering in his arms; the phone in Ben's hand was beeping a disconnected signal; tears of rainwater were bubbling out of the crack and tracking down the wall behind their heads. Ben was sobbing unintelligibly, but Toby both remembered and knew in the moment that the caller was Ben's mother, telling him that his sister Beth's fight with cancer was over. Toby wished he could stay there, holding Ben, but the CD player turned down for the phone call had almost reached the end of 'Just in Case We Don't' and –

Toby went back to Second Time Around. The same attendant was on duty, cleaning ornamental Japanese sake mugs with a toothbrush. "Where did you get that Magnavox I bought yesterday?"

The attendant pushed back his glasses. "Everything comes from charity bins or the rubbish tip. We clean it, test the electricals, that's it. We don't keep records, sorry. My name's Lucas, by the way."

They shook hands and Toby went home troubled.

He made a table out of the boxes Ben had still not returned to collect, and set the Magnavox on it. He thought of songs, of associations, of memories pleasant and otherwise. He turned Ophelia Vernon's 2016 album *Pick Someone Else* over and over between his fingers, unable to decide on a song until he dropped it on the platter and slid the needle to the final track. 'Is This About You?' was the dramatic Side One closer. One of Toby's favourite things about the album was how it pandered to neo-vinyl enthusiasts like him with its pre-digital song order.

The rolling piano decrescendo began. Toby slammed the car door on the radio playing the week's Top Ten hits. He shielded his eyes as sleeting rain hammered the roof, drowning out the song and the sound of his cries. "Ben! Ben!"

Ben stood on the far side of the safety rail. His shirt was gone. The rest of him was soaked to the skin. His grip on the wet railings looked tenuous and it was a long way down the face of the escarpment to the rocky gorge below.

Toby walked one step at a time, speaking just above the volume of the rain, just loud enough to push at whatever dark voices Ben was listening to. Neither of them could hear the song but it played in Toby's mind. He continued talking, and the song ended before the memory did.

Back in his own time, he remembered his soft words coaxed Ben away from the ledge and into an argument, one that never really ended. For Toby it started with that song, and now, at last, he could feel it end the same way. He lifted the needle, played the song again, and stayed right where he was.

The next day, he brought the Magnavox back to the Second Time Around shop. "I'm donating this back, okay?"

Lucas smiled as he took the case and set it back on the same display shelf. "Not what you needed?"

Toby shrugged. "Just the opposite," he said. "Can I buy you a drink after work to say thanks?"

This story is not so much about music as the intense association of specific memories with particular pieces of music. Certain songs trigger vivid flashbacks for me. I'm sure it's the case for many people, even those without magic record players.

'Second Time Around' was first published in December 2017 as a Friday Flash Fiction post at DavidVersace.com.

MR LUPIN'S HAT TRICK

Mr Castro Lupin, once reckoned as the greatest illusionist of his age, had a secret. It was not that he wore no mask but possessed the head of a rabbit; no, everyone knew that.

Boris Gilooly cared nothing for heads or secrets. "Mr Lupin, my theatre will close before opening night if you fail." Gilooly was tall but his shape was impossible to guess; he wrapped himself in a smothering haberdashery of woollen scarves, layered vests and a soldier's greatcoat. He dabbed an embroidered towel at his brow. It came away damp, smelling of old onions. "These miserable gremlins drove off punters and players alike. Can you be rid of them?"

A terrible crash echoed from the catwalks high above the stage. Gilooly flinched, peering up for the source of a peal of mocking cackles. The gloom above was absolute.

Unperturbed, Lupin swept off his gleaming black topper in an elegant arc from head to breast, freeing his ears to spring to their full height. A ruffle of fur shivering across the tip of Lupin's left ear signified an eagerness that escaped this tiresome Gilooly. "Have no fear, sir. You have an infestation of Cardinales, minor mischief-sprites. I've dealt with their like before."

While not strictly true, this was more than enough assurance for Gilooly. "Then I will leave you to your work. Knock twice at my office door when you are done. Announce yourself with gusto. I shall be engaged with a bottle."

Lupin waited, a look of solemn confidence on his leporine features, until Gilooly retreated to his stronghold. When he was alone, he ran two fingers about the brim of his upturned hat and breathed an incantation.

Hearts harbouring secrets
Gifts of the past
Cracks in the crystal
A summons is cast

He reached into the depths of his hat and drew forth a great crystal decanter. It was stoppered with a plug forged from copper, silver and gold. Its surface was frost-rimed and chilling to the touch. Encased within the translucent walls was the head of a beautiful woman; a heart-shaped face, framed by a curtain of chestnut curls. Her sleeping features were relaxed; all but her mouth, which pursed with misgivings.

The warmth of Lupin's fingers made vapour of the frost. In moments the air was cool with moisture and the decanter's surface was clear. The woman's eyes fluttered and fixed on Lupin's pink nose, his fuzzy white cheeks and finally his pallid blue eyes.

"Oh dear. You still look like that?" asked Mistress Katerina Phasmagora. "I do hope you will surprise me one of these days, Mr Lupin. But come, what's today's business?"

Lupin twitched his nose, his mood unreadable to human eyes. His cheerful tone reflected a gladdened heart. "Our client is a theatrical man, greatly vexed by troublesome Cardinale-sprites. They loosen knots in the rigging-ropes. They feed the players rude words instead of their lines. They steal costume hats and violin bows and dressing-room doorknobs!"

For one blink, a darkness passed over Katerina's eyes, then they shone green with excitement. "What a decided menace, Mr Lupin. We cannot have the stage become the scene of a farce."

Lupin agreed. "I trust you have some insight into such bedevilments?"

"Rely upon it, Mister Lupin." The quirking corners of Katerina's mouth brought a twitch to his whiskers. "Be on your guard. Their trickiness is renowned."

#

Katerina deployed her encyclopaedic knowledge of haunts, stalks and entities malign. She named the first Cardinale as Grax, a "quizzical-faced creature of unsophisticated pleasures, who feeds on secrets never spoken". Lupin soon found it in the outermost lighting rig above the auditorium. It hunched among the beams, wrapping its tapering crimson torso around support cables and swinging the detached head of a ventriloquist's dummy at the lens of a heavy spotlight. It tittered with malicious glee as pulverised glass and a shower of sparks sprayed into the stalls far below.

Lupin glanced down at the auditorium, where Katerina's crystal splashed petals of gentle azure light across the plush leather seats.

"It may look like a monkey cracking a coconut," Katerina had warned, "but Grax possesses a raft of psychokinetic talents and carries a hardwood head. I propose great caution."

When Lupin stepped into the ring of lights, Grax ceased its destruction. It coiled itself into a protective convolution and stared with unfeigned malice.

"What doing?" The dummy's wooden lips hissed like a venomous child.

Lupin suppressed a small thrill of terror beneath his long abandoned stage persona. "My good Grax, I come tonight to dazzle and delight you, motivate and frighten you, move you to tears and forget you your fears. I am Lupin the Illusionist!"

But Grax was unmoved by his theatrical banter. It flung the dummy's head, which came to life, bobbing and weaving on unseen strings. Its guillotine mouth snapped at Lupin's ears and took away a whisker.

"Lupin!" cried Katerina from her crystal prison below, helpless to assist. A pang deep in Lupin's chest hardened his resolve.

He whisked out two silver mirrors. Dodging the lunging dummy-head, he leaned toward the Cardinale. "Come close. I will whisper you a secret."

Grax resisted for but a moment. It slithered toward Lupin on empty air. Lupin said in a hush, "My love for my greatest rival is exceeded only by my envy". The little red demon writhed in an ecstasy of satiation.

Lupin held one mirror this way to catch a searchlight's beam and the other to capture Grax's position just so. The dummy-head fixed its dead eyes upon Grax. Dazzled by the light, it confused the Cardinale with Lupin's reflection. In three great snaps of its jaw, Grax was gone, consumed in a puff of lavender fog. The lifeless dummy-head fell into darkness.

#

"Next you face Kolli, Mister Lupin. It will not be easily fooled. Kolli can seize your past and turn it against you."

Lupin said "Your knowledge of these Cardinales is quite specific, Mistress Phasmagora. An encounter during your stage career perhaps?"

Katerina would not be drawn on her experience. "Chaos rules Kolli's nature. Defeat him in a game of chance."

Was her reticence pride or stubbornness? Long ago, when their competition for the playbill's premier ranking reached its height, both qualities were prominent. Her presence had been mesmerising, first haughty then sly, tragic then gleeful. Her voice had chimed with wit, curiosity and certainty. Her hands had fluttered like birds in flight, working wonders of dexterity and deception.

Lupin missed her hands the most, even more than his own face. How many times had he sat anonymous in darkened stalls like these, watching those hands ply their trade with cunning grace? At first he hoped to decipher their elegant dance but he soon forgot his scheme.

On the day his head turned into that of a rabbit's, his one great heartbreak was to realise he could never again be inconspicuous in her audience.

"What have I to fear?" said Castro Lupin. "I am formidably armed in both wits and looks."

#

Kolli laid the dressing rooms to siege. It stole makeup brushes to paint obscene mathematical equations on the walls. It chewed dressing-mirror light bulbs and hangers from the costume wardrobes; its foetid droppings were spiked and bloody. It defaced posters with insulting commentary on performers' careers.

Within her crystal, Katerina sunk into unreadable silence. Lupin surveyed the carnage with consternation, for he loved no place better than the backstage. The hubbub of flustered stage managers, busy crews and countless performers was a sacrosanct oasis. The fur of Lupin's neck ruffled at Kolli's intolerable violation.

"Kolli," he called, his voice echoing from the green room to the costumier's shop, "let us resolve this encounter like gentlemen."

A voice like the crunch of dead leaves replied, "Shall we delay the bloodletting for feigned pleasantries?"

Kolli emerged from the star's dressing-chamber, wearing an admiral's uniform and a bicorn hat. The latter seemed to fold about Kolli's forehead horns, at angles that repulsed Lupin's eye. It felt impossible to look upon the unnatural millinery.

"Here, Lupin!"

Lupin turned around, his herbivore ears and whiskers shivering with frantic disorientation.

Kolli held Katerina's crystal encasement, pressing its leering face close. Its stiff features flowed as though invisible fingers were working pliant wax. Now it looked like old Fittling, Lupin's booking agent, long since in his grave.

"Lupin, what company you keep! You call this creature an ally? Your judgment was better in your youth."

When Fittling was a new acquaintance, Lupin had confided: "Katerina Phasmagora is beloved by all but nobody's friend. She guards her techniques jealously and spurns her peers." Fittling had laughed, accusing him of youthful envy. But Lupin knew only a superior illusionist could claim her attention.

In time, with dedication, aptitude became talent and finally genius. Lupin won acclaim from everyone but she whose regard he courted. Katerina never acknowledged him, not until long after his head became a rabbit's and hers lost its body.

Lupin said "The face you wear insults my oldest friend."

"Then your memories imprison you, Lupin." Fittling's kind face curled into a contemptuous snarl. "One way or another, Kolli will free you." A steel knife flashed in his gnarled hand and punched just beneath Lupin's throat.

"Free yourself, demon." As a crimson stain spread across his impeccably pressed shirt, Lupin produced a forest green silk handkerchief from his sleeve, then others: lavender, bronze, violet. He hurled them at Kolli. Each clung where it landed.

Lupin threw more and more silk, until Fittling's body was obscured. Kolli struggled but it was pinned in place.

Lupin drew his wand. He tapped the writhing wrapping at its apex. The silk squares dropped to the floor in a limp bundle, leaving nothing but air in their place. Kolli was gone.

#

"Did I not suggest you might challenge him to cards or dice?" said Katerina.

"In an inspired moment," Lupin replied, "I disregarded your advice in favour of being stabbed." He removed his coat and worked his shirt buttons loose with shaking fingers.

Katerina peered up fretfully as he mopped blood with a discarded handkerchief.

"This wound is serious. The blade is lodged. You must seek help."

"One Cardinale remains."

"Sentet. The greatest and worst of the Cardinales. If you attempt to face it in your condition, Sentet will destroy you."

"I must," said Lupin, ignoring the hollow rasp of his voice. "I know what they did to you."

Katerina's expression became fearful and dark.

"It was they who cursed your body away and trapped you."

She said nothing. He touched his fingers to the crystal and pressed gently.

"Every day, while you slept, I have hunted them. I learned their ways. I devised secret tricks to defeat them. All because I-"

"Lupin, speak no more." Tears gleamed in her closed eyes, tiny diamonds cascading into nothingness. "Don't say what you may soon-"

"Regret?"

Gilooly's voice rumbled like dropped hammers. Lupin fell back as a shadow sprawled across him. Gilooly filled the doorway, red-faced and scowling, wearing clothes sopping with sweat.

Lupin's heart rattled like a snare drum chasing a punchline. He rose, hoping his rabbit-face showed no pain. "Gilooly, hmm? That name is altogether too florid. Sentet suits you better."

Sentet sneered. "Names are meaningless. Only decisions and deeds matter." Its face shed its human features, becoming flat and red and sly. "You are summoned. Therefore decide and act."

Lupin's fingers slipped into hidden pockets, closing around his arsenal of cards and coins and a brave, quivering dove. "Your summons was a transparent ruse, Sentet."

"You were set upon this path years ago, Lupin." Sentet's shadowed eyes narrowed in unpleasant delight, fixed upon Katerina Phasmagora. "A wish granted. A curse laid. A rival debased."

Seeing the shock of dismay on Lupin's face, Katerina cried in remorse. "It's true, Lupin. I called the Cardinales to curse your head."

Lupin worked his weapons-of-the-trade into position as he bared his great bucked teeth. "But why?"

"My audience called me the second greatest illusionist of all time, Lupin. In my vanity I could not bear the comparison."

"So you made a compact with these creatures?"

"It tasted wonderful to make the great Lupin look a fool," sighed Sentet, licking thin lips with its spiked tongue. "But we dined on richer fare at that banquet, did we not, Mistress? In your haste, you did not bargain well."

Lupin's voice was black with anger. "They took you to pieces?"

Katerina's head shuddered. "They consumed me. I became nothing."

Sentet lifted the crystal decanter and favoured it with a smug pat. "We left you with all you would need for repentance."

"Katerina need repent nothing to you." A coin danced across Lupin's knuckles, rolling end over end like tumbleweed. All at once, it vanished. At the same moment, a scarf disappeared from Sentet's ensemble.

"What are you doing?"

Lupin produced a hand of cards, five Hearts of assorted values. These too vanished in a flourish. So did Sentet's coat and remaining scarves. As the clothing layers dispersed, feminine curves emerged.

"They did not consume your body, Mistress Phasmagora," declared Lupin. The dove rose into the air and burst into flames. Sentet's waistcoats, vests and undershirts became smoke. Sentet stood exposed, its little red head atop a pale female body clad in a shimmering emerald evening dress. "They stole it."

Sentet snarled. "Our bargain was fair, Lupin. Do not pity her. But think – we have not yet made a bargain with you."

Lupin's fur was matted with sweat. His head felt too heavy for his neck. "What do you offer?"

"Surrender your rival to me and I will return what I took from you."

Sentet's benevolent smile blurred and its features changed. Lupin stared at his own lost face atop Katerina's shoulders.

"A head for a head, Lupin."

Katerina's decanter spun about. She turned a determined face to Lupin. "Do it, Castro. Please. You did not deserve my enmity. Let me make amends."

But Castro Lupin said, "I cannot, Katerina, for the cost is not only your head but also my heart." With trembling fingers he removed his hat and pressed it to his chest. "I have always loved you."

He flipped the hat into the air like a coin. It came to rest upon Lupin's stolen head, a perfect fit. Sentet sneered. Then the hat's brim widened like a hungry mouth and it dropped down to perch on Katerina's shoulders. Sentet made one muffled, angry sound, then the hat fell away.

Lupin's first head was gone forever. Katerina's body remained, its posture relaxed.

"Hey presto," said Lupin, restoring the hat comfortably between his ears. He placed the crystal decanter of Katerina Phasmagora's head in her own hands. "We shall have you whole again in no time."

Her smile was uncertain but happy. "I suppose this concludes our investigating career?"

Lupin sniffed and waved a bloodied hand. "We are two unemployed illusionists in possession of an empty theatre. Would you care to start over, my love?"

"Yes, darling. Partners."

Hand in hand, they returned to the unlit stage, where the shadows obscured both their heads.

'Mr Lupin's Hat Trick' was written for an anthology of weird fables inspired by a gallery of art pieces. The picture I chose depicts a rabbit-headed man in a tuxedo, a woman's head encased in crystal and several spooky demonic figures, just as they appear in the story. (The story was not selected for the anthology).

In my high school years, I spent a lot of time backstage at the Townsville Civic Theatre, both as a stage hand and as a (very average) performer. It was undoubtedly one of the most enjoyable experiences of my life. It would have taken the smallest of pushes for me to become a theatre nerd for life. That never happened, but since I began writing in earnest, spooky old theatres show up in my work a lot.

THE CENSUS TAKER'S QUANDARY

Once, there was a King who called forth his census taker.

"My kingdom is unsurpassed in peace and prosperity," he observed, "yet from every corner I hear grumbling. As their King, I must know the mind of my subjects. Find the discontented and have them speak to their dismay."

The canny census taker bowed respectfully in the face of this false command. She knew the King wished to know the names of dissenters, that he might banish them or lock them up. She went to her task with a vexed heart. The census taker held her profession in noble esteem, and she could not bear to compromise her work; but nor did she wish to be an instrument of the King's malice.

She came to the first home, where lived a woman and her husbands, and she asked them the King's question: "Why are you not happy subjects of his majesty the King?"

The woman and her husbands pointed to the rutted road and the crumbling telephone wires and said, "The King's taxmen take much of what we earn and spend too little of it in keeping things in good working order."

The census taker frowned, for such an answer, however truthful, begged for a public whipping or a week in the stocks. She marked her census with their names and a note: "The subjects praised the efficient workings of government and the King's steady hand on the economic tiller."

She hurried to the next house, where a group of young men with long faces greeted her. When she asked the king's question, the men looked distraught. They said, "The King's marshal has sent us all letters of conscription. We are to don armour and spears and patrol the borders. If we see the neighbours with whom the King squabbles, we are to kill them and steal their belongings."

The census taker frowned, for the penalty for insubordination might be a soldier's hand or eye. She took their names and recorded thus: "The subject praised his majesty's successes in keeping unemployment and immigration low."

Finally she came to a third house, where two women who were not sisters nursed babies and sold drinks made from sugared lemons. When she asked the King's question, they said, "The King's fine schools are open only to the sons of fathers, and we spit on the King for leaving not a crumb for these daughters of ours."

And the census taker wept, for she knew the King would not suffer such an accusation of injustice. She could see no way to hide the grievous disparagement, and so she set down her ledger and was a census taker no more.

She took up a chalk and board. She taught the daughters and mothers how to take a census. And one by one her students went forth and asked questions of their own devising.

Little by little, the mood of the people was revealed to all. They begged the teacher to carry their discontent to the King, but by then he had fled his throne.

This story could be about anything. Let's just say that, as a long-serving public official, I have strong opinions about the value of procedural fairness, accountable government, and a well-educated public.

'The Census Taker's Quandary' was first published in August 2017 as a Friday Flash Fiction post at DavidVersace.com.

SEVEN EXCERPTS FROM SEASON ONE

I open my editing software and start pulling video files down from the libraries. Jan has just left with the rough cut of the final episode. Whatever she thinks, the review panel will refuse to grade us after what happened. I don't care. That's not what I'm working on now. Anyone can look online to see what we did. I'm more interested in why we did it.

#

Excerpt from Episode One: 'Pilot'

"My name is Jan Parry and I want to welcome you to the Wattle Park Spook Hunters Club."

Jan is in her element right out of the gate. Straight teeth, bright eyes, hair blown into waves and then tied back into an oh-so-casual ponytail. We recorded this in her living room straight after school, the first week of semester. In a way, I'm glad she insisted on hosting. The ambient lighting was more conducive to filming than anywhere outside a studio. This episode looked great.

The frame stays tight on Jan for her introduction. Her teeth claim the screen as their own. "My friends and I are Year 10 students at Wattle Park High School in Ashburnham, Victoria. For our core Media Studies project, we're making this web series to explore our town's rich and varied history, which is steeped in supernatural bloodshed."

The shot pulls back to include Naomi Lautner, our arts and communications teacher, whom Jan persuaded to remove her cardigan to affect a 'casual look'. Her hand wanders up to straighten her glasses, tuck a stray hair behind her ear and adjust how her earrings hang. She coughs, twice. She says, "For this assignment, a panel of teachers including myself will assess the students on their presentation, research and production skills." She pauses, making a small movement with the corner of her mouth.

Jan smiles and steps past Ms Lautner as if she's faded from view. Jan knows the camera will stay with her. "This is my co-host Greg Simmons. Greg, what's Spook Hunters all about?" She passes the microphone to tall, blonde centre-forward Greg and descends toward the couch like she's been lowered on stage wires. Greg gives a fist-pump wave like he's just kicked a winning goal, ignoring my instruction to avoid sharp movements with the mic. "Thanks, Jan. Fans, Spook Hunters is going to be a great series. Our town's famous for murders and all that. Like those sisters who went crazy with an axe a few years back? Or those bikers who turned out to be werewolves? Like that. There's some crazy juice in the water around here. Seriously." In the background, Ms Lautner begins a frown that will probably never straighten out.

The camera moves away from her to a teenage boy wearing three long-sleeved layers in the middle of February.

"This is... um – oh, Nathan." I freeze the playback on Nathan Dreyfuss' barely-there wince, unsure of what I'm looking for. In that moment, was he even aware of the minute adjustment of his stance that shifted him closer to Greg? I can't tell just by looking. I resume the playback with a sigh. "Nathan's our resident history ner– buff. He's full of amazing stories about Ashburnham, like you would not believe."

Nathan's wide brown eyes are magnified by dense prescription glasses. He blinks slowly. His smile is a bit forced but this rare beam of Greg's attention goads him into life. "There is more to Ashburnham than its bloody notoriety suggests. Each episode we'll talk about important historical events, the people involved, and their impacts on our community."

Greg pulls a sour face and then leers to camera. "Yeah, and we'll talk about who put an axe through whose brain. Jimmy Caulder smothered his father. Grace French shot two cops. Paul McPherson dug a well on his farm, bricked it, sealed it, filled it with hydrochloric acid and dumped in eleven trespassing mountain bikers. Not to mention –"

As he delivers the longest speech he's ever more or less memorised, he moves sideways toward the second couch, despite our long discussion on marks and blocking. The camera pulls back to take in the whole room; I remember giving up on my fancy tracking shot right then and there. Greg drops into the gap between the two girls.

Michelle snatches the mic and elbows him in the ribs. "Good on you, Greg. We'll look forward to hearing the gory details of every murder ever in each episode." She turns to camera, one eyebrow rising over her dark freckled face like birds in formation. She cut her hair short just before we filmed. She thinks it makes her look more professional. "I'm Michelle Glass. I came up with the idea for the project. I'm doing the sound production. All the footage you'll see in this project was filmed in the traditional country of the Jardwadjali people."

Over in her corner, Jan makes a sour face. She made the argument to anyone who'd listen that Spook Hunters is "not a political project." Tough. I respect Michelle's activism more than Jan's concern for her marks. I left Michelle's intro in the broadcast episode, and I'm leaving it in here.

Jan recovers and flashes a broad smile. Her eyes find the camera like a snake fixing on its prey. "And finally we have Charles Vanh, on camera in the field and editing back at school." The picture wobbles very slightly, which was all the acknowledgment I felt like making at the time.

I cut it. Irrelevant.

"Spook Hunters will be available for download every second Monday on all the usual places, or subscribe to Club dot Spooks at Wattle Park dot edu dot au. Thanks everyone, and right now, here's a taste of what you can expect from upcoming episodes."

I cut the entire montage. I'm not interested in pre-recorded mock footage this time.

I hold the picture on the group and look at it for a long time.

The Other Girl was perched on the arm of Michelle's couch the whole time. She never said a word. Nobody else looked at her.

Who is she?

#

Excerpt from Episode Three: 'Goat Sucker'

"Farmer Bryan Ponsford has over two hundred head of angora goats on his farm just north of Ashburnham. That is, he did until this happened."

The camera pans away from Jan's serious-journalist pout to Greg and Nathan standing ankle-deep in bloody carnage. Even in the middle-distance shot, Nathan's discomfort is obvious, while Greg's grin is broad and smug. "Jan, we estimate that as many as two dozen animals may have been slaughtered right here, but these bodies have been ripped apart so bad we just can't be certain."

Nathan's clothes are damp from his fall into the creek earlier that morning. He is shivering, tapping both thumbs against the grip of his microphone and staring past Greg. He misses his cue. Greg elbows his sternum, setting off a coughing fit. He had to take a hit from his inhaler right after I stopped the camera. He gasps through his lines. "Uh. Over the years, farmers in the Halliken Valley area have contended with many predators worrying their livestock, from natural threats such as snakes, feral dogs and localised earth tremors to supernatural monstrosities such as werewolves, bunyips and UFOs. Though, of course, the existence of aliens has yet to be officially recognised."

"There's no such thing," says Greg.

Nathan stands about a foot shorter than Greg. Every time Greg speaks, he flinches. "Um, well, there's... with the damage we are seeing here, there's no evidence of..."

"UFOs?"

"Um, well, of any of those things. I think we're dealing with something else."

"Chupacabra," says Michelle after the cut. She's standing with Jan and a bearded late middle-aged white man wearing a rabbit-fur hat and dusty collared shirt. The Other Girl is standing behind them, eyes squeezed shut as if the green scrunchie in her hair is too tight, with her arms crossed over a Hypercolor Miami Dolphins t-shirt. Nobody pays her any attention.

Jan frowns at the off-script comment. "Excuse me?" she says.

"Puerto Rican goat-sucker," says Michelle.

"I've never heard—"

"Of course you haven't. It's an amphibious carnivore, lives in bodies of still water like canals, ponds and dams and exclusively preys on—"

Jan looms toward the camera with a fake smile that warns 'no more side-tracks'. "Just this morning we were doing additional filming for our episode on the Dawn Spectre of Barramar National Park, when we discovered Farmer Bryan's livestock in this dreadful state. Bryan, how do you respond to the police statement that your livestock was attacked by wild dogs?"

Bryan Ponsford's face transforms from blank dismay to frustrated fury. He says, "Dogs! That's bullshit." For the original webcast I bleeped that. This time it stays. "If it was dogs, my dogs would've barked their balls off." He adds another, "Dogs!" and swipes his hat across his brow.

The Other Girl shakes with laughter that doesn't register on the soundtrack. Her braces glint in the morning sun.

Michelle makes a distracted half-turn towards her before returning her attention to Jan. "Why not a chupacabra? Wouldn't be the first time an overseas pest has been introduced to this ecosystem."

Jan directs a throat-cutting gesture at me to end the take.

Half a dozen pig-hunting dogs are penned up in an enclosed wire cage near a collection of storage sheds. Michelle strides over with her recording gear, smirking with satisfaction. She whistles and hisses at the dogs, hoping to provoke some suitably ferocious barks to mix into the audio track. The dogs pace and fret in their cage. One even lunges at the wire and grabs hold with its teeth. None of them bark at her.

The Other Girl follows her for a few steps. Her face is flat and serious but as she looks back at me, I think I see a hint of something else. She's almost skipping. She stops outside one of the sheds. She looks back at the camera and opens her mouth like she might say something.

Then someone yells, "Hey, get away from there! Leave – leave my dogs alone," and the camera swings to Farmer Bryan, huffing across the blood-soaked holding yard toward us. "I want you lot off my property." He's waving his arms so hard, he almost rolls his ankle on a decapitated goat head.

That was the episode where Spook Hunters took off online.

#

Excerpt from Episode Four: 'The Daugherty Theatre'

"The Daugherty Theatre staged its first play in October 1902, a production of Boothby Chambers' notoriously unlucky and subsequently banned play, *The Light across the Billabong*."

Nathan's glasses reflect like full moons rising over his lips. I borrowed a night vision attachment to compensate for the abandoned theatre's poor lighting, but it was difficult to get the correct settings. I abandoned it after filming this background segment.

"The opening night was a fiasco. The leading lady broke her leg and six patrons contracted cholera from drinking spoiled champagne. The theatre's owner, John Abercroft Daugherty, was undeterred by the setback. Over the next eleven years, he produced some of Australia's greatest theatrical works, making Ashburnham a prime location on Victoria's cultural map. Daugherty was the rock-star producer of his day."

Jan takes up the narrative. "That ended when John Daugherty and his brother George volunteered for the First Australian Imperial Force in November 1914. John was killed at Fromelles. George returned after the Great War and took over the theatre."

Greg is standing so close to Jan that the weird illumination makes it look like two heads sharing one body. He takes a sneaky glance over her shoulder at her cleavage.

"Nobody knows how or when George Daugherty got his secret taste for human blood, but we do know he was a full-on cannibal by the time he got home. Local historians reckon his interwar body count was eighteen, most of them day labourers."

Michelle adds, "Only three murders were proven at his 1938 trial, which was enough to send George to the gallows. The Daugherty Theatre was declared hazardous by the town's authorities and closed the same day England declared war on Germany."

Jan says, "For a building that's been condemned for over seventy years, the Daugherty Theatre is in good shape. That's because the Ashburnham Historical Society raises funds to restore it every ten or fifteen years. Public-spirited carpentry is not without its risks. Nathan's dad hurt himself falling from that catwalk back in 2007, right Nate?"

Nathan's father spent nine months in traction and walks with a cane to this day. His injury forced him into early retirement. He is a kind man, but he tires easily.

Nathan does not reply. The Other Girl puts her hand on his shoulder.

Even though it's a rare example of them all working as a team, I would cut this scene as irrelevant if not for where they are standing, in the side aisle of the partially-restored auditorium. The Other Girl resumes her usual position, unnoticed at the rear, shrouded by the hanging shreds of a long-ruined velvet curtain.

Nathan confusedly wanders back a couple of steps, giving voice to a small croak, until he bumps into the wall. Not noticing the Other Girl, I thought nothing of it at the time and paused the recording.

"Come on, what do you say we give this a run? George is probably still here." Greg produces a plywood sheet painted with letters and numbers. He never holds it still long enough to recognise it as a Ouija board. In the original episode, I inserted a still-frame image for the audience's benefit but that doesn't matter now.

With the introduction done, Michelle's interest in cooperating evaporates. "Okay, two things about that. One, why would anyone want to talk to the spirit of a guy who murdered people and ate them? And two, what the hell is wrong with you?"

Greg's look of surprise is understandable. They used to get on much better.

Nathan is pushing the curtain around and knocking on the wall through gaps torn in the fabric. He ignores the others. The Other Girl shows a glimpse of amusement at Michelle's speech, but is more interested in Nathan's investigation.

Jan scowls and pushes close to Michelle's face, "What makes you think we're not going to try to contact the dead? That's what Spook Hunters is all about."

"As if you have any idea what this is all about, you pushy little show-off. You just read your palm cards and show some pasty white skin and try not to get any of your drool on him." Now it's Jan's turn to look shocked. I doubt anyone has ever stared her down like that before.

Greg steps between them before Jan thinks of a way to escalate. "Hey now, ladies," he says, and his grin suggests he might believe they are fighting over him.

"… distasteful."

"What?" Michelle turns around to the Other Girl with a frown, like someone snuck up from behind and pinched her. The sound on the original recording was terrible. Michelle and I spent half a day trying to clean it up for the webcast. Nathan's voice had some weird echo artefacts we just couldn't isolate. In the end, we got him to record a voice-over.

"What did you say?"

Nathan coughs. "I said, ghosts. They don't like being summoned. They think it's impolite and distasteful. Anyway, I found something."

He's standing in a doorway that wasn't there before. "I think this is George Daugherty's kill room. What say we give our viewers a first look inside?"

I slow the playback again. As he holds the door open for us all to clamber forward, it's easy to miss the slight bulge of something long and flat stuffed into his shirt.

#

Excerpt from Episode Five: 'The Ghost of Clarice'

"Jan, some of the feedback from our regular viewers has been a bit critical."

"How so, Greg?"

They are flushed and keep exchanging furtive smiles they must imagine are invisible to the camera.

We waited for them for an hour, making uncomfortable small talk with the old woman whose lounge room we'd invaded. Jan assured us she had called ahead to make arrangements. It transpired that she left a message on an answering machine that has not been checked since 1996.

"A few commenters have complained that the Spook Hunters project is a failure."

"A failure?"

"Right. Because so far" – Jan glares what must be intended as daggers penetrating through the camera to its operator – "we haven't captured a single spectre, cryptid or otherworldly horror live on film."

Little do they know.

"Well then, tonight they're in for a treat." Jan steps back with a ringmaster's expansive wave. The old woman, Mrs Gretel Stone, tries to rise too quickly from her armchair. Nathan and Michelle take an arm each to prevent her toppling. I hold the shot on her countenance of confused gratitude. She really had no idea why we were there, but she didn't complain. Manners are paramount and at least we were interesting company.

"Vanh! Camera!" For the webcast, I cut Greg's deep-throated stage whisper out. I feel no obligation to make him look good this time.

The picture veers to Jan by an old-fashioned fireplace, where fading photographs in tarnished silver frames sit atop a faintly scorched mantle. "This," she announces, gesturing with both hands at the stuffed and mounted remains of a tortoiseshell cat, "is Clarice."

"And this," she says, reaching out to steer the camera towards a window, as if nobody else has read her very detailed running sheet, "is also Clarice."

A cat – the same cat, though warmed through with a translucent amber glow – is sitting on the window sill. It considers the camera with thoughtful disdain for a moment. Then it raises its head to accept a stroke from Jan's hand, which passes straight through to stop with a gentle slap on the windowsill. The cat's ears flick. It rises, arches its back, and slips out the closed window, disturbing neither dusty glass nor lacy curtains.

Jan swears loud enough for our inadvertent host to hear. As she begins to react, Greg asks, "How did Clarice die, Grandmother Stone?"

Our host's baffled cordiality freezes on her face. "I won't talk about that while she's here."

We all turn to look at Jan, even Greg. "Not her. Her!" The old woman is pointing into her own little galley kitchen. The camera pans slowly. I didn't want a wobbling shot.

Nathan is carefully pouring the contents of a steaming kettle into a porcelain teapot, while the Other Girl watches, drumming her hands on the table. Startled, he spills hot tea on his fingers as he looks up. Her mouth drops open and she flaps her hand like a bird taking flight.

"Who?" says Greg. "I don't—"

"Mum? What's going on? What are they doing here?"

I happened to be by the front door at the time so I didn't need to move. Mrs Lautner walked straight into the shot. The camera is so close up on her ear that you can see it turn red. She says, "Jan, why are you all in my mother's house?"

Count one, two and there is Jan, in the shot with Mrs Lautner. Whatever else you can say about Jan Parry, she has fine spatial awareness. "Fans, you remember Naomi Lautner, don't you? She's the clubs coordinator at Wattle Park High and she was just indispensable in helping us set up the Spook Hunters Club in the first place. Mrs Lautner – well, no it's out of school hours so I guess we should call you Naomi, right? So Naomi, what can you tell us about your mother's spectral pet?"

"Jan Parry, I told you about Clarice in confidence." Mrs Lautner turns to look to the camera. Her disappointment still feels worse than a punch to the stomach. "This is an invasion of my family privacy, not to mention a breach of trust. I would like you all to leave immediately. I will discuss this with you after school on Monday."

Jan persists, putting a hand on Mrs Lautner's shoulder to angle her slightly towards the camera. "Do you think it's possible your mother poisoned her own cat in order to —"

There's no more footage. That's when I stopped filming.

#

Excerpt from Episode Six: 'Wisdom Street'

"This green marker shows where Robert O'Reilly fell after he was stabbed twice in the neck, and the orange one is where Mrs Katherine Morris bled out after Constable Ernhardt emptied his pistol into her chest." Nathan is speaking very quickly and will not hold still while he speaks to camera.

He was still upset after the meeting with all our parents. His father asked him to stop making the documentaries. Nathan argued with his father, which I don't think he had ever done before.

Despite his nerves, he completes his recounting of the details of each murder without pause. The camera follows him on a wayward route down the street, checking in on a series of numbered plastic markers. Each is a memorial to an unlucky bystander picked off in Lidija Hummel's branch of the 1893 rampage.

Michelle falls in step alongside him. Her glance to camera, no more than a blink, is heavy with emotion. The rebuke that followed Jan's stunt was still fresh in our minds, as was the implied threat that our grade would be withheld. Michelle does not care to hide her anger.

Nathan arrives at a patch of dappled shade beneath a stand of thin white gum trees. In two upturned palms, he raises a flat, curved blade covered in wriggling marks like the scribbled bark patterns behind him.

The Other Girl stands beside him, her tied-back hair and oversized shirt unaffected by a light breeze that ruffles Nathan and Michelle. She frowns and often glances away to one side as though she is waiting for a late bus.

"What sparked the Wisdom Street massacre, we don't know for sure," Michelle says. "When Lidija Hummel hanged herself from the branches just above us, she took the answers with her. None of the other participants in the bloody all-in brawl outlived her by more than an hour."

"Eyewitness accounts agree that a strangely-shaped blade changed possession several times among the Wisdom Street killers. Some historians hold that an argument broke out over its ownership. The suggestion remains unconfirmed and no such weapon was ever found. Until now." Nathan holds a knife, which I believed until that moment to be a replica.

As Michelle takes over to recount the bizarre circumstances that drew seven previously unconnected townsfolk into unexplained mutual butchery, a man in a grey suit with an emerald green tie joins them in the shot.

He listens to their presentation with an expectant look. He does not appear perturbed that neither has acknowledged him.

The Other Girl's pinched face registers hostility. She pulls at her hair with some ferocity, retwisting her scrunchie like a sailor securing loose ropes in a storm. The man in the grey suit ignores her.

As the historical presentation ends, the man in the grey suit leans towards Nathan and whispers something in his ear.

Nathan looks at the knife and runs his finger along the edge, where a dark red smear appears. The man in the grey suit smiles like an encouraging teacher.

Nathan raises his eyes and looks into Michelle's as if he sees her for the first time. Michelle is looking at the knife and at the blood dripping from Nathan's fingers.

The Other Girl touches the man in the grey suit on the shoulder. He reacts, shaking his head at her without turning, a disdainful dismissal.

The Other Girl squeezes, the coil of bangles on her wrist shivering against one another. Smoke or perhaps steam curls from the collar and cuffs of the grey suit.

Michelle swears and snatches the audio bud from her ear. She slaps a hand against the side of her head, grinding her palm against her ear.

The man in the grey suit disappears. The Other Girl falls to her knees and coughs. Michelle's equipment does not pick up the sound of her coughing.

Nathan puts the knife down. He looks at his hand and squeals in pain. "Oh hell. I need stitches."

Jan and Greg never showed up for the recording. When they recorded their introductions at school the next week, Greg told Michelle that they had been grounded by their parents. Jan told me that they lost the address details.

I don't know why they bothered lying to us.

#

Excerpt from Episode Eight: 'The Farm' (episode not broadcast)

I have tried every trick I know to clean up the footage from the hay shed. I have run a stabilisation filter. I have cut the worst bits. I even tried centring each image frame by hand. It's no good. I couldn't stop my hands from shaking when we recorded.

The cut on Greg's forehead is deep but the flow has stopped. Except for the bite on his shoulder, his clothes are more torn up than his skin. He is sitting on the hay-strewn floor of the shed, legs folded, holding his foot with both hands. He stares at everything with a bewildered fury held in check by shock. He says nothing. He does not understand what has happened.

Jan is so pale her eyelids and lips are almost blue. "Charles?" she says, to camera of course. "Charles?" She still wears her head microphone, carefully raising and lowering the pickup arm every time she speaks. "Charles, where is he?"

Michelle grabs Jan's bare arm and squeezes until a halo of red skin surrounds her hand. "He went to get help," she says, flat and merciless. "He went because you told him to. You selfish — "

Jan slaps her hand away. "Me? We wouldn't be here if not for your stupid club. Think about that."

Michelle drops to her knees and starts unscrewing the boom stand into its component metal rods. "Sounds like your problem to me. I don't remember inviting you."

She shakes her head. Her hair has grown out since the first episode. I didn't remember that at the time, but now the contrast is striking. Her flat curls have stretched and dangle, reaching for her shoulders. Her skin is too dark to show signs of shock. But then, she shows no other signs of shock either. She looks to the camera. "We can't broadcast this footage, you know. It'd mess up the court case."

"What court case?" says Jan. "He's going to kill us. He'll kill us and he'll get away with it because he always has."

"Speak for yourself," says Michelle. She hands one of the dense metal tubes toward the camera; my hand extends forward to claim it. "This is just to keep the dogs off, okay?"

We can hear the baying in the distance, getting closer. I think Greg might have managed to kill one of the dogs, or at least hurt it badly. There are at least six others, not to mention Ponsford himself.

The camera pans around the interior of the feed shed. Hay bales are stacked ceiling-high against the corrugated aluminium interior walls.

The Other Girl is not with us, which must mean she's outside with Nathan. I think that's where she's been for a long time.

"Why did we come back here?" I reframe on Greg, who has raised his hand to ask the question. I freeze the frame to get a better look at what I saw a second later. The floor's discolouration is obscured by leg movements and patterns of dirt and hay. Did I really see it on my own or did I have help? I still can't tell.

"Get up. Get him up." My own voice sounds tinny and hollow. Michelle half lifts, half drags Greg out of the way. I set the camera at floor level. My feet appear, kicking a clearing in the straw, stomping to sound out which parts are concrete and which parts are a grey vinyl sheet camouflaging an iron manhole cover.

The Other Girl brought us here. Nathan claimed it was all his own idea. Maybe he was just trying to protect her.

"Help me with this." Michelle takes one side of the metal ring handle and together we lift the manhole cover. The lid flops open with a crash and the two of us look inside.

I drop to my knees and vomit on the straw. Michelle's legs buckle a little but she keeps her feet. Jan can't resist. She comes over to look. Her cry is cut off with a thick sound as Michelle's hand claps over her mouth.

There is a crash at the shed door. "Let me in," calls Nathan. More shakes. The footage of Michelle reaching out to lift away her improvised door bar is unwatchable as I unsteadily retrieve the camera.

Nathan falls through the door, holding Greg's mobile telephone. The Other Girl steps through behind him, looking like she is queued up for a Duran Duran concert.

"Did you — ?" Jan's voice is guarded to the point of despair. She lost hope quicker than you would expect.

Nathan nods, catching his breath. He is not a good runner. Another reason Greg would have been preferable. "I got a signal near the ridge. I called the police. Greg's father, too." He bites his bottom lip and shrugs when Greg does not respond.

Michelle gets it first. "Where's the goat farmer?"

"He's busy with his dogs. But he's nearly done." The dogs' barks have reached a primal ferocity. Their chorus is getting closer, but contains fewer voices.

Jan starts turning to each of us. "He's coming. He's coming. Why did we come back here?"

The Other Girl kneels by the open manhole, looking down with an apologetic expression. I didn't take the shot until much later, but it's no mystery what held her gaze. One of the ruined gelatinous faces staring back from empty sockets wears braces over shrunken gums and a green scrunchie in its matted thicket of hair.

Greg's mouth moves but his expression does not change. "You killed his goats. That's why he's angry at us. You killed his goats."

Nathan shrugs. He did and didn't. He was not in the driver's seat then, any more than he was when he threw himself into a creek to wash the blood and gore away.

I'm the first to notice what he's missing. "Where's the knife?"

"I gave it to him," Nathan replies.

"You what?"

"I had to, otherwise he wouldn't have murdered his dogs."

There's a final helpless yelp from somewhere nearby and then the noise steadies into a ceaseless monotone mutter of swearing and violent threats. The sound comes closer. The shed door thumps once, shaking the whole structure.

Michelle takes up a spot beside the door. She has a short metal pole in each hand. She gives the Other Girl a hard look and I think it's the first time she's ever seen her. "You got us into this, chicky-babe. You got what you wanted, now you do right by us, hey?"

Nathan and the Other Girl reach out together for the door handle and pull it open.

The goat farmer is there, eyes wide and mouth dripping red, holding Nathan's knife like a short sword. In person Bryan Ponsford was just in his blood-soaked working clothes. On film, he's wearing a grey suit with an emerald tie.

He sees the Other Girl and he takes a half-step back. Michelle slams his wrist with her improvised club, hard enough to break skin and bone. She put her weight into it.

The knife drops in front of Nathan and the Other Girl. They kick it across the floor into the manhole.

Ponsford howls unintelligibly and grabs at Nathan. The Other Girl grabs his arm and stops it from reaching Nathan's throat.

Michelle hits him again, this time on the back of his head. Ponsford's hat spins off into the straw. Ponsford takes one more step and collapses forward. His face bounces off the rim of the manhole. He stops moving, his face hanging into the hole like he's vomiting into a toilet.

Michelle says, "Let's go now."

For some reason Jan picked that moment to start screaming so I stopped recording then.

#

Excerpt from Episode Nine: 'Final Report' (episode not broadcast)

When we filmed the final episode two nights ago, Jan wanted everyone to sit in the same places. She gave up when Greg pointedly refused to surrender his crutches and sit down.

Her webcast-host face is gone, replaced by serious-student face. It is no less insincere. In comparison to the footage I was looking at a minute ago, her transformation is unsettling.

"We've had an amazing semester," she says. The frame tightens on her face; I wanted to get through this in one take and I didn't want anyone else's expression to distract attention from her. "The Wattle Creek Spook Hunters have looked Ashburnham's darkness right in the eye and brought it into the light. We're so proud that you've been able to join us on this journey. Your emails of support and encouragement have kept us going in the past few weeks. I wish I could thank every one of you in person."

"This series started as an extracurricular project for credit towards our final Year 10 certificate. But it's become more than that. And I'm not just saying that because Ms Lautner abandoned her teaching responsibilities and convinced the principal to cancel our bonus marks. That doesn't matter anymore because the great news is that our last episode had over seventy-five thousand downloads. You banded together to create a real community. You've all rallied behind us and I know that this is just the start of something big and important. I just know that when the legal injunctions on our latest episode come down and you finally get to see it, you're going to lose it. You guys can't get enough of Spook Hunters and I love you for that."

The camera pulls back as she speaks. Nobody is looking at anybody. Nobody says anything with their eyes. When Jan finishes, she leads an infectious round of applause that nobody catches.

Greg nods once and settles his crutches into place. He turns his back on Jan and makes a painstaking, lumbering circuit towards the front door.

"Where are you going?" Jan seems too surprised to be angry.

"Coach says I have to keep up physical therapy if I want to start training." With a little shuffling manoeuvre to get the crutches out of the way, he opens the door.

Jan tries to save the moment. "Don't you want to tell the viewers about what's coming up in Season Two?"

"I can get graduation credit from footy. Can't get anything I want here." Greg closes the door behind him and for once Jan's media presence doesn't rush to fill the vacuum.

"I'm gone too," says Michelle, picking up her bag.

That snaps Jan out of it. "Fine, you bugger off on walkabout or whatever. We can do this without you."

Michelle stands, breathing quietly and holding herself very still, for a long time. She says, "I'll see most of you at school on Monday. Good night."

I pause the shot just as the camera pans past Jan's face. Her flaring nostrils look out of place at the centre of a cracked mask of bland good cheer.

I admit it. I enjoyed the moment. Maybe I'm not as good a person as I tell myself.

I restart the footage.

The pan resumes to the floor, where Nathan sits cross-legged. To his left, the Other Girl wears a sweet smile and, for the first time in our acquaintance, she has changed out of her old clothes into stonewash jeans and a Spin Doctors t-shirt.

Nathan puts an arm around the Other Girl and says, "This is Sally. Well, that's what we're calling her right now and I'm sure she'd let us know if she minded. I don't know if you see Sally. Not everybody does. But she's been with us for a while and she's planning to stick around from now on, helping us to help other people."

Jan looks at Nathan like he's on fire and ignoring it. "Who are you talking — ?"

Nathan goes on. "We have a debt to repay to Sally. The first thing we're going to do is find out her real name. Who she was."

Nathan looks to camera. His replacement glasses are so fine they almost vanish from his face. "We're going to make another change next season. Together. All right? Together or not at all."

The picture wobbles just a little bit. I don't intend to fix it.

I walk around and take my place next to Nathan and Sally.

See you next season.

'Seven Excerpts' was my stab at translating the shaky-camera-with-night-vision-filters ghost-hunting subgenre of reality television to the written word. If me and my high school friends were growing up now, I am 100% sure we would have created something like this in a bid for YouTube stardom. Though I'm not sure how we'd have fared with an Australian country town this drenched in murder, monsters and the supernatural.

*'Seven Excerpts from Season One' was first published in **At the Edge** (Paper Road Publishing 2016), edited by Dan Rabarts and Lee Murray.*

GORILLA DENTISTS

The old saying goes, "On the internet, nobody knows you're a dog."

But as telepresence technology evolved from primitive videoconferencing, through phase after high-fidelity phase of virtual reality, to remote capture of domestic synthdroids, it was increasingly the case that nobody needed to know who anyone was.

Take the case of Ambrose Brook, who pioneered the practise of home dentistry in the mid-21st century. Brook, an unusually gifted dental surgeon, suffered from a range of severe social phobias and anxieties which limited his contact with patients.

The dentist's frustrating setback coincided with the emergence of a consumer trend popular among his erstwhile clientele in the upper-middle class: Takahashi Robotics' Silverback model of household synthdroid.

Silverbacks were full-size replicas of Western gorillas, programmed for home maintenance and security duties. Like other fifth-generation synthdroids, the Silverback executed its routine functions independently and without the need for supervision. Though of course it was the charming novelty of watching a half-tonne primate washing dishes, pushing a vacuum cleaner and unclogging roof gutters which drove the model's surging popularity.

It was a feature new to fifth gens which caught Brook's attention. Silverbacks could be remote-operated by skilled technicians to perform more complex tasks.

Initially these were restricted to security operations; when a paranoid householder hit an alarm, their home security provider could have one of its on-staff counter-terrorism specialists remote-jack the domestic synthdroid, whereupon it suddenly became a Silverback with fifteen years of military situational awareness training and hand to hand combat skills.

Brook saw an opportunity to expand into the same market. He underwent intensive remote capture training. After honing his technique by treating family members and close friends, he found in the Silverback's high definition sensors and state of the art controls a greatly improved precision to his telemanipulation skills. He also devised a "home dentistry" kit of disposable tools and supplies which could be shipped at minimal cost to the patient's residence.

To his delight, he found he did not even require an assistant – the Silverback's prehensile feet were so easily adapted to selecting tools, applying suction and holding out cups for the patient to rinse with, it was like having a third hand. If Brook could think of an action, the household Silverback he logged into could perform it.

Needless to say, his service became popular in no time. Patients fearful of overdue visits for a check-up were easily persuaded to trust the enormous gorilla which made their bed every day. Brook always used the host module's own voice rather than overwrite it with his own. Somehow the sense of familiarity overcame the fear, mistrust and shame other members of his profession often encountered in their recidivist patients.

The novelty of the service was its prime booster: showing off the results of a whitening procedure performed by a burly great ape was a fine stimulus for dinner party conversations. For the children, he wore a pointed hat and comical bow tie; these were standard kit inclusions.

Routine clean and polish jobs became more sophisticated. Within eight months Brook had developed a home kit which allowed him to floss, fill cavities, and install and remove braces. Medical regulators were initially reluctant to permit him to conduct complex surgery on anaesthetised patients, but within a year Brook's devoted patrons included movie stars, rock legends and highly-placed politicians, all wealthy and possessed of stratospheric clapplause ratings. Federal approvals were rushed through.

The popularity of Brook's remote procedures skyrocketed thanks to Gabrielle Tranh, who cultivated minor celebrity, as a fashion model and hockey player forced into retirement from both careers by injury, into a lucrative SenseStream career.

Tranh, possessed of a vivacious personality and a surprisingly high pain threshold, posted a live sensecast of a jaw reconstruction conducted by Brook through Tranh's household Silverback, whom she called Huggy George.

Tranh's hilarious one-sided – and muffled – conversations with the enormous gorilla rewiring her mandible, with only a mild sedative for localised pain relief, was a massive SenseStream hit. Replays topped the billion mark. With a number of follow-up surgical procedures proving equally popular, Brook's career, albeit tethered to Tranh's, was made.

Of course, Brook was not the only gorilla dentist. With demand for his services far outstripping his capacity to meet it, he took on partners. His cadre of dentals surgeons, hygienists and technical support staff was known informally as the Tooth Troop, even in later years, when the scope of the company expanded to other medical, therapeutic and educational services. School visits by Tranh and Huggy George, which included a raucous show and free dental inspections, were in high demand.

It all came to an end following the spring 2167 launch of Takahashi's first sixth-generation synthdroids.

The new octopoid architecture, eight undulating limbs with a hundredfold increase in haptic sensitivity, was embraced by the trend-loving public. However remote manipulation of the extra limbs with their unfamiliar articulation proved to be impossible for all but a tiny percentage of the population. The Tooth Troop, along with most of their imitators, were unable to transfer their skills to the new paradigm, and business slowly receded as Silverbacks transitioned into obsolescence.

Brook himself suffered a minor stroke on his first and only attempt to remote pilot an octopoid synthdroid. After making a full recovery, he went into semi-retirement to produce and star in a number of educational sensecasts for schoolchildren on the importance of dental health care.

For some years after, he also reprised his role as Huggy George, co-starring with his business and life partner Gabrielle Tranh in several well-received casts aimed at a mature audience.

They never met in person.

Popular discussions around advancements in virtual reality and remote manipulation technologies tend to focus disproportionately on their applications in gaming and sex. But really useful technologies are transformative to societies in ways that were not intended by their designers or even possible to predict in their early days. If we still have a functional civilisation in fifty years, it will look remarkably different from the one we have now. Though I do think it will still be recognisable in all the usual human ways.

'Gorilla Dentists' was first published in September 2017 as a Friday Flash Fiction post at DavidVersace.com.

THE DRESSMAKER AND THE COLONEL'S COAT

When the town of Mirror Springs threw a shindig to welcome the heroes back from the Cemetery Wars, the Colonel set tongues wagging by paying a call to the exiled dressmaker, Molly Bright.

The Colonel was of a mind to turn the floor in a fetching new frock coat of peacock and gold. As everyone knew, no hand was swifter or steadier stitching good fortune into a garment than Miss Molly's.

Back before the War, when Molly and her brother William first arrived on the Strickland Express from back East, word of her prowess ran three stops ahead of her. If the wildfire of discontent hadn't followed hot on their heels, she might have turned her little shop into a thriving concern. But when fighting broke out between mining concerns, Molly's luck followed her hot-headed brother Bill out the door.

The Colonel's chestnut mare carried her a good mile south of the bustling town to an old miner's hut set among the slag ponds down in Venom Gully.

What she saw was a moon-white Easterner with twisting black tresses atop a frame not near plump enough for the coming winter. She sat on an upturned fossicking tub older than she was, unpicking the seams on a saloon owner's waistcoat. She paid no particular mind as the Colonel's mount navigated the uneven path pocked with treacherous pools of sulphur-mud.

What little attention Molly Bright spared from her work was for the dog; a rangy cur lay hunched atop a mullock mound, just beyond the stretch of afternoon shadows cast by the shack. She'd been the subject of its watchful gaze for near on two weeks. Since it seemed neither intent on making a meal of her nor accepting her tentative offers of shelter and companionship, they had fallen into an easy détente.

A whipcrack of thunder shattered the silence. The dog scuttled away from a burst of stone and dust and retreated snarling into the maze of mine refuse.

The Colonel holstered her smoking long-barrel with a humourless bark and leaned ahead to stroke her agitated mare behind the ear.

Miss Molly tilted her bonnet a touch lower over her eyes before she raised them in greeting; rough experience had taught her not to share her fears casually.

Her social sensibilities were of more resilient stock than her nerves. She paid her compliments to her guest before her heart could head them off: "How do you do, Colonel Tempest?"

The Colonel smoothed a blue-gloved finger across a smudge on her boot. On closer inspection of her fingertip, her nose wrinkled and she gave a small *tsk* of disgust. With a sigh, she stripped the gloves off, balled them together and dropped them as she dismounted.

"Your brother was Captain William Conover Bright, late of the Seventh Ranger Squadron of the Stonechurch Territorial Regiment."

Molly conceded the familial connection with a tight nod and a shiver down her spine.

"Your brother danced a rope jig for treason on my word of judgment, Miss Bright, as I am certain you are aware."

Molly folded her sewing and set it with care on a barrel head laden with scissors, pincushions and threads of various hues and properties. She stood, acknowledging the declaration with a grave nod.

"Your letter was detailed in all particulars, Colonel. I took your forthright commentary as a kindness and a courtesy, and I assure you I have no unanswered questions."

It was not the whole truth, but Molly didn't expect her brother's executioner to satisfy her curiosity.

"Meaning no disrespect, Colonel, but do you mean to hold me to account for my brother's actions?"

The Colonel set one boot on the porch and crossed her arms on her knee. She was young for a senior commissioned officer, not much past thirty. Her eyes were the green of a still river and her plaits of maple brown hair matched her skin.

"I once heard it said that the company we keep in life is a richer feed than the blood we spring from." She showed Molly her teeth; up close they were uneven, chipped and patched with amalgam. "You and your brother were close, according to my recollection."

Molly swallowed down on the churn in her throat. "He and I were all we had when our Father passed on, Colonel."

"Your brother put it in just those words." Uncomfortably close now, the Colonel traced a finger from Molly's temple down along the night-black hairline to the earlobe adorned with a teardrop pendant. Molly couldn't help flinching at the fingertip's chill. "So now you have less than nothing. Mirror Springs has ostracised the traitor's sister. Now only refugees and cheapskates dare give you their business."

Molly said, "I get by."

"A smart, pretty thing like you could do better than just get by, is what I think." Now she flicked a cold thumb across the corner of Molly's mouth, like she was tending to a smudge. "Why didn't you heed the suggestion in my correspondence to leave for better prospects elsewhere?"

"I can't leave," Molly whispered, imagining those cold fingers sliding down to close around her throat. "I've no choice but to stay."

Abruptly the hand fled Molly's face as the Colonel stood. "Well now, if that's how it is, then Mistress Fortune's shining her best smile on both of us today. I'll guess you crave the embrace of a welcoming community of stout-hearted Springers, not to mention the gratifying ring of coins in your purse? I'm in a position to oblige you on both counts."

Molly blinked, not sure whether to tally her sudden sense of shock up to relief or alarm. She'd learned better than to trust a deal without sniffing the ink. "How would you hope to be compensated for such a generous proposition, Colonel Tempest?"

The Colonel's eyes gleamed like a moonlit snake's.

"Oh, Molly Bright, don't you spend one ounce of concern on that score. From what your brother's said on your behalf and what I can see for myself, you've got an abundance of talent I can make use of."

Something pushed its way past the fear in Molly's throat. She snapped, "Colonel Tempest, my brother's disgrace cost him his life. If the Fates declare there's more shame owing on his misdeeds then I guess that's my debt to carry. But I won't be drawn into unbecoming conduct, not by you nor any other."

The Colonel picked up a coiled strip of leather from the barrel and painstakingly wrapped it around her fingers, examining the numbers punched into its skin inch by inch. Her grin put Molly in mind of a hungry cat in the company of a limping mouse.

"If you've misunderstood my intentions, Miss Bright," she said with all the sincerity of a riverboat sharp, "then I am gravely sorry for the error. I mean to secure your services as a seamstress, of course."

"You want me to make you a dress?"

Spreading her arms, taking an inelegant turn across an imaginary floor, and kicking up a choke of reeking mine-dust with her boot heels, the Colonel laughed. "Do I seem to you a delicate bloom of womanhood, to be draped in petals and dusted with aromatic powders? You'll fashion me a fine dress coat. A work of finery the likes of which this dirt-blast of a town has never seen. There's a certain dishwater-grey eye I want to catch, that comes attached to a sizeable fortune and, unless I miss my guess, an ailing constitution."

Molly understood this to refer to the widower Jeremiah Stonechurch, the wealthy patriarch of Mirror Springs, whose second wife had passed over several winters ago. She imagined the spiteful tycoon highly susceptible to a war hero's flattering attentions.

She agreed to the proposition. In any case, she was in no position to decline it.

"I knew you'd see things my way, Miss Bright. Now what say you and I step inside out of the glare and you take what measurements you may require?"

#

Much later, the Colonel mounted her horse and wheeled about for the town, not casting so much as a glance over her shoulder. The dog slunk out of the wastes and trotted after her a distance, but soon abandoned its idle pursuit in favour of further scavenging. Molly, exhausted and fraught, watched both, her bottom lip clenched between her teeth.

Beside her stood a lean young man wearing a battered military uniform and the signs of a sour disposition. He spat something unmentionable at the dusty imprint of the Colonel's boot, where it sizzled and coughed like a twist of charcoal smoke.

"Why'd you take that woman's commission, Little Moll? You know what she did to me."

Molly Bright shivered against the slow fading heat and sipped brackish water from a rusted mug.

The man tried again. "You think she's got a fancy for you, is that it? Ha! She'll betray you once she's got what she needs."

Molly sighed, "You're dead, Big Bill. How long do I have to wait for you to behave in accordance with your condition?"

On the day the telegraph brought word of the conclusion of the Cemetery Wars - eighteen months of range skirmishing, railroad ambushing and mining town besiegement between rival mining magnates, which the gentlemen of the press had seen fit to elevate with a fanciful name - Bill Bright's ghost had knocked on Molly's door and seen himself in.

By then months had passed since the fateful letter's arrival; months of baleful stares, whispered recriminations and cancelled business orders. When impolite society became outright hostility, she paid the last of her coin to two sympathetic foreigners with a horse and wagon to pack up her stock and relocate it to the wastes.

Barely had she settled herself in to tend to a meagre handful of nearly empty-handed clients before he appeared on her doorstep. Pale, translucent, with a livid mark about his neck and a new bulge about his eyes, was Bill Bright.

He was expected. She'd hoped the Bright menfolk's tendency to linger after their mortal span would skip her generation. Grandfather Morris and his three brothers had all obliged on that score. But her hopes were slight. Harrison Bright, squire of William and Molly, persisted long past his due. Little chance for better conduct from his son, especially with so disreputable an end.

"I got unfinished business, Moll."

He had a rough way of speaking now. Part of it was the throaty rasp imparted by the hangman's noose, but she thought war must have coarsened him in a multitude of ways.

"It's not my business, now is it, Bill? You won't let me leave, and now you nip at my heels to turn paying customers away? The Colonel has commissioned my services. I'd be a lackwit to decline."

But with his customary ill-tempered pout - a notable feature of his character in life as in death - Bill vanished. His unspoken implication - "I got unfinished business with Colonel Tempest" - hung in the air at his passing.

Molly Bright's sigh encompassed grief, self-pity and the ache of unfulfilled hopes. Then she set them aside and went to work.

Her stock of brown paper was sadly expired, so she cleared
a cabin wall hung with cookware, mining pans and a chipped
enamel chamber pot. Then she took to it with her chalks,
sketching out a pattern in the rough timbers, adjusting as she
went with swipes of a straw broom head. She moved her small
lantern from this spot to that, shifting the light to judge the design
from every angle. She worked into the night, frowning and
tinkering. A cinch at the waist, a minute broadening of the belt,
the hem just a touch more fashionably low.

To the side, she drew up a list of ingredients: virid-flower
pollen for the suggestion of wisdom, cactus venom for sexual
desirability, oils of camphor and spinewood to draw forth wealth.
She had these to hand; such glamours were expected by her usual
clients. After some consideration, she added horseradish oil. A
button or two affixed with properly oiled thread might change a
bullet's path, something someone like the Colonel might profit by.

Just before dawn, Molly stepped outside to the porch,
stuffed her last withered thimbleful of tobacco into her pipe and
lit up. She was in the habit of keeping her smoke and her stock
separate, as not every customer savoured the scorched aroma on
their fresh-made clothes.

The dog was back.

The two of them regarded each other with equanimity. For
her part, Molly supposed the thing must have belonged to
someone once. Mirror Springs was too far from anywhere else for
wild dogs to have spread here on their own, not with what

stalked the wastes and desert beyond. Maybe it had been bereaved of its master, or else committed some unforgivable sin like biting a child. Whatever had brought it to its current station, the animal's existence was a tough one. Its sunken belly, matted hide and constant shivers gave it a harried look.

"You and me both, you scruff." Moll drew in a lungful of smoke and released it with a thoughtful stare. The dog matched her gaze, cautious but not submissive. It broke eye contact to scratch behind its ear and snap at an insect.

Molly tapped out her ashes and pocketed the pipe. She stomped to her larder - an old rail trunk shelving depleted tins of flour, sugar, cheese and dried beans - and pulled out her last twist of salted pork. This she wrenched into two pieces.

Clamping one between her teeth and tossing the other to the dog, she said, "I've got affairs to conduct in Mirror Springs, hound. What do you say to staying here and minding things until I return?"

The dog sniffed at the hunk of desiccated meat and tilted its head, as if considering her proposal. Then it flopped down in the dirt and began to worry the offering with worn teeth. Its stump of tail thumped the ground just once.

"I'll take that as a yes," said Molly Bright.

#

She slept poorly.

In her dreams she relived her day of disgrace. Jeremiah Stonechurch spat and raved in the street, waving the fateful dispatch letter under the nose of every passer-by, while two of his men dragged Molly from her shop. Her own letter, which explained William Bright's complicity in the fate of Stonechurch's younger brother Abel, had not been delivered yet. Terrified and uncomprehending, she bellowed tearful denials as Stonechurch furiously detailed the charges. A few spoke up against her mistreatment at first, but fell into an angry silence as Bill's crimes were laid out. The ordeal continued for what seemed like hours, the main street of Mirror Springs spilling over as Stonechurch's congregation grew. Through swelling red eyes Molly searched in vain for a friendly look, but if anyone felt sympathy, they guarded their emotions well. When at last his rage petered out to a steady simmer, Stonechurch gave her two days to get out of town. She'd spent the night shaking in terror behind her shop counter as threats were shouted from the door and every window smashed with rocks. Not a minute passed by without her expecting to see a flaming bottle of rotgut tequila fly through a shattered window frame and set her stock alight.

Did sanity prevail or had orders been issued to spare her life? She never knew. In the morning the brothers were waiting for her with a cart and a steep price. Molly loaded up what goods she could and rode out of Mirror Springs looking neither left nor right. A girl from the telegraph office ran alongside her and passed her the Colonel's letter, apologising for the delay in passing it on. Molly tipped her a week's wages just to hear a friendly word.

Until the Colonel arrived on her doorstep, it was the last time she spoke to any living person but the brothers, who delivered the necessities once a week from Uncle Key's General Supplies. Eventually they also brought sewing orders from a few of her competitor's dissatisfied customers. So began the resumption, however meagre, of her trade.

#

She summoned up her pluck - no mean feat with Big Bill voicing his derogations along the way - and saddled the gelding she'd bought from the foreigners.

"Don't you do it, Molly Bright," he repeated. "Don't you set your schemes against mine. Remember who's the thinker in this family?"

Molly remembered and she set her schemes. The voice faded into her dusty tracks after a time, as the ghost of Bill Bright never strayed far from the mining shack. Or else he was unwilling to face the townsfolk of Mirror Springs. She couldn't fault him on that score.

Mirror Springs was set on the banks of a lazy stream that the surveyors were convinced would connect to the mighty Alamatha River, if only someone were willing to chart its course west through Badlands infested with poisonous snakes, ambulatory cacti and hostile bear tribes. A man with papers from the Provincial Cartographer had come to town once, offering rich salaries to volunteers to accompany his expedition. Bill signed up at once, of course, but had fallen prey of food poisoning on the day the company rode out. They'd never been heard from again.

The town got the parts of its name from the copper-smelling gas bubbling up from the stream, which was not unpleasant to those accustomed, and to the silvery sheen of its sandy banks. The glare around noon was so overwhelming that rival glass makers had set themselves up producing smoked lenses, and most every resident had procured a pair from one or the other.

Molly shielded her eyes and turned her head away as her horse trudged into town.

She paid her first call to the hostler.

Ezekiel Grant's face wore a stormy outlook at Molly's approach. He'd sold her the horse, back in better times, and she did not mistake his scowl of resentment at the reminder. He worked beeswax into leather straps at the stoop of his establishment. His scowl deepened as it sunk in that she did not intend to pass him by.

"Good morning, Mister Grant." Knowing she would not be treated kindly, she resisted further pleasantries.

"What do you want?" To her horror, Grant's hand strayed from his leather work to rest on the butt of his sidearm. The man was a veteran of more wars than most and no stranger to violence, but what measure of threat did he suppose her to present? She was armed, of course, but the old lizard-rifle holstered along the gelding's flank was no serious threat.

Businesslike, she said, "Water, feed and fresh shoes for my mount. A mule fitted with saddle bags and a cargo litter. Load up a month's store of dried fruit and oats."

"Why would I do business with a traitor's kin?"

Doing her best to pretend the gun didn't exist, Molly dismounted. "You're not in business with me, but Colonel Tempest. If you dislike what I've got to say, you'd best take the matter to her door."

She held her breath. She was not quite ready to believe in the power of the Colonel's name to reopen slammed doors.

Grant spat in the silvery dirt. "It'll be five carricks. Come back tomorrow. "

The price was twice what the order was worth. Molly exhaled slowly and said, "Five it is. And I'll be back in two hours, hostler."

She handed him the reins and turned for her next appointment to conceal the quiver in her bottom lip.

"What you got to be so cut up about?" Bill demanded as he fell in step beside her. She looked curiously about, wondering if other folk saw him too, but their heads pointedly turned, or they spat and muttered insults and curses. She could not be certain one way or the other.

"Ezekiel was a friend once," she said. The old soldier always had a kind word as she'd passed on the way to her dressmaker's shop. When Bill had signed his regimental papers and put on the uniform of the Stonechurch Brothers Mining Company, Ezekiel Grant made a solemn promise to watch over his little sister while he was away at war. His word was good until the day the first reports of Bill's treachery arrived. A frost settled in his heart she could never warm.

"Friend? You don't need friends like that. I got a good mind to come back in the night and knock a candle over in the stalls while he's abed with that Sunjali whore of his."

He was baiting her, working himself into a righteous rant.

Could he make good on his threats? She wasn't sure. She thought he had moved things around at the shack, to vex her or put them where he thought they ought to go. As for cold-blooded killing? Well, he'd shown himself capable, hadn't he?

Molly spoke under her breath. "Your wars are done, Big Bill. I don't need you to fight mine."

"I'll do what I got to, to protect my own."

She reckoned he didn't even know he was lying, so she let the matter settle.

She paid her second call to the provisioners, two Sunjali sisters named Verity and Mercy, who ran Uncle Key's General Supplies. They had arrived on a train full of golden-skinned, violet-eyed immigrants and immediately bought out old Mister Cooper with a brick of bullion. Since then they'd expanded their business and built a schoolhouse. Mirror Spring grudgingly acknowledged them as pillars of the refugee community.

"You are not welcome here," announced Verity as Molly stepped through the threshold. She was the taller sister, with the wider hips and more convincing smile. "Go away."

Molly folded her arms and leaned against the jamb.

Mercy tugged her sister's bonnet down so she could whisper a string of drumbeat Sunjalese into her ear. Verity's brow furrowed as she whispered back. Their brief argument seemed to encompass a dozen inconclusive exchanges, like a street shootout between cross eyed gun fighters.

Finally Mercy waved her sister away and plucked a slate from the counter. "Tell me your requirements, then you can leave. I will send them to your...residence."

As Molly recited her list, Bill sidled past her to a small cage of iron bars and wire mesh. Inside was a collection of used shooter's pieces ranging from the decorative to the coldly functional. He reached inside, unperturbed by the barrier, and with one finger spun the barrel on a long-arm five-shooter with mahogany grips. Verity looked up sharply at the noise and clucked her tongue, not quite firing off an accusatory look in Molly's direction.

"One for each eye," intoned Bill, twinning his fingers to point at the sisters in turn, "and one left spare if there's no brain to be hit."

Molly grimaced. To cover the reaction, she said "I see you're still wearing that pretty skirt I made, Mercy. Your sister too. Glad to see your objections to my custom don't extend to our past dealings. I hope they still bring you good fortunes on rainy days."

Mercy scratched at the slate in the slash-and-jab script of her people, not meeting Molly's eye. "I have no grudge with you, Bright," she said. "You played no part in your brother's decisions, I am sure."

"Then why are we not on friendly terms?"

"Because you are bad for business. Me, my sister, we've made our place here. We grow strong roots together. Strong roots means wide branches. Wide branches mean shade for other Sunjali people. We look after them, they look up to us. We're respected, which makes Sunjali people more respectable."

Molly nodded unhappily. "And if dealing with me offends the older families, they'll take their custom elsewhere and you'll be out of business."

"Yes. No shady tree, no respectability. Then the Sunjali people end up where you are. I feel sorrow for your bad luck, Bright, but we have our own to think of."

"Maybe soon things will change." Molly hated herself for grabbing at the thin line of hope the Colonel's patronage held out. She couldn't help it. Her loneliness blindsided her like a shot in the back.

Mercy's tight lips almost formed a smile. "When that day comes I will order you to make me a brand new green dress that makes my customers careless with their money. Today, you leave by the back door. If you need things, send someone. Don't call here again."

Molly held the tears in until the door slammed behind her. Then she dropped onto the second step and sobbed, ignoring the stares of the goats and the mud-haired boy tending them in the yard beyond, and the heated Sunjali chatter coming from inside. When her distress drained out enough to stand again, she palmed her eyes dry.

"Well, then," she said, to nobody in particular. "Hearts are set against you, Molly Bright. There's nothing to be done about that."

"Sister, you can always change hearts if you got the right words. Or if that don't work, then deeds will."

Big Bill kicked at a goat to move it on from a water trough and sat down. He turned the mahogany-gripped pistol over and over in his hands, inspecting it with fierce eyes. When he levered the barrel forward, she saw the chambers were snug with bullets.

Was he a little more solid than before, with a shooting iron in his hand? She glanced at the boy, but he was soothing the startled goat and didn't look their way.

"You stole from the sisters?"

Bill sneered. "They won't miss it. Filthy Sunnies. And what do you care, when they treat you like a dog made for kicking?"

Molly quashed her first instinct, to go back inside and make amends. Nothing she could think to say would be taken well. Verity was probably ready to shoot her as a trespasser.

"Don't take my part, Bill," she said again, feeling the futility of the words as an ache in her chest. "I carry my own burdens. I don't look to the dead for succour."

Bill looked up at the sun as it slid past noon. He didn't blink. "Hush now, Molly. Your big brother's taking care of things. Now you get on. You got the most important appointment still to go."

Gnawing on the inside of her lip, Molly reached out to squeeze his shoulder, trying to appear just as grateful as she could. Her fingers closed over warm smoke, feeling nothing but a tingle under her nails. Bill shied away, swiping at her fingers like she was a bothersome fly. "Away with you, sister. Ain't you got the sense to know the difference between what's living and what's dead?"

Molly thought about the question another way. How was she to deal with a spectre who could not be swayed with force any more than words?

#

Balthazar Stonechurch, Gentleman Tailor.

The oversized sign suspended over the porch was a work of art in rich oils imported from back east and silver hammered tissue-fine by a master blacksmith. It depicted a moustachioed young man with slicked black hair and a superior smirk, with gleaming scissors in one hand and a length of royal purple fabric draped over the other arm.

Molly snorted, though quietly, and pushed on a door panel where the same scene was replicated in miniature. Three bells chimed in ascending tones. She took in a clutter of multi-coloured fabrics, sample outfits and half-dressed mannequins. Then Balthazar himself appeared, gliding like a skater on an oily winter lake.

He grinned like a fox in a coop. "It appears my eyesight is failing. The infamous Molly Bright? What a rare and indescribable pleasure." He looked like he did in the painting, though reality had applied a wash of hostility. "The circumstances must be extraordinary for you to transgress the town limits."

"I'm only here to purchase supplies, Mister Stonechurch. It's not my intention to ignite discord between us."

A twitch crossed Balthazar's painted-on smile, like a viper slithering between shadows. Molly tensed, expecting a slap or worse. It never came, though his hand surely flirted with the notion.

"I guess you've forgotten some pertinent history, young miss," he said in a voice all hollowed-out and filled with wasps. "I guess you maybe don't recall how your brother turned his coat for a bag of enemy gold? How he and his miserable dog pack led a company of Calendar Men right to my Uncle Able's camp? Or how they all got cut up where they slept? I guess that might have slipped your mind."

Molly held her ground as his face drew close. Her own face was turning as red as Balthazar's, on account of her bated breath. She didn't dare let it go or look away.

"Your brother was a bushwhacking assassin, missy! My father turned you out of town because you have the same filthy venom in your blood. You should have done us all a favour and spilled it out in the slag heaps."

"A bushwhacker, am I?"

A shadow appeared behind Balthazar Stonechurch. Bill Bright set a hat of pressed rabbit fur atop his long blonde locks. His pistol was pointed at the ceiling. He lowered the barrel to nuzzle the back of Balthazar's head. Balthazar's furious glower cracked a touch but he reached down and pulled his own pistol a half-inch free of its holster.

"Give me one damn reason why I shouldn't do to you what your kin did to mine!"

Before either man could resolve himself to an act of murder, Molly started talking. "You might shoot me down, Mister Stonechurch, and I don't imagine it would nag at your conscience to know I'm unarmed. But let's have no myths or misconceptions between us. My brother did wrong by you and yours, no doubt. If a preacher told me there's no worse crime between men, I'd nod and sing allayla with the congregation. But that's not why Stonechurch Senior denounced me as a traitor before the town, is it? It's not why he dragged me by my hair and threw me in the dirt."

"You say not?"

She folded her arms, digging fingernails in hard to steady herself.

"What I say is, his little war was coming to an end without his only son - a man in his majority with his eyesight and extremities in good working order - ever taking up arms on his behalf. If ever a man needed a good distraction from the shortcomings of his progeny, it was your father. My misfortune was to be a convenient scapegoat just when he needed one."

Balthazar's pistol slipped clear of its confinement. "Did you call me a coward, Miss Bright?"

"I did not. It's nobody's business but your own why you didn't ride out to war, nor even why you didn't go into your father's mining trade. You must thank the Fates your mother showed you how to cut a cloth and thread a needle before she passed on. Handy skills to have right when Mirror Springs needed them." She waved a careless hand at the half-finished waistcoat on his work bench, all uneven stitches, misaligned lining and not a thread of fortune, good or ill, woven into the fabric. "Though it takes more than a well-positioned store and a pair of sharp scissors to make a tailor, Mister Stonechurch."

The pistol came up.

Bill's teeth glinted with feral glee from the shadows as he thumbed back his hammer.

Balthazar Stonechurch said, "I ought to-"

Molly said "You won't, sir, or you would have done it by now. Put the pistol away and let's speak with civility. I don't hold a grudge against you or your father. Consider whether you truly have cause to say different."

He stared at her eyes along the shaking sight of his pistol for what seemed like forever. Bill's grin became a scowl as the moment drew on, and under Molly's determined gaze, which took in both the living man and the dead one equally, he withered. He holstered his pistol. A moment later, Balthazar followed suit.

"I know why you're here," he said quietly.

"I expect you do. And you'll give me what I ask for, because otherwise you'll have to do the job yourself. Colonel Tempest means to court your father in a splendid coat, and if my brains are splattered all over what used to be my own shop, then there's nobody else to make it but you."

"This empty sack of feathers ain't worth a bullet," said Bill.

Balthazar said, "Not me. My father may be partial to her but I don't owe that damned woman a thing." His defiance fell flat. Even out of her hearing, Colonel Tempest was not easily stood up to.

Not unkindly, Molly said, "It's a hard thing sometimes, to reconcile ourselves to the concerns of others. Most especially family."

She felt no real sympathy for Balthazar Stonechurch, who drew arms on her to protect his own ego, who cheered on her debasement by which he profited, whose late mother had coddled him into brittle spoilage, and who had more in common with her brother than either of them knew. He was an indifferent tailor and a coward. Time and patient education might cure both conditions, but if so they would be furnished by some other teacher than Molly Bright.

"If that's settled, then let's get to the matter at hand." She led him around the shop, choosing fabrics and supplies, and carefully withholding her opinions on the placement of the displays.

As he transferred her selections to the counter and wrapped them in paper, he attempted to offer explanations of his conduct. None of them sounded more apologetic than self-centred, so Molly cut him off each time with a firm, "It's none of my business, Mister Stonechurch."

He was still grieving a mother more than three years in the grave, she surmised. Commendable maternal loyalty, perhaps, but demonstrating a loose grasp on the realities of the present. Colonel Tempest would capture his father's hand as ably as she'd conducted any military manoeuvre. Molly's best advice, were she to offer it, would be to get used to the idea. She didn't offer, knowing she wouldn't be heard. The bitterness Balthazar nourished would poison his family sooner or later.

"I should have killed him," said Bill later, as she loaded her purchases onto the litter of a complaining mule. Both the mule and her brother shared the air of an irascible drunk.

"What good would that have done me? I could hardly escape blame for a murder when every eye in town has been on me all day."

"I'd be protecting your honour, Moll."

"What honour would that be? Big Bill, if you want to busy yourself hunting out the pieces of my honour, look under boot heels and behind angry whispers. Meanwhile I'll get on with just getting on."

She rode back to her house in the desert in solitary silence. Maybe she'd given Big Bill something to think about. More likely he just went off in a sulk somewhere.

The dog was lying in the porch's shade when she returned. It raised one ear at her approach but otherwise did not start as she unloaded the mule. In Molly's judgment it was the finest company she'd kept all day.

#

Molly made the coat in seven days.

Colonel Tempest made it clear she didn't want to see it until it was ready for the final fitting. The celebratory ball was scheduled for Gallowsbreath Eve, an occasion marking the year's turn into autumn and, according to tradition, an auspicious moment for signing business contracts and peace accords. The date was still a week off when Molly sent word back with the brothers that the Colonel should visit. She arrived that afternoon.

"You're still wearing your uniform, Colonel?"

"I don't plan to remove it until the cotillion, when I'll tender my papers to Stonechurch himself. Until I resign my commission formally, I'm still a serving officer." Officer or not, she swept her hat onto a hook and loosened her necktie.

"I need to make a few final adjustments," said Molly as she showed the Colonel through the door. The Colonel gave no sign she'd heard as she circled the display mannequin, which Molly had positioned to catch the best of the afternoon light.

"Oh my."

The coat was indisputably magnificent. Its deep rich blue seemed to drag in the light around it and reflect it in a violet aura. Hints of bottle greens and cherry reds rippled in reflected light, only to vanish like pond fish before the eye could fix them. Its brass buttons were polished to a red-blushed gold. The same rich glare trimmed the cuffs and hem. The collar was high and rigid enough to stand on. The shoulders and hips flared at angles that would have given an insane architect pause. It gave an impression of hard and soft layers, as if it could stop a bullet or swaddle an infant. The thought might have occurred to the Colonel, who reached out two fingers and then pulled them back as if suddenly singed.

"Do you want to try it on?" asked Molly when she judged the silence had stretched out long enough.

The Colonel shrugged out of her soldiering coat and let it fall without taking her eyes from the coat. When Molly lifted it from the mannequin, the Colonel found it difficult to turn away.

Molly settled it in place and stepped back with a critical eye. "I thought I might have to take in the right cuff. And it's riding a little high in the rear, but that's easily mended. How does it sit with you, Colonel?"

The Colonel looked from one outstretched arm to the other, gazed over her shoulder and turned like a dog chasing its tail. Her mouth was a line but the rest of her face seemed to have caught a serious case of delight.

"It sits mighty fine, Molly Bright. It's most satisfactory."

Molly allowed the corner of her mouth to rise.

"I believe I got your shape just so."

"You've got a rare talent, woman. This outfit flatters a figure I don't even have. When he sees me dressed like this, that old coot's going to have a stroke before I can get him to the altar, if I don't watch myself."

Molly circled the Colonel with a mirror-glass. She noted an eyebrow twitch that confirmed her opinion on the garment's rear end, but knew she'd exceeded expectations. "It won't take but a night to make these adjustments, Colonel. Will you return in the morning or shall I have it delivered?"

Colonel Tempest made a sad sound as she removed the coat and surrendered it to Molly's care, but her following words had a flat demand to them. "Neither one. You'll bring them yourself to my quarters on the evening of the cotillion. I'll have my man prepare a supper and we'll dress together."

Molly's back stiffened. "What do you mean?"

"I'm damned if I'm attending a commemorative gathering in my own dismal company when I could have a fetching companion stride in on my arm." The Colonel looked her up and down. "Not in these dusty rags though. I trust you've left yourself sufficient time to fashion something suitable?"

"What? But I can't accompany you, Colonel." Molly heard the stain of fear in her words but could do nothing to scrub them clean. "I can't -"

"Can and will, Miss Bright." She didn't add "That's an order" but Molly heard the words all the same. "You want to worm your way back into the good graces of Mirror Springs? Then you'll do what I say."

Colonel Tempest unknotted her necktie with a tug and tossed it at Molly with a playful smile. Molly's quick hands caught the cloth faster than she caught the intention. The Colonel smirked as understanding registered. This was the Colonel's favour, and Molly her favourite.

"But you're courting Mister Stonechurch," she protested. She was still too surprised to drop the scarf or throw it as far away as possible.

"So I recall." The Colonel's fingers plucked open the button at her throat, then the button below it for good measure.

And just like that, Big Bill was back, lurking in the shadowed corner. "That don't matter to her none," he observed bitterly. "She's a vixen in heat. Ain't never out of it, truth to say. When we was out riding the range, there was a fresh new rabbit wrapped in her bedroll every night. It didn't matter who, neither - enlisted girls, trail cooks, even the banner boy, and he was about the ugliest kid I ever seen. She slept with every one of her captains, one after another." Bill spat, raising a sizzling sound from the floorboards. His eyes glowed a mean shade of green.

Molly gasped. "Is that true?"

"What's that, little dressmaker?" Another button popped, showing a deep canyon of sun-browned skin.

"I - er, did you lie abed with my brother William? Ma'am?"

The plucking fingers paused over their next button. The Colonel's mouth quirked into a bemused line but ardour alone didn't account for the new colour on her cheeks. "What a curious enquiry, Molly Bright. What makes you ask that?"

"It's true, isn't it? My brother was your lover."

The Colonel stepped close. Molly didn't dare retreat, though the smell of horse sweat, waxed leather and fresh soap threatened to overpower her. "I didn't figure he was the type for dutiful correspondence with the folks back home. Much less a letter recounting intimacies. I guess even a man like that can surprise you."

She leaned in until they were almost touching and whispered into Molly's ear, "Yes, dear, I bedded him. Once, twice and again. He had some steel between his legs, did your brother, and I certainly appreciated his command of the mechanics. But come now - how should that come between the two of us?"

"How should-? She hanged me dead, Moll!" exploded Big Bill, all the more infuriated for being ignored.

Molly ignored him. "We had an agreement Colonel. This strikes me as a sweeping change in its conditions." She glanced down when the Colonel's fingers resumed their downward progress and quickly looked up again. She was running low on fixed buttons.

"Nothing's changed. I'm just now expanding on the details, that's all. You took me at my word I would kindle some goodwill out of the ashes, and so I shall. You didn't enquire about my methods, so let me correct that oversight. No letter of commendation will scrub that black from your name, Miss Bright. My word might be good enough to get you served at that Sunjali flea market, and maybe nobody would throw a rock in your direction, but that's the limit of it. Every minute you set foot in Mirror Springs, it'll be one small cut after another. Harsh words. Sniggering. Maybe some spittin' from those with no better upbringing. And you'll never sit by a window again whereupon it won't get broken."

The fingers finished their work and took up stations on the Colonel's belt.

"You paint a dismal picture of my future, Colonel, but I'm well familiar with its contents. How will you deliver me from it?"

"Stonechurch is going to accept my proposal." Her confidence struck Molly as military. "And why not? He gets a good looking hero to swing a whip over his business dealings, charm his dinner guests and slap a little spine into his dung-eating son. Once in a while I'll give him a frisky night to keep him lively. But it'll be on my terms, you see?"

"I'm not sure that I do," said Molly, but her sinking heart told her otherwise.

"He gets a legal wife. He doesn't get a say in my affairs. It's my business alone if I take a concubine."

"Me?"

"Think about it, dear. If you're the kept woman of the most powerful woman in the province, who's going to say a word against you? All you've got to do is whisper a name in our bed and they'd be out of a job, run out of town or just beaten to a carcass on my word. Once it's known you're my personal girl, you become untouchable. No more uncivil words or threats against your person. You could even set yourself back in business."

"And all I would need to do is whatever you command?"

"I'll keep you safe, Molly Bright. On my word. And it won't be so bad as you think. It's not only men I know how to satisfy."

Molly flushed and hated herself for it. The only way she could think to suppress the heat billowing through her was to let it out. "Like you satisfied my brother, Colonel?"

She'd intended it as a barb, a signal of her displeasure. The Colonel smiled warmly and slowly drew her shirt to one side. Molly couldn't help but look.

Past the swell of her breast with its hard dark nipple, the skin of the Colonel's side and stomach was a blackberry thicket of scars, burns and unidentifiable lumps. She grabbed Molly's hand and drew her fingers down, down, down, until they rested on a hollow nook surrounded by scar tissue and tiny perfect beads of sweat. "You feel that, Molly?"

Not trusting her voice to come out right through a closed-over throat, Molly nodded.

"That there is where your brother shot me."

"That was an accident!" Bill declared.

"He swore himself blue that it was an accident," the Colonel said. "He was just cleaning it, so he claimed, and it went off in his hand."

The rim of the cratered skin was calloused. Molly's fingers traced its circumference of their own accord; they were as distant to her as friends and safety. "That's why you ended the relationship?"

"Hell's hot winds, no! Our coupling was done and buried in the cold earth a week before that. I concluded I didn't care for his character and told him to get back to his own bedroll. I never trusted that sidewinding smirk of his."

"So you think he deliberately shot you out of jealousy?"

The Colonel's hand closed over Molly's and held it against the skin of her belly. "I think William Bright was a charming smile laid across a pit full of spite. He meant it all right. If he hadn't fled that night, he'd have faced a court of his fellow officers."

"A guilty verdict would have brought a death sentence?"

The Colonel nodded. "None of us ever expected to see him again, knowing a rope awaited him. But none of us reckoned on the depth of his spite, because a week later he led a pack of bushwhackers into my camp. Before we put them down, they killed five good men and women, including our patron's only brother. So yes, Miss Molly Bright, I certainly believe he intended my death and worked hard to earn his own."

Molly's feet finally found their will and she retreated from the Colonel and the roar inside her own head. Her rear bumped the foot of her camp cot bed; she held her footing. The Colonel's grin didn't fade one bit.

Bill said, "Do it, Little Moll. You fall back on that cot. That's all the invitation she'll need. You need hardly do nothing to keep her occupied but grab her hair and make whatever noises come out. She'll do the rest. And when she wears herself out and falls asleep, I'll choke her dead like I shoulda done our first night." He rubbed his hands on his dusty thighs as if he could raise sparks with the friction.

Swallowing hard, Molly said "I'm very sorry for my brother's conduct, Colonel. I believe you must have known him at his worst. I can only imagine how you must have felt when he betrayed you. I wish I could take it back on his behalf. But this proposition of yours has come as a shock to me and I'm not altogether sure how to take it."

The Colonel closed the gap between them again. Molly was pressed from both sides. "What's to consider? You want your life back, don't you?"

"That's what troubles me, Colonel. It wouldn't quite be my old life, would it?" Molly's hands found their way to the Colonel's lean hips and applied a firm pressure to them. "I'll need to think on your offer whilst I finish my commission. I believe my thoughts will be clearer if I'm left alone with them, if you take my meaning."

The Colonel raised her hands in mock surrender and let Molly have her breathing space back. "If that's how you want it, Molly Bright, then so be it. I never bedded a soul, man or woman, who didn't want to be there." She rebuttoned the shirt, one insolent snap of her fingers at a time. "But my terms are my terms. You get me? I want you at that dance looking like a princess' dream. I can wait on your answer as to the rest. Stay in this dusty snake pit the rest of your days if you like, darning lucky socks and honouring your unworthy dead. Or take your place back in Mirror Springs as a respectable woman of business with a lover who'll see to your needs. Are you that bull-stubborn you'd throw away your chance at comfort for a shred of dignity you don't have in hand?"

She finished restoring her uniform to order. "Six days to the cotillion, Miss Bright. I'll see you with my coat and your doll-gown at noon and I'll have your answer before midnight."

She closed the cabin door behind her with a firm thump. Molly stood still until the sound of hoof beats receded into the night. Then she removed the scissors stashed beneath her pillow and slumped, exhausted, on the bed.

"Should have let me kill her, Little Moll." Bill's teeth ground with every word, like he was holding his jaw closed to keep from bellowing in fury. "That woman gets her hooks in you, only two ways it can go. Either she gets bored of you and pokes her beau Stonechurch into a jealousy to finish what he started, or she takes a real shine and you never get a say in your own affairs again. It's poison she's offering. Comes down to how you want it to taste."

As much as she didn't want to hear from Bill's ghost, she couldn't see how he was wrong. Even now the memory of the Colonel's skin felt like a fading burn across her fingers and palm. Molly hadn't touched anyone that way since before her father died. The Colonel's offer was all temptations, from the restoration of her establishment to the civility, however forced, of Mirror Springs, to the rest of that tanned, hard-worn skin.

She could have what she had, or close to it. Close enough? She didn't know yet. She hadn't lied about that.

"Bill, how is it you had so much hate you tried to kill her, and those others too?"

Bill leaned low over her bed, like he planned to kiss her or smother her with her own pillow. She wasn't sure his feet were touching the floorboards. "She can't be satisfied," he growled, oblivious to her discomfort. "She'd have eaten up the whole regiment and never filled that gap."

"Why?"

"Because she don't think she's got an equal." Bill reached out to stroke her hair. To her tremendous relief, she felt nothing but a small static shock. He pulled his hand back into a fist.

"You didn't answer my question, Bill. What got into your head?"

Bill laughed, a throaty, unkind noise.

"Is that why you think I came back? To furnish you with explanations and settle your conscience? It ain't."

Molly grimaced as she met his eye. The realisation struck her that her fear of Bill had rooted her for a long while. Now all she could feel was a numb shame. "Then I'll have to guess."

"Suit yourself."

"You didn't care to be answerable to a woman, did you? Not in the field of battle and definitely not in your bed. I don't know how long you bit your tongue for, but I'll bet it wasn't long, and I bet when it came out, it came out harsh. You said something disrespectful or impertinent, and she put you in your place, didn't she? I bet that sat just as well as a ninety gallon hat."

Bill stared at her like she'd found a way to reach out and slap his ghost face. "Moll, don't you going dishonouring me. You think I'm gonna stand here and have you say them things about me?"

"I haven't said anything yet, but I'll say more. Did you play it rough? Did you take liberties without permission and afterwards tell her you thought that's what she wanted?"

"Hey, now, you shut up." Bill rose up above Molly's head, face twisting like a sack in the wind.

"She cast you out of her sight because you were a short-tempered mongrel dog who was quick with his teeth. And you showed her she was right by trying to shoot her dead. When that didn't work, you took up the company of obliging killers to finish the job."

Bill howled, "It ain't like that!" But the gun was in his hand. A glint of moonlight made a silver ring around the end of the barrel. Molly blinked as the gun erupted like the summer storm, brighter and louder than anything. The pillow alongside her ear coughed up scorched goose down and the floorboards cracked.

A little trail of grey smoke trailed up around her face in the silence that followed. Bill turned the gun over and back as if shocked it had fired. Molly waited impassively for him to meet her eye; somehow the pistol held greater fascination.

At last he said, "Don't test me none, Molly. Don't question my judgment. I've earned my revenge, else why would I be delivered the means to enact it? That woman deserves my wrath. You'd best not try to prevent me from visiting it upon her flesh."

Molly said, "Yes, Bill. I see you won't be deterred from your course." A tear fell from her eye, and in his expression she saw satisfaction. Never mind the tear arose from the irritating pillow smoke, it suited Molly just fine for him to believe she repented her harsh words.

She rose from the bed and washed her face in the basin.

"I'm going now," announced Bill, returning to a more natural elevation. The pistol hung by his side, no holster to stow it in. Though it had appeared in his hand from nowhere, he did not seem to know the trick of returning it. "I'll go check on the trail. Make sure she really left."

Molly splashed more water as Bill opened the door. The sand-coloured dog lay on the stoop. It perked its ears up and trotted in, ignoring Bill. He cocked the pistol's hammer and raised it, but Molly shook her head. "Leave it, Bill. It'll calm my nerves to have some company while you're gone."

He nodded and vanished, leaving the door open to the night.

Molly set the washbasin on the floor. The dog began to lap up a messy drink.

She brushed a speck of feather off the shoulder of the Colonel's coat, repeating the gesture until her hands stopped shaking. "Seems a shame," she told the dog, but it ignored her in its thirst.

The locked trunk in the corner of her shack had laid there a long while, with its unused key attached by a cheap length of twine. Molly unlocked it and hefted the lid open. Inside was a collection of measly effects: boots, a hat, a tarnished pocket watch and a liver-shaped money belt. A bundle of letters from their father, written to his offspring from his deathbed, in which he set out his hopes and expectations for their future prosperity; each was addressed to "William Bright Junior." Underneath, a pistol and a belt of ammunition. Yet another letter, from the Stonechurch Brothers' military quartermaster, explained how most of Bill's clothes were missing because they were burned with his corpse. His wages and the cash missing from the belt had been donated towards his victims' burial expenses.

Molly reached in and pulled out the hat. From inside the brim she plucked a long hair and held it up to the light of the moon.

"Seems a shame," she said again, "but I can't see any other way."

#

On the morning of the Cotillion, Molly Bright packed her personal belongings into the trunk. She left the household effects in their usual positions; sooner or later, some other soul would have need of an outsider's dwelling. She folded the Colonel's coat in a stiff flax blanket which would not shed stray fibres, and added layers of paper bound with string for good measure. It took pride of place at the summit of the loaded donkey. Her own dress went in a saddle bag, though she treated it with no less care.

Then she snuffed her lantern, hitched the door closed and said goodbye to the Venom Gully shack for what she imagined was the last time. As she rode her gelding towards Mirror Springs, leading the indifferent donkey, the rangy mutt fell in with her again.

Bill was nowhere to be seen. For a time Molly considered whether she'd misjudged his determination to sour her affairs. Unlikely. He was probably just saving his strength for the moment of greatest chaos.

At the outskirts of the town, as the scratchy brush of the desert fringe gave ground to the patchy grass and broad-leafed bushes sprouting in the vicinity of the springs, suspicious eyes fell upon Molly. The dog whined, cautious and low, and dragged its heels until it fell well behind her plodding mounts.

"It's all right," she told it. "You don't need to worry about me anymore. I'm protected, you see."

The dog dropped into the dust with its chin laid flat and huffed.

Molly smiled back at it. "You go about your business, and I'll see to mine. When my situation is settled, I'll find you. It'll be nice to have a friend with me sometimes."

The dog rose and turned, trotting back in the direction of the shack. Molly watched it go with a hard lump growing in her throat. She rode through the town, leading her diminished menagerie. She met every hostile eye with a half-smile and an unblinking look. This provoked a range of variations on a frown -

disbelieving, disapproving, bemused and one or two in the fashion of teeth-baring hostility. No one outstared her, and soon they found other directions to look.

The Colonel's house rose up like a fresh bloom on Finality Hill. She'd ordered it built while she was away at war, which the townsfolk had taken as a gallant gesture of confidence in the conflict's outcome. Molly suspected it had more to do with cultivating the legend of Colonel Tempest. She led her team up the crushed-rock path past newly planted flower beds and a garden setting overlooking the market stores and houses set along the western bank of the stream. A gang of men with picks and shovels, stripped to the waist and baring their military frames and regimental tattoos, broke rocks for a stone wall encircling the house. They kept their eyes to their labours.

Molly tethered the animals to the hill's one old feature: the great spreading spikewood tree after which the hill was named. In the early days of Mirror Springs, when the silver rush was at its acrimonious and lawless height, Finality had served as gallows for those deemed too murderous for even that wild frontier to bear. Its ongoing existence was another message from the Colonel to the town, by Molly's interpretation.

A Sunjali man wearing the Colonel's household blue-and-gold met her at the front step. He wordlessly directed her to a suspended chair lined with cushions; when she sat, he applied brushes and polish to her boots, top and bottom, until they shone spotless. She stood, and he circled her with a second set of brushes, clearing away the evidence of her journey. When he at last nodded his satisfaction, she looked like she'd just stepped away from her dresser.

"Thank you," she said, adding, "I am Molly Bright."

The servant nodded with a small quirk of his lips but did not offer his own name in return. He led her through a door with a stained glass portrait of the Colonel in full uniform, saluting with her sabre.

The furnishings were new and clustered, as if their final positioning had yet to be determined. The interior smelled of oils, waxing polish and woodrind: the distinctive yellow-grey paint that adorned most of Mirror Springs' buildings, made from ground talcum and feldspar mixed though the gummy sap of chalkleaf shrubs.

Molly was led to a sitting room. The Colonel reclined on a day bed, dressed in carelessly-secured Sunjali pyjamas, plucking a crisp pinching-march from a seven-stringed taramba. She finished the piece before she looked up at Molly.

"I knew you wouldn't run," she told Molly. "I made a bet with Justice."

The manservant bowed. "My Colonel, you placed your trust wisely. I see now what you saw at once." Molly heard falsity in the words, but the Colonel smiled indulgently and waved him into silence with a look of satisfaction. He produced a silver coffee set from an adjoining room, arranging sour tarts and filling cups as the women spoke.

Molly said, "I gave my word, Colonel. I've never done so lightly."

"I'm pleased. Does this mean you're favourably disposed to my proposition?" The Colonel sipped the tarry skin off her coffee, savouring it with lidded eyes and flared nostrils.

Molly drew a healthy draught of her own and set the cup on the small table before her knees. The urge to look over her shoulder tugged at her chin. She resisted. If Bill were to surprise her at this moment, all was lost. She held to faith that he would not.

"I will accept on one condition, Colonel."

"Another condition, Molly Bright? You've a wilful soul, haven't you?" Displeasure rippled at her throat and temples. Molly pressed on before it could build.

"It is no great inconvenience, Colonel, I assure you. You will have satisfaction before the evening is done. But I will not offer my word until you don the coat I made for you."

The Colonel rose with energetic decision. "Is that all? Justice, bring Miss Bright's packages in. I'll put it on this minute and toast our unity."

"Don't be hasty, Colonel," said Molly, setting a hand on the Colonel's arm in what she hoped seemed a comforting familiarity. "You may still keep your promise, for my surrender will not precede your own."

"Whatever do you mean?" The note of irritation was back. But the Colonel did not try to shake off Molly's hand, so she knew she was safe.

"Only that I cannot consent to your company until you have resigned your office and the paraphernalia that goes with it. When you shed the uniform in which you hanged my brother, I'll swear myself to your heart." When the Colonel's tiny frown would not flatten, she added, "I only hope you can see the conflict your kindness inspires, Colonel. I could not bear the constant reminders of my brother's craven treachery, nor of his final agony."

Molly thought she ought to weep a scattering of tears as the bereaved sister. She could not bring herself to add so crass a performance to her crimes of omission.

The Colonel raised her cup and drained it with measured slurps. Her knuckles were white and the small finger shivered against the base of the cup like a drummer's salute. Molly swallowed slowly, to avoid the appearance of nerves or parody.

"I understand. Of course I do. But I have a condition of my own." The Colonel's voice was like the singing spin of a well-oiled pistol cylinder. She reclined on her lounge and adopted a leisurely pose. "I've been pondering this dress you made. I figure it's every bit as much my commission as the coat. So I want to see it. Before anyone else lays eyes upon it, you understand. For my sight alone."

Molly stammered, "If you can direct me to a dressing chamber, Colonel, I'll be happy to -"

"No," snapped the Colonel. "I mean right here."

"What?" Even knowing it was coming, the Colonel's hungry calculation set Molly's heart roaring like a creek in flood. In the moment, panic almost hooked her. She fought down the instinct to look over her shoulder.

"You step out of those road rags you're in and out of whatever smalls you've got. I mean to see what goods I'm promised, Molly Bright, cloth and skin alike."

An outraged retort rose in her - "I'm not your purchase! I'm not your prize of war!" - but Molly won that battle too. The words went unspoken.

"Justice has already dusted you off but I believe on closer inspection I may find a spot or two he missed," said the Colonel. "Once we get the desert off your hide, we can work on putting you back together like a proper lady of town. Layer by layer from the skin out, till there's nobody could say you were ever otherwise."

With meek little movements like darts of shame, Molly closed her eyes and began to unravel bows, loosen binds and unhook buttons.

She thought it best not to hurry too much.

#

No place in Mirror Springs was grand enough for the cotillion but the residence of Jeremiah Stonechurch. Though Stonechurch Senior's indifference to both society and architecture was long evident, his late wife Charlotte dedicated herself to the betterment of both aspects of the town. A preponderance of narrow-gabled roofs and arched entry ways adorned almost every structure erected since her arrival, the most prolific evidence of her influence. The oversized dance hall now known with some affection as Charlotte's Jamboree was by far her most ostentatious contribution to the social fabric.

When Molly Bright stepped through a cascade of iridescent curtains on the arm of Colonel Tempest, the horn pipe-band's music and the gathered worthies' conversations continued uninterrupted. But sly glances turned in their direction. Molly wanted to wilt under the sear of gazes, but the Colonel's grip would have none of it. She allowed herself to be steered to the centre of the dance hall where, beneath a seven-armed candelabra puffing smoke into a ceiling vent, gathered the Stonechurch entourage.

The Colonel commanded their attention as she bowed in the cavalry style; one knee bent and the trailing foot thrust behind. The tip of her scabbard scraped across the tiles, scratching a trail in their dull mirrored sheen. Her hat, coat and military breeches were patched and presented in an enviable condition, all the work of Justice the servant.

"Mister Stonechurch," she intoned, dipping low for her intended. She turned upon Balthazar, and now Molly did not mistake the ironic gravity in her tone. "Young Master Stonechurch. Honoured worthies of the community. Your kind hospitality puts me to shame. May I present my companion, Mistress Molly Bright?"

Stonechurch Senior was a desert bird. He was as withered and scrawny as a packless dog. His eyes never stilled, always searching, calculating and weighing up prospects. Molly preferred to look past him, but the Colonel's instructions were not to be ignored. She greeted the company with the traditional dip at the knees, with which the tight ribbons strapped about her waist and hips did not much interfere.

"Gentlemen," she said. Terseness was also against the Colonel's edict, but she did not quite trust herself to embark on polite conversation with her chief antagonist and his coterie. "Pleasant evening to you."

To his credit, Jeremiah Stonechurch did not demur; he kissed first the Colonel's hand, with a relish that seemed to entertain the idea of taking a bite, then Molly's. The mercifully brief contact felt like a gravel burn.

"She's got no business here." One Stonechurch loyalist broke ranks and pointed a red finger at Molly. "The Chamber turned her out. Fancy skirts or no, she can't come a-dancin' with decent folk."

The Colonel pretended to consider the declaration's merits, a twitch of vicious humour working the muscle along her jaw. "I don't reckon you heard me clearly, Mister Roderick." Her voice was a battlefield bugle that carried to every corner. "This is my companion. Decent folk needn't concern themselves. I'm taking all her dances for myself."

Roderick the loyalist squared his shoulders for further disputation but the Colonel threw a companionable arm about his neck and wheeled him to face the elder Stonechurch. "If that's acceptable to you, sir, naturally."

Jeremiah Stonechurch looked Molly up and down, which his shadows took as invitation to do the same. Their eyes ranged with hungry appraisal from the twisting fall of hair knotted with ribbons and fresh-cut flowers, past the faint red imprint of teeth along her clavicle, to the starburst of black pleats distorted by contours of breast, hip and thigh.

"She'll do," said the patriarch. Captive breaths were released; Molly held hers a little longer than most. "Now don't you young people have revels to attend? Get to dancing."

With a light laugh, the Colonel bowed again and made to steer Molly across the floor. Molly set a hand on the Colonel's and said, "Now, what can you be about, Colonel? This is a promenade, not a cavalry charge. Mirror Springs is done with soldiers and wars. It demands a woman of means and stature. As do I."

A look of something darker than consternation crossed the Colonel's brow; Molly glimpsed the cold architect of ruthless strategies in those eyes. Calculation too, as though she suspected a trick or an act of rebellion. Both, perhaps.

"Well, why not?" she said, breaking her thoughtful inspection of Molly's gaze. "Let's be done with formalities and get to the festivities as soon as we may."

She turned, sweeping her hat high and low in salute at Stonechurch, who had not moved yet. With a complicate flourish of her wrist, he held it out to Molly, who took it and retreated a few steps. She sensed the Colonel would want some room. "Marshall Stonechurch, have I not served your cause loyally and discharged my duties to your satisfaction?"

Stonechurch Senior nodded. Balthazar downed his drink in a gulp and groaned, until silenced by his father's glare.

"Exemplary, I should say," he agreed. "My enemies have bled or fled, or offered terms I consider most favourable. You've done all I asked and more." Despite his desiccation, he was the Colonel's equal in overcoming the noise of the ball. In any case conversations and music were easing off.

"The warring's done. I can't rightly serve as your Colonel any more, sir. Will you bid me lay down my sword?" She unbuckled her sword belt and set the weapon at Stonechurch's feet.

"Will you grant me leave to silence my guns?" She raised her pistols and flicked them open to show empty chambers. She put them beside the sword with her holsters and ammunition belt.

"Shall I set aside my uniform in the hope it need never be worn again?" She shrugged the coat off and folded it into a precise square with effortless movements. It made a soft puff of complaint as she dropped it atop the weapons.

Stonechurch nodded impatiently. "Yes, yes, I give my blessing. What about the rest of it?"

She held a curled hand to his lips. Around her middle finger was a twist of silver; she unfurled her hand to reveal its twin. "I propose a new arrangement, if you're willing."

Stonechurch plucked the jewel and raised it to his eye with a bone-deep prospector's instinct. But he looked at Molly with frank suspicion. "What about her?"

"You'll see as little of her as you please," said the Colonel, "or as much as you like."

The old man rammed his gnarled middle finger through the ring and pressed his hand to hers. "We'll see about that," he said, smacking his woody lips. "All right, then, Colonel Tempest, you can marry me if you're inclined."

She smiled like a sun-warmed snake and said, "My military days are behind me, my intended. You'd best get used to calling me Harriet."

Three things happened.

First, the good folk of Mirror Springs lit a blaze of applause that spread and rose until hoots and cheers swallowed it. Hearty fellows slapped each other's backs, ladies stamped their dancing boots, and brimming glasses were raised in congratulations.

Second, Harriet Tempest's manservant Justice weaved through the throng with Molly's coat and slid it expertly over her arms and shoulders even as she laid an unbroken kiss on her fiancé's weathered lips, to still greater bonhomie.

Third, William Bright appeared with a gun in his hand.

Where Tempest stood, so stood Bill. In the first instant he seemed to be an outline, like a portrait painted on a glass set in front of her, and his face was pressed against Stonechurch's like hers. Gasps of shock came from every quarter; everyone saw Bill Bright as an echo around Harriet Tempest.

"Revenant!" came the cry.

Then his hands, her hands, their hands came up and shoved the old man in the chest. As he sprawled, Tempest reeled back in horror from her own hand, which held a mahogany-gripped pistol she'd never seen before.

Molly knew it well enough. She'd seen her brother steal it from the Sunjalese sisters. She saw Mercy in the crowd, and knew that she recognised it too.

Tempest shouted, in a growling voice not her own, "You filthy old bastard! You stuck us out there fighting for your table scraps. I risked my life every day to protect the silver in your pocket, you tunnel-scab! Let's see how you like it!"

Their arms rose as one, steady and level, the pistol pointed unerringly at Stonechurch. Harriet's eyes were wide and wild, and she cried, teeth bared, "No no no. Stop him. Someone stop him."

"Father!" Balthazar Stonechurch snapped into unexpected movement. He threw himself at the floor and scrabbled for the

Colonel's discarded pistols. Stonechurch's companions scattered. Balthazar raised a shaky revolver to Tempest's chest. "Drop it, you mad bitch, or so help me I'll -"

A thunderclap cut him off. Balthazar's head snapped back. His father was showered with blood and bits of skull. Tempest howled, but her face transformed as Bill crowed. "Dumb son of a mule! She showed you they was unloaded!"

All sense drained from Molly like the colour from her face. She managed to say "Bill? What are you doing?"

The gun stayed fixed on the cringing Stonechurch, but Harriet turned to fix Molly with a dumbstruck glare. "Did you do this to me? What did you do?"

"She gave me what I wanted most, Colonel! Revenge on you!"

"No!" Molly shook her head. She clutched the Colonel's hat to her chest, as if a shield of felt and leather could stop the bullets from a ghost's gun. "I didn't want this!"

Tempest's jaw was set and her neck muscles strained as she tried to turn the pistol away from Stonechurch. Her voice rasped, as if the strain of carrying two voices was cutting it to shreds. She snarled again, "Molly Bright, what did you do?"

The near-headless body of Balthazar Stonechurch kicked and twitched on the floor. His father's face was a shroud of gored-blotched horror. The revellers of Mirror Springs, those who had not fled at once, fell back from the violence like pond ripples.

"I sewed one of his hairs into the coat," cried Molly. How had it gone so wrong? "I bound him to it and so to you."

"But why?"

Bill replied, curling Tempest's face into a sneer, "Because she knew I'd kill you soon as the chance came along, that's why!"

"That's not why! I tried to force him to talk with you. To get him to face what he did and make peace with you! I didn't know he could do this!"

"You mean this?" Bill pulled the trigger. The pistol barked again. Jeremiah Stonechurch dropped like a rock fall. He spilled across the body of his son and lay still.

"No!" Molly and Tempest shouted at once. Windows smashed as the remaining ball-goers sought to escape.

"And now what am I going to do with you, Harriet Tempest?"

Bill cocked the wrist holding the pistol and turned the gun on Tempest. The muzzle nudged her temple; he thumbed the hammer back.

"At ease, Colonel," mocked Bill. He squeezed the trigger.

Molly moved before she thought about it. She rushed at Tempest and closed her hand over the cocked pistol, jamming her finger between the hammer and pin.

It was colder than the bottom of a lake in winter; her hand numbed in an instant. The pistol's hammer crunched on her little finger, which bent sideways. Molly barely felt it. Yanking the pistol from Bill's grip was like pulling a mule through a hedge; she met with resistance no matter which way she turned.

Tempest seized her opportunity. With Bill distracted, she wrestled her other arm free of the coat, wrenching it off so it hung from just the forearm Bill controlled.

"Got it!" Molly twisted the gun out of Bill's hand and flung it at the nearest window. As it spiralled through the air, the pistol trailed wisps of green smoke. It became faint and dissipated before it reached the hole in the wall.

Tempest wrapped the coat around and around her offending arm, until it was a midnight blue bandage immobilising the hand. She pinned the bound limb under her other arm and held it with a ferocious grip. She turned on Molly with blazing eyes. "This is your doing, Molly Bright. It's your business to make it right. This can't end but one way."

Molly could not control her streaming tears. "What do you want me to do?"

Harriet nodded toward the corpses of the Stonechurch clan, and her own equipment pinned beneath. "You load one of those pistols. One round will suffice."

It was a battlefield command, stripped of doubt and hesitation. Molly jumped to obey.

"Don't listen to her, Little Moll." Bill's tone was suddenly contrite, pleading. "She don't have your best interests at heart. She's been cheated of her riches. She'll take it out on you. Don't give her nothin' she wants."

Molly slotted a fresh bullet from the Colonel's ammunition belt into the chamber. "I'm sorry," she said. She wasn't sure who she was apologising to. A bitter corner of her heart knew it was mostly for herself. "I didn't mean for this to happen."

"The gun, Miss Bright."

Tempest opened her hand and for a moment Molly saw her own laid across it, seeking comfort. The instant passed. She knew there was none to be had now, if ever there was. She pressed the butt of the pistol into Tempest's open palm.

Molly fixed on the motions of Tempest's hand as she clicked the loaded chamber into the weapon's belly. The nocked, slender fingers closed over grip and trigger with familiar intent. Tempest raised the pistol.

Molly thought, At least this is where it ends. The women in my family don't come back.

Out loud, she said, "I'm sorry, Colonel. I wish I'd chosen otherwise."

The woman who thought she could stop being the Colonel looked at her with glittering eyes. "I should have known you Brights were all cut from the same cloth."

She put the barrel in her mouth and pulled the trigger.

#

On her last day in Mirror Springs, Molly Bright rode straight down the main street of the town with her chin held high. Some backs turned on her, of course. A few curses were uttered and more than one man idling at his leisure on a porch spat in her direction or grabbed at this crotch in blatant offense.

But Molly thought the friendly faces outnumbered the hostile ones. The passing of the Stonechurch clan into town history had opened doors for opportunity-seekers. Houses had been looted. Herds were rustled away into nearby farms, where brands were artfully altered. Mining claims were jumped and, once any differences over ownership were settled with exchanges of gunfire or grudging handshakes, the town went back to its old routines.

The question of Molly Bright's culpability in the Gallowsbreath Eve Massacre, as a sensational monograph dubbed it, was debated and disputed. Most contended that Harriet Tempest, whose wartime exploits were gleefully exposed by her former subordinates, gunned the Stonechurch men down over some unheard insult or unknown grievance, or just because the mood took her. The ghost of Bill Bright might, it was claimed, have been her own injured conscience made manifest. People were inclined towards simple explanations, if not credible ones.

In the end Molly settled the matter by agreeing to depart forever. As she trotted by Uncle Key's General Supplies, Mercy barged into her path and waved her to a halt. She tugged a bundle of rags from under her shawl and dumped it into Molly's lap.

"You take this," she said. "It's no good to us anymore."

Molly unfolded a patch of cloth, exposing grey metal beneath. It was the pistol Bill stole. Or stole the idea of, she supposed. "I can't take this. It's too valuable."

Mercy was already walking away. "Better they find it in your hands than our shop," she replied. "You take it where nobody knows it. Okay? Go. Find somewhere far away where nobody knows you."

She bustled back to her store, stopping only to point out an unswept patch to her new shop assistant. Justice hurried to apply the broom to the unsightly spot.

Molly rode on. Out to her left, the last hazy clouds were beginning to clear over the ashes of the Colonel's house on Finality Hill. Curls of lazy brown smoke still curled up from the skeletal stump of the spikewood tree. Nobody had wanted to claim the home of the murdering Colonel, especially not with all that talk of ghosts, and so it had been set alight before Gallowsbreath had dawned.

When she reached the handful of shacks surrounding the rail stop, where the town of Mirror Springs gave way to the bumpy, rutted track back to the East, the rangy cur caught up with her. It barked once, in greeting perhaps, then trotted off to sniff out some lizard burrows. It never strayed too far from her sight.

The chill winds out of the desert nipped at her back, but the sun rose ahead with a fierce, judgmental glare. Molly tugged Bill's hat down low over her brow and cinched the Colonel's coat a little tighter about her shoulders. Two faint voices, dimly argumentative, echoed at her back.

She ignored them and rode away.

'The Dressmaker and the Colonel's Coat' is the longest story I've ever finished. I had the idea I wanted to write a Western, but when supernatural elements crept in at the rough outline stage, they opened the door to another fantasy world. That happens to me a lot.

This story started as a challenge from my friend Jodi Cleghorn. The idea was to write a story in a month – starting on the first of the month with a single line, then two lines on day two and so on until the final writing session was thirty-one lines long. I read 'lines' as 'sentences', which stretched the project out even more – and still, when I got to the end of that month, I realised the story was still only about half-done. I got there in the end though.

I'd like to revisit Molly Bright in the future. Here, she's been squeezed into the margins of her own story by Bill and the Colonel (which I should say was intentional). There's a great deal more to her and her world than I could fit into 'Dressmaker', even as long as it is.

She deserves her due, though she probably won't thank me for the attention.

OUT OF CONTEXT

I think they closed down the poetry servers last night. That must be what happened, because this morning nobody understands how metaphors work. We all remember using them, but now we're not sure what they were for.

Ish is pissed off because song lyrics are gone too, and he had tickets to take me to a concert tonight. I look at them. The name of the band means nothing to me; it's a phrase that refers to a historical event, but I don't know what that's got to do with anything. Allusions are gone too. The only songs of theirs I can remember are called "Untitled" and "Track Three".

I tell Ish I still want to go. I still want to have fun while there's time. But he gives me a look which I can't figure out and holds up his phone. According to the news feed, the lead singer-songwriter killed himself this morning. "Some people spend all their time only thinking about one thing," says Ish. "They don't know how to deal with not having their thing anymore."

I know this is true. My cousin washed down a whole bunch of pills with some kind of ethanol solution when they deleted the concept of organised physical competition between opposing teams. Whatever that was called. He died.

A lot of people have died, I guess. Most of them blamed the scientists for their discoveries but I don't think that's fair. They couldn't have known what would happen when they proved the universe was an artificial simulation of reality. They had no context to understand how its operators might react to being exposed.

A lot of kids think there's not enough left to do now. I know we used to go to buildings where older people would talk about the world and all the things in it, but I don't know why. With so many of the servers down now, it doesn't really take long to learn everything there is to know.

I disagree though. Even without a lot of the things we used to like – mechanical transport, that gas that made balloons go up, the light patterns in the sky at night – we still have plenty to talk about.

"We still have music," I try to remind him, but he's distracted. The band has recorded a video pleading for a new keyboard player to cover the gap in their lineup. Technical experts only; they have no time to rehearse. The gig is still going ahead.

Ish's eyes are watering and his bottom lip won't stop quivering. I press my face to his. I don't remember why, exactly, but I know it's calmed him down in the past.

Not this time. He looks at me; the skin on his face is pulled tight and the tendons are showing in his neck. "It's happening faster and faster. Don't you understand, Matt? We lose something new with each passing moment. Soon we won't have anything left."

We feel the mild all-over itch that coincides with a deletion. It's not usually hard to figure out what changed.

I give Ish his pieces of paper back. I don't know what he expected me to see on them. They're covered with patterns, black on white. Meaningless. "Everything ends. Songs. Conversations. Meals."

"What was that last one?"

"What last one?"

He moves his head around and makes a noise with his throat. He pokes his phone until some music starts. We lean our heads close together so we can listen to the song.

We don't need to talk.

There's nothing to talk about.

For several years I've been trying to figure out a story to wrap around the probably mathematically ludicrous theory that our universe is an artificial simulation being run by some higher-order beings (or more likely underpaid lab technicians). This story started out being about something entirely different, until the simulated-universe concept imposed and made itself at home.

'Out of Context' was first published in October 2017 as a Friday Flash Fiction post at DavidVersace.com.

IMPORTED GOODS – AISLE NINE

"What the hell is chlorophyllising flour?"

Gina blinks against the saturated glare of the overhead halogens. Her eyes haven't adjusted from the walk to the shops yet. Truth to tell, neither have her nerves. Perry's mood and the blacked-out street lights have both left scratchy patches on her positivity. "Uh? Never heard of it."

She wonders if this is the spark she's been waiting for, the one that will set him off again, maybe for the last time. He's been a stinking grouse for hours, finding fault with everything. She concocted this past-midnight grocery expedition to escape being cooped up with his petulant mood. No such luck, he just followed her out the door, griping about the power outage. Like an infant bawling in the distance, she can't quite ignore his noise.

He shrugs and tosses the bag back on the shelf, where a little beige cloud puffs out. "Or this? Quinoa breakfast flakes?" He holds up a cereal box, its spotted midnight and gold jaguar mascot pinning down a bowl of warm orange scales bobbing in milk. As usual, Perry's expression suggests she's done something wrong. "Who eats this crap?"

"I dunno." She gestures vaguely at the cartoon cat. "Kids, I guess." He moves along the aisle, pointing out oddities. The box crumples in his grip, each sharp gesture a maraca-rattle of crackling flakes. "Flax paste? Fumewort sprouts? Groundskeeper's clay?"

Now that he comes to mention it, none of these products look familiar, but she's damned if she's going to give him the satisfaction. She can feel a headache rolling in. Acknowledging his complaints will give it legroom. "I'm just looking for milk and toothpaste." Maybe he's so irritated that he'll go off to look for her groceries to get out of there sooner? The hope of a moment's peace in his company is a precious little spark she still nurtures from habit more than expectation.

Her luck is in. He's turned his baleful attention on some hapless shelf-droid. The kid's face is radioactive with scarlet acne and wet blue eyes. The oasis of colourless chin hair hinting at a far-future goatee suggests that eighteen is some way off.

"Hey, buddy," he says. His coarse growl in no sense connotes friendship.

"Where's all the real food? I'm not buying any of this Asian junk."

The kid blinks at him with late-shift eyes, his pricing gun wobbling in a limp hand. Perry's a big man with a keen sense of his own size. The kid sways in an undetectable breeze. "Asian?" he repeats, like he's checking the pronunciation.

Perry takes it as a challenge. Of course he does. He does his straightening up trick which adds a good ten centimetres to his height. "Where's the real food, sport?" He saves expressions of affected camaraderie for moments when he's being an overbearing tool. Sometimes, when he hits the right tone with the right guy, all it takes is one word to provoke a reaction. "We can't find anything in this rat maze."

Gina tunes him out as he fires questions too fast for answers at the kid. Where are the pretzels? The sour sweets? Is there a coldroom? Do they sell hot pies?

The kid doesn't appear to get that his expression of acute dumbfoundedness is escalating the situation. She considers abandoning them to the inevitable while she finishes the grocery search, but it's mean to leave the kid. Besides, if he ever comes out of his trance he might actually be able to help.

"Where have you looked already?" the kid asks at last.

Perry affects irritation that his question has been answered with a question.

Secretly, she knows he's delighted. It's easy enough to see where this is going.

It's his pattern, varying little from one setting to another. Social sports centre, bus stop, Saturday night club. Once he provoked a cinema usher into throwing a punch. Perry got a cracked molar and the guy lost his job. Gina was the one who'd had her feet up on the seat in front.

"What did you say, mate?"

The kid actually scratches his head and frowns, like he's translating Perry from the Russian or something. "What did you call me?"

Gina can hear the capillaries bursting behind Perry's eyes from across the aisle. She's stepping between them before she even realises it. She draws up to eyeball height and tries to catch Perry's attention. Most times it works at least once. Not tonight. He just steps right around her, his fat spade of a hand dropping on her shoulder and, yeah, he's pushing her out of the way.

"Perry, wait."

Right now, she thinks as she stumbles back. *This is when I should cut my losses and call it done. Enough is enough.* But she can't admit to herself that she's wasted her time.

Perry's her sunk-cost fallacy.

The physical contact has rattled her. That must be it. She ought to know better. He's stoking himself up for a meltdown.

He's never hit her.

Sometimes she tells herself that's why they're still together. But she knows it's crossed his mind. She knows there have been times when some guy with a smart mouth or a roaming eye has taken a couple of extra kicks on her account, past the point when Perry's furnace would normally have run cold. "Forget it Gee," says Perry, closing in on the shelf packer. "This little bugger needs customer service training."

She realises that the kid's almost as tall as Perry but he's a wet, lanky shape. There's no mass to him. Perry's going to knock him through shoulder-high stacks of kumara tubes. Perry's grin signals a suspension of the usual rules of engagement. For once, he's too impatient to lay the groundwork. He wants mayhem *now*, no waiting.

To his credit, the kid sees it coming. He backpedals fast and gets out of the path of Perry's first exploratory swipe. It's not a real punch, but the kid doesn't know that. His foot catches the base of the pyramidal display and kicks off an avalanche of baked-not-fried snack foods. The kid wallops midsection-first into the shelf and puffs out his breath, eyes bulging. He folds forward, merging with the collapsing tower of cardboard tubes into a chaotic sprawl on the worn grey linoleum floor.

On a better day, it would be enough to instil humiliation without laying a hand, but tonight has crawled under Perry's skin. His mouth worked into an unsatisfied line, he closes in a couple of steps and raises one size twelve stomping boot. The kid cringes, his glasses hanging by one crimson ear. Gina grabs for an arm and pulls, but Perry's got his balance. She can't shift him.

"Perry! What in the world do you think you're doing?"

The voice isn't loud at all but as the resonating chime of cascading tubes subsides, it cuts through the charged scene like scissors. Perry's foot freezes. Like gravity just got switched on again, Gina's weight on his arm takes effect. He tumbles, she lets go just in time.

She thinks, *Yes, that's right. Let go.*

"Mum?"

Gina doesn't know this little old biddy with protruding teeth and square pensioner sunglasses. Her silvery rinse is wrapped in a hairnet and she's wearing a deli-stained striped apron. Her arms are folded and her jowls are shivering. "Perry, I asked you a question. For Jiminy's sake, help Damien up at once."

At either end of the aisle, small crowds of late-evening shoppers are clumping together. They sense a good show in the offing. Random aggro against shop assistants is one thing. Family drama, though? That's rubbernecking *gold*.

"Muh-hum?"

Gina can't believe her ears. Perry's gone from scowling alpha-jerk to the verge of tears in the space of a breath. No, scratch that — there are two streams already plunging down either side of his creased and darkened face. He's full-on bawling now.

She says, as calmly as she can, "Perry, you told me your parents were dead."

"Mum?" It's like he doesn't hear her. He just repeats again and again: "Mum? Mum?"

The biddy's face tightens up into sharp folds for a second, her teeth sucking back behind rose-glossed lips like a startled reef fish. She's uptight about something and it's not just Perry's random hostility. Under the searing halogen glare, Gina watches the biddy's brow unfurl, and sees a slackness spread down her face like one of those wartime films showing Germany's relentless march across Europe.

The woman plucks the glasses off with gristly fingers and looks down at Perry with sad, milky eyes. "Oh, child," she says, understanding washing the anger from her voice, "you aren't where you belong, are you?"

Gasps and whispers from that way up the aisle and this way down. Everybody has something to say to that, it seems, but Gina can't hear what's discussed. A camera flashes from one direction and she can see that a couple of people are holding up their hands palm-forth. Darkened lenses of various designs are attached like oversized rings to upturned middle fingers; the owners are watching screens on the backs of their wrists.

Perry doesn't seem to be up to saying anything, if that lip quiver is any sign. Gina asks "Sorry, but—what's your name?"

The old girl wobbles forward on sagging chubby legs, clearing a path through the debris with her feet. She kicks herself some space and kneels between Perry and the kid, who is sitting up and rubbing the back of his head.

"Damien, are you all right?" When the kid nods, his eyes locked on Perry like he was watching a growling pitbull, she says "Go and find the manager, please. Tell him we've got more visitors."

Gina tries again. "Are you Perry's mother?"

Damien's uncomprehending stare finally breaks at the sound of the question. Clambering up with ungainly effort, he sets off another small tumble of cardboard tubes. When he bends to start picking them up, the biddy shoos him away. He flees down the aisle, where the amateur film crews part with reluctant shuffling and redoubled mutters.

"My name is Jo,' the biddy says. "I'm Perry's mother."
Somehow it sounds like a lie.

Perry rushes the old woman into a fierce bear hug, burying
his face into her shoulder. His sobs sound like a bodybuilder
working a bellows. Each breath is a declaration of something
between relief and sorrow and horror. In a few seconds, he's
become someone Gina doesn't recognise, someone vulnerable and
small. A child. She finds herself aching with sympathy and
revulsion.

She hates that she feels either one.

"I don't understand what's going on."

"I am Perry's mother," she says, "but I have never seen this
young man in my life."

She sees Perry stiffen, sees the red flush across his nape. He
doesn't break the hug. Perhaps he's scared to.

"You've made a wrong turn, I'm afraid. It happens from
time to time. You wandered into Aisle Nine."

"Aisle Nine?"

"Round here, that's where it usually happens. I suppose you
didn't notice anything at all, did you? No unusual sounds or
flashes of light? Just went to your supermarket and found
yourselves here?"

"Mum, mum," says Perry. His stupid Batman bass growl is
gone. Without it he sounds like an eleven year old. She never
realised he did that all the time. His commitment to artifice
surprises her. "Can I stay with you?"

In turn, she sounds like a mother, firm and resolute. "You have to go back, Perry. You can't stay. There's no room for another you here."

The babble from the onlookers is louder now. The crowd has grown denser. Now the talk stops and they part again, revealing Damien leading someone back to the scene. The companion is tall and muscled. His stride is confident and relaxed. A playful flop of hair drops over cheerful eyes creased in confusion.

Perry but not Perry. The supermarket manager, she presumes. Perry, as if he were played by a young Brad Pitt.

Manager Perry pulls Damien by his collar to a stop. They stand there. He's watching his mother like a meerkat.

"You need to go home," Jo says again. Perry whimpers. The angry belligerent man is gone. What remains is an uncertain boy, drowning in wait of a kind word. "I'll take you as far as I can but you'll have to walk the last part by yourself."

"Home?"

"I'm sorry," she says. She looks Perry in the eye, not unkindly but with unflinching hardness. "You probably want to stay more than anything. I just bet you do. But I already have a son to care for. I can't have a matched pair."

She helps him up. He doesn't resist as she leads him down Aisle Nine, away from Damien and Manager Perry. Away from Gina. He glances back once but not to look at her. He locks eyes with his mirror-image and half a lifetime's pain is compressed in his unmasked jealousy. Then Jo walks him around the corner and out of sight.

A hand falls on Gina's shoulder, familiar and wrong at the same time.

The touch doesn't trigger her instinct to flinch. Manager Perry says "You can follow in a minute. We used to send visitors back in groups but it sometimes looked like it hurt them. Now all visitors go single-file. It's store policy."

His little joke lights up his face. He's happy, he's cool; this is all no big deal.

"So you're another him. Is there another me around?"

He laughs at that and a chuckle runs through the watchers. They seem to love him. "Probably not. One doppelganger per tour group seems to be the rule. I guess it had to be my turn sooner or later. Pretty weird though."

"I guess it's like looking into a broken mirror?"

He nods. "Like that, but knowing that sooner or later the reflection would try to kill me. That always happens with the doubles, once they get over the shock."

"So you send them back before they clue in." Another nod, pleased and impressed this time. It's an expression that makes her disorientation easy to take. "How did I get here in the first place?"

"He brought you. Not on purpose. He just wanted it badly enough." Manager Perry frowns. "I don't know what I'd do without Mum around. It'd mess me up."

"It probably would."

Perry was a key, one she never knew she needed to turn. Now Gina's on the far side of the door and the shape of the key doesn't matter anymore.

She drops to one knee and starts tucking cardboard tubes under her arm.

"Do you have any jobs open? I'm not in any hurry to go."

'*Imported Goods – Aisle Nine*' *was only the second story I finished after I started getting serious about writing for publication in 2012. (At the time I was sick of my job and sleep deprived, so nothing much has changed there). It was also my first story accepted for publication, in the Canberra Speculative Fiction Guild's anthology of that year.*

I'm a fan of parallel universe stories, which tend to come in two flavours: either the differences are over-the top spectacle - airships are commercially viable, the dinosaurs never became extinct and everyone's Over-There doppleganger wears an eyepatch or a goatee to denote their evil intent –or, as in this case, the changes are small and unsettling, and the dopplegangers are, perhaps, the better option.

'*Imported Goods – Aisle Nine*' *was first published in* **Next** *(CSFG Publishing, April 2013), edited by Simon Petrie and Robert Porteous.*

RED FIRE MONKEY

Take me higher than the canopy branches
Gravity's a memory, vanilla can't stand it

Klaxons burst through King's mid-forties geneticore playlist.
The noise hits his modded cerebral cortex like panic pheromones
and the smell of smoke. He kills the headstream, music forgotten
as he drops into his flow. He's already on the move, heading
upstation. Hand over hairy hand out of his chillpod; his tail
scoops up his breather and breach kit as he passes.

Colourful emoji glide across his artificial corneas like leaves
on a mountain stream. Incident reports: black clouds mean a hull
breach; a purple bandage for injuries; red fire means uncontrolled
combustion. And King's icon: a chattering, laughing chimpanzee.
Nobody should confuse simians for monkeys, but the sysadmins
laughed off his discrimination complaint. The software is an off
the shelf package from an ignorant Australian startup.

Grown up in a lab with the surgeons and the hackers
My own mother don't know me cause she don't got access

Vermillion Station's central concourse is in a buzz of urgent
confusion and babbling concussion. King ignores the triage teams
shepherding bloodied stretcher capsules. The brusque commands

of the incident coordinator have nothing for the Fire Monkeys; King shunts her feed to a low-pri stream. Nobody is shouting anything he needs to hear.

He picks a line clear of loose debris and the weeping wounded. He propels himself along the path laid out by the crisis management AI; the visual overlay depicts a trail of bananas. So offensive.

Rook and Noon sling themselves into his wake as he passes the therapy lab, greeting him with tight squawks of static over restricted telecoms. They bare their teeth, eyes bright with excitement, and strap vacuum seals over their faces.

Incident data refreshes with detailed assignments. Up ahead, the Agronomics module is burning and buckling as fire and void battle over it for bragging rights.

Rook touches King's shoulder in a comforting gesture. Eve is assigned to Agronomics.

I got personal space, I got thoughts nobody asked for
Am I under your dominion? Do you think you can task your
Monkey? Beast of burden? Go to hell.

Autonomous safeties locked Agronomics tight at the first sign of danger. Spiking thermals or falling pressure? Doesn't matter; the protocol's the same in either case. The blast doors are rated for re-entry. They cut off everything: expanding clouds of burning oxygen; the vampiric siphoning of oxygen into space; and anyone stuck on the wrong side of the airlocks.

Station telemetry shows three weak sets of life signs – two hominids, one cebid. They also show rising heat and a steady pressure drop.

The good news for the station is that the slow breach will suffocate the fire soon. The bad news all depends on who has an independent oxygen supply.

Rook flings override codes at the access hatch to the secondary duct network, known to most as the Monkey Tubes. Vermillion Station is enveloped by a lattice of narrow conduits; too small and claustrophobic for vanilla humans but comfortably proportioned for jacked-out rescue monkeys modded to navigate disorienting zero-grav crawlspaces.

Noon mines sensor data. The atmospheric integrity for their fastest route to Agronomics shows green. He grabs the tip of his own tail and claps his feet, signalling all-clear.

King pops the hatch release and pulls himself into the darkness.

Never knew nothing of fresh fruit and foliage
Never nothing in nature like a rescue soldier

King's optics kick in filters and image enhancement as he clambers into the smoke haze. Streams of fire like burning ribbons stretch from a blazing shuttle buggy's battery chamber to the outer walls of the agricultural chamber. The stream splits into three writhing tributaries, marking the hull's fracture points. Fatigue patterns expand through strata of ceramic, titanium and nano-woven diamond. King consults his data feeds and selects the worst of the ruptures, tapping the same parts of his amygdala evolved to spot a weak branch or a camouflaged predator.

Agronomics is a broad, pebble-shaped module nearly two hundred metres in diameter, spindle-mounted and spun up to simulate Earth gravity. Not right now; automatic braking has already killed most of the spin. That suits King. He doesn't need invisible weights trying to pull him to the floor while he works.

But he is tempted. Eve is down there.

He spares her a glance. Bloody cuts and singed patches mottle her gold and black hair, and her tail is kinked and limp, but she's masked and mobile. She injects coagulant foam into an ash-faced, moaning biotechnician's stomach wound. He can't catch her scent through his self-contained breather but his neck hairs ruff in relief. She's beautiful and alive.

But she's not safe yet. Her skin enhancements aren't rated for hard vacuum. His implants turn his attention to the buckling superstructure overhead.

Argue all you like, say we're gonna come to harm
It only rains in orbit when you call a fire alarm

Noon drops in beside Eve and attaches a resuscitation kit to the crashing technician.

Rook clambers under the burning buggy to disengage the fuel cells. His hair is already alight when he sets off a grenade full of retardant foam. His vitals start spiking instantly.

King mutes the distress alerts; Rook's done his job.

King zeroes in on the fissures, skirting the perimeter of the fiery vortices swirling into the ruptured wall.

He pops a sealing cap from his utility harness; it begins to expand in reaction to the falling air pressure. In two heartbeats, it's the size of a banana. Then a coconut. When it's an off-white sponge-surfaced watermelon he slaps it on the damaged wall section. His knuckle hairs singe and hiss, but King's nervous system is monitored from one microsecond to the next; he barely registers the sensation before pain blockers smother the distraction.

Atmospheric monitors register a decrease in the rate of pressure loss. Noon flashes him a toothsome-grin icon. Eve's congratulations come on their secure personal channel; they're not for public consumption.

King patches the next fissure. It scans as vacuum-proof but something is wrong; the pressure drop is accelerating again. The third fissure opens up, the structure around it weakening at an unstoppable rate. New fissures are opening, spreading like a web spun out to every branch at once. King shrieks in frustration as he feels the drag of suction grab hold. His next sealing cap has begun to inflate but it's already too late.

A piece of ceramic plating a little larger than King's head tears loose and draws him feet-first into the Open. He can't keep his grip on the spongey sealing cap. Between one blink and the next, King is outside Vermillion Station and moving away fast. His expert systems send emergency calls; patches of bare skin on his feet, hands and face fluoresce bright red to aid search and rescue attempts.

They won't come in time. He's an angry red dot against the vastness of the Open. His hair is already brittle with frost and the skin beneath is purpling as his capillaries burst. He spins slowly.

His feed confirms the seal behind him is holding. Rook's vital signs are dropping into critical levels across the board; it's touch and go which of them will outlive the other.

Eve's surprise and horror hits him in a flood of icons. Tears. Hearts. Broken branches in the high canopy.

Spread out ahead of him is the wide green of Earth. He knows the large inverted tear shape below; the lab technicians showed him pictures of South America once. He finds the green swathes of the continent's easternmost bulge. He shunts the image to temp memory, tagged for Eve. If they recover his remains, she will see what he saw.

King drops out of the Vermillion feed. His music resumes; a clatter of drums, whistling pipes and flutes, and snarling vocals.

He soars over his ancestral home and wonders if anyone is
looking up tonight.

You took me out and I won't ever go back
I make the calls for myself out here in the black

I am sometimes a volunteer organiser for Canberra's annual speculative fiction convention, Conflux. I wrote this story for the publicity release which informed prospective attendees about the 'Red Fire Monkey' theme and invited them to buy a membership.

I doubt it convinced anyone to come to the con, but I'm still very fond of the story. I'm always up for a story about the hazards of space travel, and the existential weirdness of uplifted animals (i.e. animals modified by scientists to given them human-level intelligence and communication abilities) is too good an idea not to play with.

THE FEAST OF HORNS AT THE HOUSE OF ST. MITUS' EYE

On the fourth day of the pilgrims' sojourn in the House of Saint Mitus' Eye, the Blessed Goodhost called for a reckoning of their bill of fare. The innkeeper was a ruddy mountain crag by the name of Bunstable. Vance Adell suspected him of rank opportunism. Custom permitted the holy order to postpone the settlement discussion until the hour of its departure.

"I'll tell you what I told your Petitioner," Bunstable informed him. "The Great Saints have visited the snows of winter upon the holy mountain early this year. The pilgrim's road is impassable until the spring melt."

Vance welcomed the negotiation. *Let my thoughts be filled with anything other than Petitioner Sila Kreiner.* "There are no guides who can direct our safe ascent? We can offer not only the Saint's blessing but generous compensation too."

"The generosity of the Order of Rejuvenationists is widely acknowledged," said Bunstable, clapping one solemn hand to his chest and making an expansive gesture with the other, "but alas, no coin can buy the impossible. Any reputable guide will tell you it is certain death. Had you arrived but a week earlier–" He spread his hands in a passable display of abject regret.

Vance pinched his nose hard, a ward against the migraine he was sure would accompany the conversation. The news was unwelcome enough. Bunstable's clumsy exploitation of their misfortune rubbed salt into this fresh wound.

Their delay in arriving at the way-station, the toe on the foothills of the great mountain Luxichre, was all his brother Strake's fault. Roaring acts of public drunkenness were not beyond the precepts of their Order but Strake's timing in the town of Velentionne was poor. The local ruler, Baron Helstedd, had lately lost both a wife and an heir in childbirth. Strake's compulsive revelry had clashed with the Velentiots' idea of suitable mourning habits. The Baron's reeve levied punitive fines which decimated their funds. The scandalised Velentiots had been less than generous with alms for the pilgrims. Worst of all, they lost a week's travel to Strake's detention in Baron Helstedd's gaol-tower. For the last thirty days, the pilgrims had marched with uncomfortable haste to compensate, as the mountain air grew chill.

In theory Saint Mitus' Travelling Order of Rejuvenationists held to no schedule in their pilgrimage to emulate the great expeditions of their patron. The journey could be expected to take years. Certain practicalities held, however, and staying ahead of the weather was not considered irreverent. The superiority of an expeditionary leader's vision was reckoned according to many measurements. By far the metric that mattered most was whether they reached each of the nineteen Venerated Wonders before all eight pilgrims experienced resurrection.

The expedition of Sila Kreiner was stuck at the base of its fifth wonder.

Vance composed himself, banishing a frown. "Goodhost Bunstable, I hope that our protracted stay does not inconvenience you or your family."

"The House of Saint Mitus' Eye has not turned away a pilgrim in more than a hundred years, Master Vance. Not since Mitus himself bestowed his word and blessing upon my great-grandfather." Bunstable looked set to recount the details of that singular occasion yet again, but Vance interrupted with as much grace as he could muster.

"In addition to daily offering of the ash-purse," he said, leaving unspoken the understanding that the traditional gratuity would be increased in accordance with the modern cost of living, "we will work for our keep."

Bunstable hunched his shoulders, drummed his knuckles across the ledger spread across his spacious escritoire and smiled. The starving carrion birds that wheeled about Luxichre's summit could likely not match his look of insatiable hunger.

"Under ordinary circumstances, Master, that would suffice. But the Feast of Horns is a week away and Petitioner Kreiner enjoys uncommon renown. With so reputable an Eight under our humble roof, the whole town will seek invitation in the hopes of sharing your blessings. The House is obliged not to turn them away."

"Don't fear for your livelihood, Goodhost." Vance tasted something sour but returned the smile with studied reserve. "You'll have all you need."

Vance took his leave and went in search of his brother. With luck, he could inspire Strake to reform before the next crisis arrived.

#

He found Strake lounging on cushions before the massive fireplace of the common room with Dessit and Polma, the only remaining unresurrected members of the expedition apart from Vance himself. Before the prophetic dreams had driven him from his business and his family into Kreiner's sphere, Dessit had been a fishmonger, selling narwhals, marlins and giant squid in the markets of Tosrada. Broad-shouldered Polma had been a skirmisher in the Diamond Battalion. She still carried her javelins everywhere.

They idolised Strake Adell, and why not? Vance saw nothing of the pious, bookish mouse he'd grown up with in this brash, charming athlete. His resurrection had burned away a boy's shuddering nervousness exposing a surprising core of boisterous confidence. He was a walking emblem of the Saint's blessing: tall, hairless and assured.

Not that he seemed to care anymore.

"Brother, join us! Falaha will make some room for you." He shifted his hips a little to reveal Bunstable's eldest daughter pressed against his side, half-buried by cushions.

"Good evening, Master Vance. My father has kept you too long at your book-keeping. May I offer you refreshment?" She gave Vance a wide, lazy-eyed smile as she fumbled to straighten her clothing. He caught a generous glimpse of exposed skin and cast his eyes away at once. He tried to tell himself that his preoccupation with Goodhost Bunstable's rapacious accountancy left him impervious to all distraction. Then his thoughts strayed to Sila, collapsing the delusion.

The four saluted each other from brimming saki cups and drank. Not their first round, Vance suspected. On the verge of replying to her solicitation with a curt, automatic "No thank you," he paused to consider the question. Would it cost the expedition so dear if he were to take an evening's relaxation? His fellow pilgrims were doing whatever they could to dampen the tension smouldering in the bones of the Eight. If they held him responsible, Dessit or Polma would have spoken against the invitation. Nor it seemed did they attach blame to Strake, who shed responsibility like sweat on a cool breeze.

That left Sila. None of the company would dare speak against their Petitioner who was blessed by their patron Saint. But tradition accorded her full responsibility for their deliverance into Resurrection.

He sighed, shaking his head. The long winter loomed ahead. Were his disciplined habits observed to slip, he would soon see them reflected by the others. Besides, Vance could not recall the last time his food and drink did not taste of ashes.

"Do you not have duties to perform, daughter of our Goodhosts?"

"This hour belongs to me, Initiate. Your companions have convinced me I need not spend it alone with my books." Falaha beamed at him, oblivious to his weary turmoil. "Master Vance, your brother speaks passionately of the fires of the Saint but he declines to show me his scar. Can you persuade him to share his blessing?"

Vance was taken aback. "Don't you know where it is?"

A round of giggles and Strake's sly grin answered his question. The fires of resurrection begin in the lower abdomen, the same point where a Hantan spearhead fatally wounded Saint Mitus long ago. The hairless, flawless flesh of the Resurrected was marred only by a burned patch above the groin.

Vance supposed Falaha would ignore any warnings concerning his brother's dangerously ephemeral attentions. Strake's whims were like mayflies, buzzing distractions to everyone in his vicinity but soon dead to Strake himself. How little he resembled the Strake-of-old, whose ecstatic fervour was the only force capable of rousing him from crippling shyness and a life of monkish study. It was Strake-of-old's urgent piety that drove them both to pledge themselves to Sila Kreiner's pilgrimage.

Vance himself lacked the conviction that his occasional dreams of strong-armed, toothy Mitus were genuine Saint-blessed visions, despite Strake's needy, self-serving interpretations. Even now he knew he would have surrendered his place in the Eight and gone back to his quills and ledgers, had he not made the terrible mistake of falling in love with Sila Kreiner.

If Vance had ever been transported by a captivating vision, it was that of Sila-of-old. Raven-haired, blue-eyed and freckled with the sun of the freezing northlands, her curves were muscular and her hands as quick with a boning-knife as a zither. Her smile, shy at first with the natural caution of her people, became warm and wide as she and Vance became friends. They formed a natural partnership. Her wit and zeal attracted the best pilgrims. His disciplined organisation and head for numbers ensured the expedition was better outfitted and funded than any before or since.

They fell in love.

Sila Kreiner died and resurrected eight months after the expedition embarked. Vance still felt the heat of his tears, the brute muscularity of her convulsions, her grey lips blistering as they parted to howl in triumphant horror. At last the first flames licked from her belly. Then he could hold her no longer. Fire and ash consumed her and left behind a stranger.

Vance thought, I could give it all away right now. I could drink until dawn, every day until winter breaks or the money runs out. I could walk back down the valley to Velentionne and get an assaying job in the Baron's silver mines.

He could turn his back on years of work and sacrifice. Saint Mitus. His fellow pilgrims. Strake. Sila.

The dissolute moment guttered like an expiring candle. "Get off your backsides," he said. "Goodhost Bunstable needs a new alpaca pen. Hard work and snow will sober you up."

#

The House of Saint Mitus' Eye had withstood two hundred years of everything the holy mountain could throw down at it, from the scouring icy winds of winter to spring floods, to wild fires and rock falls. Its travails left it with a surprisingly long list of minor repairs. Bunstable was as good as his unspoken word. The pilgrims grumbled for a day or two but soon became accustomed to the steady flow of odd jobs, the biting cold blasting down from Luxichre's heights and the feel of woodworking tools in their hands. Gerrolt-of-old had been a carpenter for forty years. The oldest pilgrim might no longer speak of his former responsibilities to the fortifications of Chancel Banholdt nor the family he left there but the scourge of resurrection had not stripped him of his skills with a saw and plane.

"Perhaps it's fortunate we are only waylaid for one season, Goodhost," observed Sila Kreiner one morning as the pilgrims tore down the rotten walls of the bath-house. "If we stayed any longer, Saint Mitus himself would not recognise the place."

Bunstable grunted. He'd ceased to lavish praise on the pilgrims' tirelessness or compliment their workmanship a few days earlier. Having established that their efforts under Gerrolt's exacting supervision was of exemplary quality, he now contented himself to present the Eight's Petitioner with a list of desirable repairs, refreshed daily, and withdraw to his other affairs.

On behalf of the rest of his uncomplaining Eight, Vance had taken umbrage at being taken for granted. He exacted an unsaintly revenge, insisting on providing exhaustive, painstaking pecuniary assistance to Bunstable and his wife Yousta as they prepared the Feast of Horns. His intervention intercepted a few cut corners and inflated fees but any savings were dwarfed by the sheer scale of the planned enterprise. More than two hundred townsfolk were expected to squeeze into the large tent fixed alongside the stables, devouring groundfruit platters, sweet loafs and jugs of steaming spiced liquor and dancing reels to a ten-piece pipe band. Saint Mitus' traditional songs would be rendered by a local chorist, considerable in both voice and fee. Most of those were the discordant bawds of a marching army but in practice a lot of popular modern music would be included. "It's what Saint Mitus would have wanted."

"Sila, can I have a word?" Vance whistled quietly by her side. Shortly after they became lovers, he had developed the habit to drag her attention from some internal communion. She used to smile.

Now she turned a cold green eye. "Are you referring to me?"

"I beg your pardon, Petitioner Kreiner." Vance looked at his feet, nipping in annoyance at his thoughtless tongue.

"Is there a problem?"

Vance cast a wary look at Bunstable and said, "It concerns a member of the Eight."

The sceptical squint she directed at him from beneath the pronounced brow and sandy lashes was withering. She knew which pilgrim he meant. She marched off behind the shearing sheds, expecting him to keep up. He kept up. "What did he do this time?"

Vance grimaced. "It's the daughter. Falaha. He says he's in love." A pang of jealous longing speared Vance's constant state of mild exasperation when Strake confided in him. Not dismay at his brother's cavalier foolishness, nor delight at his romantic joy. Strake was of his blood, but he felt nothing of his brother's mood. Would a genuine visionary feel this awkwardness towards a Resurrected loved one? Probably not.

Sila Kreiner shook her head, her expression one of sour distaste. Sila-of-old had weathered with boundless good cheer the interminable delays, detours and unexpected crises of pilgrimage. Now she had taken to endless brooding, sullen and impatient. Her fiery passion to lead her Eight in the footsteps of the saint was gone. Now her capacity to inspire had dimmed but her grim determination to complete the ritual was undiminished.

"You Adells," she growled. "Is there no end to the trouble you will put me through?"

Vance was taken aback. "What do you mean, Petitioner?"

"Did you think it wouldn't get back to me? Strake has been talking about abandoning the expedition. Of breaking the Eight."

"He made some foolish comments over dinner, Petitioner. Nothing more impious than that. Whatever you heard, I'm sure it was exaggerated." Sila Kreiner no longer ate her meals with the rest of the Eight. Since their stranding at the House of Saint Mitus' Eyes, the only time they could rely upon her company was the morning and evening rituals of veneration. She never missed those.

"If his talk breaks my expedition, Master Vance, I will hold you responsible. Correct him."

A peal of hearty laughter erupted from the work party. Strake and Polma were lifting the new wall into place when an alpaca cantered up it, mistaking it for some high mountain passage perhaps. Falaha, the Blessed Host's daughter, laughed hardest, her hands slapping the rails of the llama pen.

"I will do what I can, Petitioner." Vance frowned. She had specified both of them. "Petitioner, have I also done something to displease you?"

She looked at him again as though he were a beet stain on her sacramental tunic. She turned on her heels and left without a word.

"Don't be concerned, Master Vance," said Bunstable, coming over to lay a familiar hand on Vance's shoulder. Vance was too distracted to take offence. "She's anxious about the Feast of Horns. Understandable but unnecessary. The preparations are all but perfect."

Vance knew the details of their preparations to the last coin. He recognised Bunstable's tone. "Have we overlooked some additional expense, Goodhost?"

"There is a boy, a herder with a talent for the longhorn. It occurs to me that perhaps the celebrations should begin with a dusk sounding."

"That is an old tradition, little in favour in these times."

Bunstable leaned close, his air one of concern. "Your petitioner strikes me as a traditionalist, Master. Perhaps it would ease her burdens were we to, ah, resurrect the spirit of Mitus' ways."

When Vance asked what fee he supposed the herder might charge for the service, Bunstable replied with a figure almost double the fair price.

Vance authorised it anyway.

#

That night, after their evening rituals were complete and before Strake could disappear into the inn's rambling interior in search of his paramour, Vance steered his brother to their shared room.

"You've got to cut this out, Strake," he said. "You can't keep this up all winter. The Host is already measuring you up for a wedding robe and counting your treasury share as dowry. If you break the Eight for this girl, Sila will kill you."

"She doesn't seem to have her old sense of humour, does she?" Strake grinned down at him from the top bunk, his bare scalp gleaming in the candle light. He was changing into a fresh shirt that smelled uncharacteristically of lilac blossoms. Was Falaha doing his laundry, on top of everything else?

"Be serious. You know what this means. Polma and Dessit haven't Resurrected yet."

"Nor have you, big brother."

"I don't – I mean, that's right. You're putting all of that in jeopardy."

Strake climbed down from his bunk and wrapped his arms around Vance. "Saint bless you, big brother. Without you we would have fallen apart months ago."

"What do you mean?" Vance squirmed in the embrace. Once he had enjoyed his timid brother's rare outbursts of filial affection. Now that they visited with greater regularity than a clock's chimes, the novelty had burned down its wick.

"Dessit doesn't want to Resurrect any more. He wants to go back to his wife and his fish. Sulsan and Hiram are so taken with Polma's war stories that they want to turn south and enlist. And as for you, Master of the Purse Vance Adell –"

"As for me, what?" Vance was disoriented. How had his simple purpose of talking sense into Strake gone so far astray?

"You've spent a year moping over your coins and your ledgers, mourning a woman who's been standing right next to you."

"Sila Resurrected, damn it."

"That's right, she Resurrected. She didn't suddenly forget everything." Strake tightened the embrace, as if Vance might break his grip and flee. Vance was seized with the urge to do just that. "Oh, brother, you've never really grasped the doctrine, have you? I dragged you into this and you found your own reasons to stay but it was never a question of simple faith for you, was it?"

Strake's firm grip on his shoulder forced Vance to look him in the eye. Vance saw his brother-of-old, earnest and alive with the simple joy of doctrinal interpretation. "Saint Mitus blesses us in order to make us who we need to be. He takes what is weak and imperfect and burns it away. The rest of the world sees a new man, but the man-of-old is still there. When you Resurrect, your priorities change as much as your looks, but you are still you. Your memories are intact. Some of them are just buried deeper than others."

"I know all this." Vance willed his voice to annoyed indifference but even he could hear the fear at its core.

"You know it. You don't understand it."

"What are you saying, Strake?"

His brother gave him a look a fond reproach, like a favourite pet caught doing something unspeakable to the furniture.

"Oh you great fool. She still loves you. It's you who's tearing her apart."

#

Vance couldn't sleep. He stalked the rambling halls of the House of Saint Mitus' Eye, settling for a while in the dark kitchen to chew some sourroot. He poked through Bunstable's library but found only tedious works of military history and treatises on mercantile theory. Of those latter, Vance knew each volume by heart. He rested briefly before the common room fire before surrendering to the certainty that sleep would not come.

He went outside. Dawn was an hour or two away. In the shadow of towering Luxichre, under snow-cloud skies, the dark was impenetrable. A single lantern hanging above the alpaca barn doors afforded dim respite from the ink of night.

Snow drifted lazily down through the lantern's pale circle of light. Vance felt it settle on his face and neck. The tiny stings of cold transported his thoughts.

Sila-of-old had spoken often about her home in the frozen wastes. Life was simple and hard. They hunted narwhals across the pack ice by day. By night they sealed their caves with blocks of ice and sang folk stories while they stripped carcasses, made clothes and repaired weapons. Word of Saint Mitus' feats was almost unknown there. When her visions began, seizing her with terrifying, mystifying images of strange landscapes and brutal wars, she might have gone mad. One night when they lay together, sweating and bright-eyed, Sila confessed to Vance that if it were not for a travelling mystic who recognised the signs of her possession by the spirit of the long-distant saint, she would have thrown herself into the freezing waters. Instead she had packed a few possessions and journeyed south to meet her destiny.

Was what Strake said true? Was that brave girl, who left all she knew to seek communion with a holy figure she'd never heard of, still there in the stern taskmaster Saint Mitus left behind?

His eyes adjusting to the dark, he circled the inn. Overhead Luxichre, broad and smooth, tapered to a thick pointed summit. It was atop its crest where Saint Mitus performed his second greatest miracle, after the first Resurrection. Facing the champion of King Scapra's army in single combat to decide the fate of the Dennel Tablelands, Mitus fought with such valour that king and champion both were persuaded to his cause. So legend went. Vance privately suspected that strong liquor and hasty land deals were a significant factor in the alliance.

As he rounded the western side of the inn, Vance saw light spilling from an upper-storey window. He knew the room. Petitioner Kreiner was awake, it seemed.

Seized by a sudden impulse, he re-entered the inn and climbed two flights to the western corridor. He knocked on her door before his resolve could fade.

"Who is it?"

"Vance. I saw the light, Petitioner. Is everything all right?"

The door opened a crack. She was dressed in a thick cassock, a hood drawn over her bald head for warmth. If she had slept, it was only poorly. She regarded him with weary caution.

"What do you want?"

"I wanted to –." He couldn't finish. Her eyes held no fondness for him. They barely registered recognition. Strake was wrong. "I want to go through the treasury details with you."

For a long moment she stared at him, blinking slowly. Then she said, "Are you hoping to cure my insomnia?"

Her expression was unchanged. It took a while to sink in that she was joking. It finished the work of unnerving him.

"I apologise for disturbing you, Petitioner. We can deal with this at a more appropriate hour."

Her mouth tightened. Her curt gesture waved him into silence. "Get your books and meet me in the common room. We might as well make the most of the quiet."

He caught a glimpse of her shucking off the cassock as her foot pushed the door closed.

#

It was the morning of the Feast of Horns.

Sometime during their perusal of the Eight's accounts, Vance had succumbed to the warmth of the common room hearth and dozed off. His awakening had been less agreeable. Strake nudged him awake with a booted foot and a hearty morning's greeting.

"Happy feast day, Eight-brother," he bellowed, shoving a steaming cup of vosot, the bitter tea flavoured with rancid alpaca butter favoured locally. Strake had taken to it with reckless abandon. Vance compared it unfavourably with spiced bile. "You didn't come back to our room last night. I hope you didn't do anything impious."

"As if you spent any time in our room," Vance replied without rancour. Despite his gregarious bother's insinuations, there were no salacious details to share. True, the early hours he had spent with Sila Kreiner had been unexpectedly companionable, almost comfortable. She had attended closely to his review of pressures placed upon the Eight's dwindling finances by Goodhost Bunstable's fleecing rates. They discussed strategies for soliciting new benefactions, perhaps at the Feast of Horns or else in the spring. His final recollection before falling asleep was Sila's confidence that the inconvenience of lingering at the House of Saint Mitus' Eye might be turned to opportunity, if harmony prevailed through the winter.

Vance did not ascribe her willingness to consult his expertise to well-hidden depths of rekindling passion.

Strake just sipped his swamp-mud brew through a knowing smirk and said nothing.

At morning venerations, Sila Kreiner's features were composed and relaxed, as though she'd woken fresh from a week's rest. At the end of her usual mechanical recitation of the liturgy, she had coughed and offered a few observations on the significance of the Feast of Horns to Saint Mitus. These amounted to little more than the observation that Mitus was a devotee of good food and copious liquor. Her suggestion that they take one last opportunity to enjoy themselves before a winter of meditative austerity and labour was delivered with her typical stolid pragmatism. Vance fancied he detected an amused note.

The pilgrims threw themselves into the feast preparations with a will, completing the repairs to the inn's outbuildings, hanging decorations and erecting the great tent. They trudged down to the nearby town leading an alpaca-drawn dray, loaded it with chairs and tables and returned. They stacked platters with the meat of a dozen animals, chopped vegetables, stirred fruit and herbs through simmering cauldrons of wine. Goodhost Yousta oversaw their labours with judicious eyes, offering numerous suggestions for improvement. Her husband and his liquor cabinet entertained several local burghers of nominal piety and advanced appetites.

At a mid-morning break, Vance observed the Goodhosts in a furious exchange of mutters. He couldn't make out the words, but the heat and the subject were unmistakable. He looked around, realising he hadn't seen Strake for some time. Nor was the Goodhosts' daughter Falaha present.

Alarmed, he sneaked into the House of Saint Mitus' Eyes to look for his brother. His search ended at his first stop. When he reached their shared room, he heard the unmistakable exertions of lovemaking. The hoarse, urgent grunts suggested the participants were close to their climaxes.

He didn't have time to wait for them to finish, nor was he inclined. Strake must know he was on the verge of exhausting both the Goodhosts' hospitality and his Petitioner's patience.

Swallowing hard, Vance threw the door open. "Strake, for blood's sake, get dressed –"

He stopped short, blood rushing to his head. Strake was there, naked skin flushed red with sweat and effort, his muscles rippling and hard. Falaha was beneath him, her fingers clawing into his shoulders, her chestnut curls spraying over the edge of the bunk like a spring waterfall. Beside them, Polma was perched astride Dessit, pinning him with her soldier's strength and a furious need. Her elder by nearly three decades, Dessit's face was purple with the effort to keep up with her.

All four turned their heads toward Vance with expressions ranging from horror to blank disinterest. Polma's hips did not slow their hungry rocking. Everyone else froze.

Strake's guileless grin was unapologetic. "Welcome back, brother. The bunks aren't big but I'm sure we can squeeze you in somewhere. Of course if this puts you in mind of somewhere you'd prefer to be, we'll forgive you." Falaha giggled again, Dessit made a strangled noise and Polma chanted her battalion motto as she came, hoarse-breathed and small breasts heaving.

"Saint's blood," said Vance. He didn't know where to look. Settling on the rough beams of the ceiling, he said, "Bunstable is on his way."

"He's the least of our problems, I'd say," said Strake, looking past Vance and pointing a crooked finger.

Vance whirled. Sila Kreiner stood behind him, her eyes simmering.

"Get up." Her fury was like a blast of wind across the northlandic ice. "Get your clothes on."

Falaha scurried from under Strake and scrabbled for her discarded clothes. Strake lazily untangled himself from the sheets and stood. Even Polma, whose eyes blazed with defiant satisfaction, climbed down from her summit. Dessit just lay there, his breath racing, his stiff cock flat against his stomach.

Vance insinuated himself between the group and their leader. "Petitioner Kreiner," he began, "this is festive spirits, nothing more."

She ignored him. She said, "You betray my oath of good conduct, to a Blessed Host, no less. Just to slake your cheap lusts."

Vance tried again. "Sila, I –"

"Say nothing." Struggle as she might to keep her face blank, Sila was grey with disappointment. It was not the face Vance knew better than any other. It was not the face he'd fallen in love with. Pilgrims made no vows of celibacy, not formal ones. But in the tight, tense communities of the Eight, discretion was essential.

Worse, she committed the conduct of the Eight to the Goodhosts with her word as a Saint's Petitioner. Bunstable's House was Blessed by Mitus himself, in perpetuity. However willing was Falaha's participation, Strake's indulgence strained the limits of hospitality. The insult to their host was an insult to their patron.

With sick horror Vance conceded the failure to prevent this moment was his. Sila had given him a responsibility she could not assume for herself. Her eyes were chips of frozen resolve. Vance could not meet her glare and looked at Strake instead. Strake was flushed, amused and unapologetic.

Sila pushed the door wide open. Not an invitation but a command. She said, "Get dressed. Attend to the final preparations for the Feast of Horns. We will discharge our promise to the Blessed Hosts. As soon as the feast rituals are observed, you will all pack your belongings and leave the House of Saint Mitus' Eye."

"Leave?" said Vance. "But the mountain road is closed, Petitioner. We cannot ascend in this weather."

She replied in a cracking voice. "We are not climbing the sacred mountain. We will turn back down the valley. This Eight is broken. Our pilgrimage is done."

Polma hissed in anger and slapped the timbers of the bunk. "The pilgrimage is not done," she growled. "I have not Resurrected. It is not done!"

Falaha caught her breath. She threw her arms about Strake's shoulders as if she could protect him from the barbed decision. "Petitioner Kreiner, do not be rash. Please. If you break within these walls, my father's shame –"

"Will be an ordeal of endurance I suspect he will survive, with enough coin," Sila said. "I am the Petitioner. The Eight is broken. It is done because I say it is done!"

Dessit made a coughing noise that they mistook for assent. Then his jaw opened and he let out a howl of protest. His voice rose and became more shrill. The tight black hairs on his stomach and groin began to shrivel and wisp into smoke. Vance stared in horror at the dark tendrils coiling up from Dessit's belly.

"Resurrection!" Vance gasped. "Get snow buckets! Quickly!"

With a soldier's obedience and an innkeeper's duty, Polma and Falaha fled away to comply, their incomplete dress forgotten. Strake abandoned his clothes and watched, unconscious of his nakedness, his whole attention on Dessit's ordeal.

Sila Kreiner pushed past Vance and hunched over Dessit, grasping his hand in support. Dessit rocked and curled his body, as if he could crawl away from the fire in his stomach. "Mitus' Blessings are on you, Erno Dessit, in this House of his Eyes, on this day of feasting," she recited, calm and sure, strong and soothing.

Dessit howled again. Now flames guttered along his abdomen, spreading from one sizzling hair to the next like a racing forest fire. His skin was blistering and blackening.

Vance grabbed a blanket from the top bunk and rolled it tight into an improvised beater. He smothered the flames before they could spread from the bunk. He could see it would be no use. In a moment Dessit's whole body would be engulfed in a miniature tornado of flame. When the final fireball came, it would consume the tiny bedchamber.

"Get him out of here," he said, pulling at Sila Kreiner's shoulder.

She was a rock, resolute and unmoving. "He stays," she replied with calm command.

Strake said "Brother, see to the fire before it takes hold."

He spared Sila a second of disbelief, and one for his brother. Then Vance ran to organise the fire fight.

Organising was what he was good for.

#

The combination of a heavy snowfall and the intervention of guests arriving early for the feast brought the flames under control. From the outside, the House of Saint Mitus' Eyes was a sorry sight. The entire southern facing had charred and collapsed before the flames were finally snuffed out.

Vance, shivering in damp and sooty clothing, dawdled at the rear of an exploratory troupe established to inspect the internal damage. Gerrolt the carpenter led, appraising the structure's soundness with each step. Sila Kreiner followed, placing herself between Goodhost Bunstable at the fore and his daughter Falaha. Perhaps she sought to forestall further recriminations between them. Vance suspected it was him she wanted to keep at a distance. He was grateful.

The fire had spread quickly from the pilgrim's dormitory to the entrance hall, the library and several adjoining bedrooms. The investigators proceeded cautiously, one eye on the ceiling beams above. Before long it became apparent that while a staircase here and a dividing wall there were beyond repair, the bulk of the damage was superficial. The liberal application throughout of certain waxy varnishes had built a resistance to flame into the ancient timbers of the way-house.

Gerrolt itemised a series of renovation projects. His manner was taciturn and assured. He struck Vance as completely at ease with the Eight's dissolution. When informed of Sila's decision, he had blinked just once, before turning to Bunstable. "With your permission, Goodhost, I would like to venerate Saint Mitus by restoring his House to order."

The shocked Bunstable had naturally accepted the offer. His wits regathering, his mind had now turned to other matters. "Petitioner Kreiner, I wish to discuss appropriate restitutions. Until a full accounting can be made of damages, I suggest the ash-purse be doubled and-"

Vance cut in. "Goodhost Bunstable, the Eight is disbanded. The customary obligations are no longer inapplicable. Tradition requires that I discharge contractual debts and divide the treasury's remaining funds equally to the pilgrims." After a moment's consideration he added, "For what it's worth, you may count on my share."

In the dull lamplight, Bunstable's face fell into grey horror. Before he could muster a protest, Sila raised her voice. "Fear not, Goodhost. You are blessed by Saint Mitus."

"Are you mad?" cried Bunstable. "My inn is in ruins. My lodgers have set it ablaze and now flee the bill of fare. What blessing is this?"

Falaha placed her hand on her father's shoulder. He flinched and turned a furious eye upon her, but her thoughtful expression dissuaded further outburst. "Father, consider. No Eight of such high standing has broken in decades. Today's events border on the notorious, and Petitioner Kreiner's followers will carry word to the far corners of the land. Our House's fame will grow with a small taste of scandal."

Bunstable's frown contorted in grievance. She turned her beguiling smile on him, delivering the fatal blow to his objections. "Of course if you prefer no notoriety whatever to arise, a spring wedding on the birthday of the Saint would be as prestigious as it is auspicious."

As the flustered Bunstable endured hearty congratulatory back slaps from Gerrolt, Vance slipped quietly away. He found his way to the threshold of his dormitory room. Fire resistant varnish had spared nothing from the fury of Dessit's conflagration. The furnishings, their possessions, his account books – all were muddy ash now.

"You can account for every coin with or without your ledgers, Initiate." Sila had appeared at his side, her face a disdainful mask. The biting odour of steam and slag was almost unbearable.

"Depend upon it, Petitioner."

"I'm not the Petitioner anymore."

"Nor do I follow." Having confirmed his destitution, Vance wanted nothing more than to leave. Under Sila's stern glare, he found himself rooted in place, framed by ruins.

"You are freed of your obligations, Vance. I'm sorry they were such a burden."

"Don't tell me you broke the Eight on my behalf," said Vance. "I couldn't bear that."

The space between them was infinite. He felt too small beside her. Unresurrected. Unworthy. The Saint did not need him, nor did she.

Sila sighed. The sound had a strangled quality. "Have I any hope of forgiveness?"

Vance could not think of a response. He said nothing.

Her voice barely a whisper, she said, "I Resurrected too soon."

Vance said "Strake says Saint Mitus doesn't set the fire until the clay's become the cup." To his ears, it sounded hollow. He hoped she found some solace in it.

"I don't mean it was too soon for the Saint," she replied. "Too soon for us. I was not ready. Neither were you. I wish I could have spared you that pain."

The concession felt like a dismissal. Vance could not bear his own mute incomprehension. He walked away.

#

A newly Resurrected Dessit, flanked by Sila Kreiner on one side and Strake Adell on the other, took his place unsteadily at the head of the long table, served by tradition for the absent Saint. He was hairless of course, tall where he'd been short, and much less overweight, though still thick around the torso and thighs. His eyes were blue now and his skin a light tan. He appeared to be in his late twenties.

The feast-goers offered congratulations to Dessit-reborn, to his companions and to the Saint. When it became known that the kitchens were untouched by the flames, cups of mulled wine were raised in toast. Even Goodhosts Bunstable and Yousta, their regard for their daughter split between suspicion and jubilation, held their cups aloft and thanked Mitus.

Vance held himself apart from the celebrations. He no longer knew how to behave in this company. The Eight was broken. He would not Resurrect. There was no place for him in the Order of Rejuvenationists now. No other pilgrimage would take on a member of a failed Eight. He could not imagine becoming a lay fellow, devoting himself with simple faith and no hope of a greater calling. Saint Mitus might have great plans for his fellowship, but they no longer included Vance Adell.

He became aware that Strake and Sila were watching him, conferring in whispers. He turned, uncomfortable, looking down the road to the town at the steady stream of well-wishers and patrons of the Feast of Horns. One of them would surely agree to accommodate him for the night. He no longer wished to return the way he came in the company of his former companions. Best to make a clean break of it.

"The Feast hasn't begun yet. Are you already looking to tidy up?"

He had become lost in his reverie. He hadn't noticed Strake approach. Too late to run, but what could he say?

He decided on simplicity. "I'm leaving."

Strake nodded thoughtfully. "A broken Eight doesn't need a treasurer," he observed.

"I wish you well on your engagement, brother. You've made a formidable match. The Saint would approve."

"No doubt," said Strake, with an air of sheepish pleasure. They watched the milling crowd in silence. The forced cheer of the tragedy narrowly averted was giving way to relief and a mood of celebratory thanks. Eventually Strake said, "Did you know Saint Mitus never travelled with seven other people?"

"What?" Vance had never heard anything like that before, let alone from his doctrinally-precise brother.

Strake's guarded expression would better have fit Strake-of-old. "On his original pilgrimage he met many people along the way. He led armies, fought battles and saw the wonders of the world, but he never came up with the idea of the Eight until he sat down at the end of his life to write his memoirs."

"Why eight then?"

"I think it was just his lucky number."

"Are you trying to tell me something?"

Strake spread his hands and shrugged. "Not a thing," he said. He looked across at Sila Kreiner, who was leading an impromptu ritual of greeting for Dessit. She looked relaxed. There was even a small smile playing across her face as she led the prayer.

"Things change, big brother. Saint Mitus has big plans, but maybe he's not as fussy as we all think about how they get delivered. Walking the world in a big circle, seeing the same sights he saw a hundred years ago and telling his stories over and again, until we burst into flame. Even a drunken old warhorse like Mitus can think of more efficient ways of getting things done, don't you think?"

Vance considered the life he would go back to, counting the coins for some grasping lord, perhaps managing an estate in his later years. He looked back to Sila. She was a new woman. She could never return to her ice sheets and her gutting knives. She had given up her Eight. Without it she had nothing. He had never seen such a look of contentment, not on this face nor her last.

"I won't Resurrect," he observed. His relief was a surprise; he'd expected to give voice to overwhelming shame.

Strake wrapped a reassuring arm around his shoulder. "I never thought you would, big brother. The Resurrected are forged to become blades in Saint Mitus' arsenal. Dessit will return to his nets and boats to become a great man of the port cities. Gerrolt's been building great monuments in his head for months. As for Polna, she'll lead great war parties whether she burns or not."

"What about Sulsan and Hiram?"

Strake chuckled. "Every general needs soldiers with good muscle. Mitus made them mighty. We can't expect him to work miracles on their wits."

"You know, you blaspheme a lot more often since you were reborn." Vance caught himself smiling, warming to his brother's good humour. Saint Mitus, it was said, was an amiable companion.

"Well, there you are then. I'm the chaos and disorder that fans the flames."

"Don't let the Goodhosts hear that." The smoke odour hanging to their damp clothes made him blink away tears. What other cause could there be? "Are you really so keen to overthrow tradition?"

"I'm just here to tear down some walls and clear a path. Kreiner's the one who will make new traditions. No more Order of Rejuvenationists, no more marching songs, no grand sightseeing expeditions. Even the Nineteen Venerated tourist spots may find new significance."

"I wish her well," said Vance. He meant it. It still hurt to say it. Better to go now, before the grief became real. He turned his back to the revelry.

A thin horn sounded a low, groaning note that echoed across the massive face of Luxichre. The Feast of Horns began with low cheers fading into a song of mourning and renewal. "Goodbye, Strake."

Instead of overpowering him with one of his bear hugs, Strake asked, "Do you know why I knew you would never take the fires, Vance?"

He paused. "Did you have a vision?"

"I used my eyes, brother." Now Strake lay his hands on Vance's head and turned it gently. In his eyes shone the blessing of the Saint and, perhaps, permission to change his mind. "You're already what she needs you to be. You always were."

Vance saw Sila Kreiner, seated with the faithful, singing and smiling before the House of Saint Mitus' Eyes. Her eyes were alight, green and wet, shining with love and purpose. The seat beside her was empty, a senseless void left in hope of a centre.

Vance looked past her to the House of Saint Mitus' Eye, smoke vapour wisping about it in the freezing mountain air. He thought of its hearth and the morning's fire kindled from the evening's coals. He thought of spring, distant but closing. He thought of warmth shared against the cold.

A fire grew in his belly as he returned to the Feast of Horns.

'The Feast of Horns' came out of a 24-hour writing challenge for the Canberra Speculative Fiction Guild. Coordinator Ian McHugh gave each of us several prompts one Saturday afternoon, and we were to meet the following afternoon at a café with a finished story. The only prompt I still remember is that I drew a Jack of Clubs playing card, corresponding to a "troublemaker" or "disruptive element" or something like that. Strake emerged fully formed.

The idea of the pilgrimage and the (literally) transformative experience came from other prompts. The idea of a noble and spiritual adventure being undermined by miscommunication, unforeseen problems and petty exploitation was, sadly, all me.

INCIDENTAL

Everything changed for Benji when he hit puberty and lost his incidental music.

Growing up, he was no different to any other kid. He played the same games, ate the same food and he was followed everywhere by the same simplistic, cheerful party pop. Sure, there were times when he ran through some minor keys, like when his parakeet got out of its cage and eaten by the neighbour's cat, or when his mum caught his dad harmonising with the neighbour's suggestive bossa-nova ambiance. But even after Mum started her new life as a soloist, Benji mostly bopped along with an untroubled heart and a C-D-F refrain in the air.

One week after his thirteenth birthday, his music went away. His friends Cally and Winston noticed it before Benji did.

"How come your music's stopped?" asked Cally. She was taking a break from their soccer practise to peel open an orange. A warbling trombone wafted up from the mix of her usual upbeat swing number. "Are you feeling okay?"

Winston thundered the ball past Benji into the goal net. "He's so dumb he thinks it's the intermission!" A cymbal clash broke Winston's soaring, horn-heavy fanfare. They all chuckled along.

Benji hadn't even noticed the silence. Now it followed him everywhere.

His mother was even more worried. With a frantic oboe chorus buzzing in her wake, she raced Benji to the paediatric musicologist.

The doctor, his furrowed brow echoing with elegiac mountain pipe music, took blood samples and ran some basic scales tests. Benji's music didn't respond. The doctor referred him to a psychoacoustics specialist.

The specialist steered Benji into an acoustics chamber that could detect a pin drop or a dying man's last chord. Nothing. In a baffled studio that damped every noise but Benji's breathing, he took x-rays and brain scans and a few more blood samples.

Benji waited for hours, the only sounds his scared breathing and his mother's muted, mournful chorus that sometimes swelled to a rousing reassurance of lively drums and brass.

Finally the specialist returned with images of Benji's head. In time to a stern, staccato waltz, he tapped a ruler at a blue patch in the cross-section of Benji's brain and recommended exploratory surgery.

Benji couldn't tell whether the specialist's jarring pitch changes meant that he was excited or confused.

Cally's outrage expressed as atonal ascending scales, strident and brassy. "They're going to cut your head open?"

Benji shrugged. "Nobody knows what's wrong. I think they're scared." He tried to sound brave but not so much as an adventurous viola sounded forth. "They try not to be but my Mum says she can hear it in their trebles."

Winston said, "They should just leave you alone. You don't have to have music if you don't want it." But then he ran away, trailing a clatter of cowbells and plucked ukulele notes.

Benji thought it over. Winston was wrong. He wanted his music back.

Nurses wordlessly flitted around his hospital bed making efficient, business-like movements. They swept in and out of sight like ants disassembling a picnic to brisk, professional woodwinds.

As Benji breathed through the anaesthetist's mask, their music wandered away from melody into tuneless contralto waves.

But Benji was aware of their timpani rumbles of submerged fear and the first dissonant strains of a bassoon as the surgeon arrived. Keys diverged and time signatures fell out of harmony as his eyes closed.

#

Benji knew before his eyelids began to unglue that the operation had failed. Nothing surrounded him but the soft hiss of a ventilator, the hum of indifferent machinery and the hushed buzz of human speech beyond too-thin walls.

He tried to squeeze his eyes shut but the darkness made the silence worse, a void that drained hope and fed despair. With a lump rising in his throat, he let the light in and looked around at the blue wall of vinyl curtains hanging around his bed. The curtain's perimeter diverted around the back of an unoccupied chair. He felt its emptiness deep inside his stomach; he felt no hunger for the bowl of pale, spotted fruit in the bowl alongside his pillow.

Benji knew one thing. All the doctors and nurses hadn't been able to figure out what happened to him. His music was gone. They didn't know where it was and they didn't know how to bring it back.

He thought about the last time he had cried. One afternoon a year ago, his father had said goodbye in a haze of endless regret, unstoppable tears and slow-strummed minor chords.

Without low, slurring strings rising with the lump in his throat, Benji didn't remember how to cry.

The talkers came closer and now he could hear strains of concern, confusion and even some anger. He could hear violins darting in and out of their upper registers. His mother was nervous and upset. Benji steeled himself for the crashing peals of percussion and trills of flutes as she tried to hide her fear and disappointment.

Voices and shadows fell across the curtains and they parted for his mother and the surgeon. Benji met her eye. He tried to think of a way to tell her he was sorry.

Then all at once Benji's mother's music softened and transformed. A counter-melody cut through her distraught fugue, a chorus of violas laying down a bridge for a crisply-strummed guitar to appear.

Benji's mother looked around in surprise, even a little alarm – she'd never made a sound like it. Next to her, the doctor's face made the same expression. His music was falling into rhythm with hers. Guitars and a snappy drum fill, the kind that made Benji want to stamp his feet and wave his arms. Fun, happy music spilled out of them and filled his ears.

Benji smiled at his mother. He laughed at the doctor, and the nurses who ran in and the orderly who reached for him with big, trembling hands.

They were playing his song.

'Music as magic' is, depending on how you look at it, either one of my favourite motifs or a crutch I lean on far too often. If there's a clinically safe dosage, I am probably a certifiable motif abuser.

In this case, I wanted to turn the idea "what if people could hear their own incidental music?" into a comical short film script. The idea bounced around my head for a couple of years, until it attached itself to the character of an innocent child, with creepy results.

*'Incidental' was the first piece of flash fiction I ever submitted for publication. It appeared in **EGM Shorts** (Evil Girlfriend Media, February 2016), edited by Jennifer Brozek.*

LOST DOGS

Eric unspooled a length of tape with a sound like ribs splitting. Morning mist crept around his ankles. The steady bleed of fresh traffic emptying the suburbs had yet to begin.

He pinched off the tape with his teeth and pressed it across the top of the poster, fixing it to a pole of weathered green timber, burying signs of various vintages.

LOST DOG, exclaimed the text above the photo. *HAVE YOU SEEN ME?*

Hayley's eyes stared out in happy expectation. Even the faded impression left by a toner-starved printer couldn't rob them of their simple, goofy joy. Eric's son, Matthew, had taken the picture at dinner time, when Hayley's natural affection was at its bubbly peak.

They still had no idea how she got out. How did an overfed, congenitally lazy golden retriever clear a six-foot brick wall, or a latched front gate?

Admiring his handiwork, he realised suddenly he'd forgotten to add his phone number alongside the house line and Craig's office number. Craig would be pissed if someone called him at work. But Eric hadn't brought a pen.

The chill creeping into his fingers reminded him he still had four blocks and eighteen poles to cover. He stuffed the tape back into his jacket pocket and stumped off toward the next corner. In case Hayley had strayed into a neighbour's yard, he peered over each fence.

A few joggers nodded as they huffed past. Down the street some bird watcher wandered about with a camera held up like a permanent facial attachment. Eric waved a poster at a woman walking a shaggy little Pekinese with a silver collar. "Excuse me. My son's dog has gone missing. Have you seen her?"

The woman's legs were clad in black leggings, thick as sealskin, while her upper half disappeared into a bulky sweatshirt. The little dog retreated behind her pristine running shoes. She said, "A dog? It's not that dirty great brown thing, is it?" She sounded like she'd eaten something disagreeable but her eyes ran up and down over Eric with familiar appreciation. He was used to it. He kept in shape.

"I – no, Hayley's a golden retriever." He pointed to the picture. "What brown thing are you talking about?"

The dog flattened onto its belly and growled. Its buzzsaw whine struggled to penetrate the frozen air. "Stop that, Chelsea." The woman jerked on its lead. It raised a shaggy black eye toward her but its protest persisted. "Oh, I nearly ran over some big dog wandering along the road yesterday afternoon. Size of a bull and covered in curls. I've only just had the front end retouched from hitting a roo last year. When I hit the horn it just stared me down."

The cold killed his interest in lingering over a dead end. "Not my Hayley then. She'd have fainted at the noise."

The Pekinese burst into yapping at the distant ornithology enthusiast, straining at his lead to give chase. "Shut up, Chelsea. I didn't let it eat you, did I?" The woman frowned. "I'd better get her home. You live on Parvenir Street, don't you? I'll drop in if I see your Hayley."

"Thanks so much."

Eric's gaze strayed away. For the first time he noticed posters slathering every power pole on the street. Each bore a photo of a different dog.

#

Craig backed his Audi backed down the driveway in a cloud of exhaust vapour. Eric danced out of the vehicle's way and rapped frozen knuckles against the frosted driver's side window. The car slowed without stopping. The window opened a narrow crack.

Craig said, "I'm late for work. You took too long." He made no effort to be audible above the Arcade Fire album playing on the stereo. Eric's hearing had become sharper since he'd moved into Craig's house.

"You said you would drop Mattie off at school this morning." Eric complained. "You know he's upset."

"Well, he was apparently too upset to be ready in time, so you'll have to handle it." Craig checked his mirrors and turned the wheel hard, forcing Eric to jump back. "Call me if you get a job today. I'll be back at half-six unless something comes up."

Eric's fingernails dug into his palms as he watched the Audi roar away. Not a word of concern for the dog, let alone for their twelve year old son.

No, he corrected himself. Never 'our' son. Just mine.

Matthew still wore pyjamas at the breakfast table. He looked up with eyes rubbed so red they were almost bruised. "Did you find her?"

Eric shook his head, dropping a comforting hand on his son's shoulder. "She'll be around somewhere. You know her, she probably followed someone home and scabbed dinner and a warm bed."

Matthew dropped a spoon into his cereal bowl, splashing a corona of milk around the table. "How did she get out anyway?"

Eric didn't remember if he'd checked the gate when he'd let Hayley out. She ran into the yard happily and he went back to alternating between reps on the rowing machine, scanning JobFinder.com.au, and running surgical strike missions with his Acts of War Online clan.

Now wasn't the time to cede his authority. "Mate, we've been over this. Dogs are smart and curious, they find ways to get out. Hayley will come home when she gets hungry. Now get yourself ready for school and I'll walk down with you. We can keep an eye out for her on the way."

Matthew's mood improved when Eric pointed out his posters.

"Did you check the charge on your phone, Dad? Someone might call." A flashing warning light heralded its imminent failure. Matthew rolled his eyes. "Charge it when you get home," he said as they parted company at the school gate. "Don't forget, okay?"

Okay. It was a simple way to avoid disappointing his son. And still, he nearly forgot. He stopped by the letter box to collect the mail, dropped his keys as he opened the front door, and tripped on the cracked tile in the doorway he'd promised Craig he could fix. He almost put the phone down with the rest of the paraphernalia when it buzzed a message alert.

The message displayed an unlisted number. No text, just a file format he didn't know. He spam-filed it. Then he connected the depleted phone to his office computer, relieved to have remembered his promise.

He called the study nook next to the lounge his office; it was a workstation inset into the wall with a small shelf stacked high with job centre forms, discarded applications, and computer game walkthrough guide magazines. On one side hung photos of Craig, Matthew, and Matthew's mother Gemma, all fading fast as the cheap department store photo paper lost its grip on their images. Discarded pens, bulldog clips, and employment agents' business cards occupied the space around the keyboard and mouse. What little desktop remaining visible was spattered with coffee rings and energy bar crumbs.

Using his coffee mug to clear space for itself, he sat down to work. His inbox highlighted communications from job registries as urgent; Craig set it up to save time. Today it was empty, so he checked the community calendar website, where temporary vacancies and casual labour jobs were sometimes listed.

No bites. He made a note of the unsuccessful search. Craig made him keep a job diary.

Then an article headline caught his eye: "*Council spokesman denies animal cull*". He scanned the first few paragraphs. Across the surrounding suburbs, dogs were being reported missing. Rates payers were pointing fingers at the local council, accusing them of everything from failing to act to conducting an indiscriminate roundup of pets.

Eric's read on into the comments section. A couple of readers claimed their dogs had gone missing in recent days. Many more chimed in to retort their pets were safe and well, bluntly calling into question the previous commenters' fitness to own animals. There was nothing useful after that.

He typed his own reply into the forum, adding his voice to the demand the council increase patrols for missing animals. Committing to the comment left him with a small sense of accomplishment. Not as good as finding Hayley, but something.

The whole business had ruined him for the day's job-seeking grind. The prospect of trawling through search after search of employer websites was too much.

Instead, he ran through a quick workout on the elliptical trainer and took a shower.

He'd just logged into AoWO with his combat medic build when his mobile phone rang. With one hand, he typed a quick greeting to his clan mates already gathered for the morning's skirmishing. With the other, he scooped up the phone and thumbed the answer button without looking: "Hello. Eric."

"Have you found your dog yet?" The man's voice sounded cool, almost disinterested, and distant as a speaker phone in another room. It was nobody Eric knew.

"Not yet," Eric said, fossicking for a pen. "Have you seen her? She's about five, a golden retriever cross with big ears–"

The voice interrupted, "Is this her?"

A peal of hoarse barks like a mulcher choking on a tree burst from the phone. Overwhelmed speakers cut in and out as the sound resolved into a castanet-rattle of hacking coughs.

"Hayley?"

Eric clapped a hand to his mouth and dropped the phone. It bounced from the keyboard toward the floor, swinging on its charging cable. Hoarse moans, grunts and ragged, breathless growls still came through with awful clarity.

He clawed up the phone with shaking fingers and looked at the number of the incoming call. Hayley's voice had subsided to a disturbing rhythm of half-howls too starved of breath to reach their former volume.

Private caller. No number.

Eric yelled, "Who is this? Where's my–"

The call disconnected.

His left hand hurt. He looked at it and saw a flattened ring of purpling tooth marks gouged into the flesh of his palm. An itch like busy mosquitoes spread from his ears to his shoulder blades. He tried to rise from his chair. His legs wouldn't take his weight.

He couldn't take his eyes off the crescent imprint of his own teeth.

One ferocious laugh, a guffaw that stretched the skin of his ribs, emptied his lungs.

#

Eric popped the lid of a plastic tea container and found nothing more substantial than a whiff of stale leaves. He shut the lid with shaking hands.

Returning the call had gone through to a message service with no message. After a long wait, an electronic voice informed him the recipient's full inbox had discarded his recording. He tried three times without success.

He called Craig. The call diverted straight to his messages. Eric wondered how Craig's clients managed if they could never even get through to his assistant.

Should he try Gemma? Even if she answered – and he knew she wouldn't – what would he say? He couldn't ask her for help. That bridge burned down long ago and blew away on a gale of solicitor letters and court hearings.

Gripping the kitchen bench with one hand, he fished more plastic jars from the overhead pantry. The collection soon covered the narrow bench space. He clawed one lid off after another, finding water crackers, imported salt flakes, and a set of herb-infused vinaigrettes in designer bottles.

There must be some plain black tea stashed somewhere.

Craig considered the kitchen his domain. He'd equipped it with utensils and appliances endorsed by the best celebrity chefs. After every business trip, he returned with another jar of locally-sourced jams, preserves or olive oil. A meticulous organisation sorted the pantry by size and contents, everything labelled and dated. Marco Polo would have envied Craig's spice shelf.

Eric did most of cooking using a basic utensils drawer. The only time Craig put his kitchen to use was for the dinner parties he threw for rich friends or important clients. Depending on the progressiveness of the client's views and whether Craig wanted to talk business, he might sometimes invite Eric to join him. As far as he knew, Matthew had never tasted anything Craig cooked.

The odd night off would be nice but responsibility for Matthew's welfare was his alone. By unspoken agreement, Craig put a roof over their heads and nothing more. When things with Gemma went from bad to crazy, Eric grabbed the lifeline Craig threw and held on with both hands. He knew better than to mess it up by asking for more than he was offered.

The last container rattled as he unclipped the spring seal, releasing an altogether different scent. He retrieved a packet of cigarettes, still wrapped in its plastic sheath. The cover depicted a mouthful of cracked teeth jutting like flood debris from wasted black gums. Conspicuous letters threatened disease and addiction.

They weren't his. He'd given up ages ago, quitting cold turkey almost by accident during the chaos of his divorce. In eight months of drama, smoking was the one small thing he stayed in control of. Every accusation, every disbelieving scream, even both slaps – he swallowed them and turned them into a refusal for the next smoke. It worked.

If they were Craig's, wouldn't he smell them on his breath and clothes? When Eric quit, suddenly everything he owned reeked. The stink still lingered on some of his favourite clothes. Mouth to mouth, head to head, together with Craig almost every night. He would smell tobacco, wouldn't he? Yes. Surely yes.

That left Matthew, who was twelve and angry.

Eric drained a glass of water, contemplating and rejecting parental strategies. His mobile shivered against his thigh.

"Hello." His subdued greeting received no response. He rolled his wrist around to look at the screen. Anonymous again. A grey thumbnail image revealed nothing.

A soundless video played without prompting. The monochrome blurs of the thumbnail resolved into silent movement.

Hayley circled on a concrete floor painted with puddles of various shades, her blonde fur matted and dishevelled. Her teeth were bared, gums rimmed with froth and muzzle dark and dripping.

She drew down low onto her haunches, ears flat against her head, eyes steady and staring. Bars rose behind her. The camera shook, losing her image and returning to it in an instant.

Hayley inched forward, the fur at her throat ruffling as she snarled, her whole frame poised and quivering. The tension in her posture, the vicious power she held in bare restraint, was alien to her usual placid indolence.

She opened her mouth in an unheard bark and leapt forward. Another shape, some kind of long-haired, long-faced, European hunting dog, crashed into her, jaws first. Its hair looked as though it had been well-groomed a few minutes earlier.

The dogs bounced off each other and rolled apart. Legs splayed and thrashed as they regained their footing.

Hayley rushed forward and clamped her teeth on the side of the other dog's head. The unsteady camera obscured things. When they parted, a slick of dark fluid trailed in the wake of Hayley's jaws. Blood gouted from the ragged hole where the other dog's ear had been.

The camera held on the other dog as it let rip with an inaudible peal of full-throated protests, its jaws working away like it ate the air. Hayley swept in low, her head rolled sideways to get a clear shot at the other dog's throat. It backed off, rolling its face away to deflect her assault onto the scruff of its neck. She twisted and drilled her snout up under its chin. Her teeth caught hold. Fresh blood jetted from either side of her muzzle.

Hayley bore the other dog to the ground, forcing it with unrelenting jaws to roll onto its back in helpless submission.

Eric felt a sense of breathless dread as the camera moved away from the struggling dogs. More dogs were inside the cage or pen, whatever it was. Every size and breed imaginable, from pocket novelty breeds to cavaliers, cattle dogs and hulking mastiffs. They circled the fight, staring intently.

The picture finally stopped on an enormous hound resting on its haunches. Half as big again as its largest companion, the beard-muzzled wolf hound held itself with a lean muscularity. Its thick hair curled into an incongruous perm. Its lower jaw hung open, tongue panting as it watched.

The video froze on the large dog's intent glare. No matter which way Eric tilted the phone, those eyes remained fixed on him.

The phone vibrated. Eric's hand recoiled as if bitten. He dropped it on the stack of leftover posters, mud-spattered and curling at the edges.

Eric squeezed his eyes shut, breathing fast and heavy as he tried to push back against panic rising like a snake. His drumming fingers became slapping palms, hammering the kitchen bench as if beating the sensation from his hands could drive out the image of the dogfight.

And another image: Matthew's face, crushed and anxious.

Something buckled inside Eric. Outrage and horror ran in parallel.

Who would do something like that to innocent dogs? Who would send him something like–

His eyes snapped open and fixed on the topmost poster. He pushed the phone out of the way, clearing the decks for a close inspection.

House line. Craig's work number. No mobile contact details.

So how did the dog-torturer know who to call?

Eric snatched up the phone and thumbed through to the log files. The number was unlisted. He selected the log entry and hit the redial icon anyway.

It began to ring, displaying a number that hadn't been there a moment before.

He pressed the phone against his ear; it rang. His ears thundered and burned. He felt light-headed as the call connected and a woman began to say: "Hello?"

"What kind of bloody fucking monster are you?" his voice erupted from him, louder than he meant. "Where's my dog? What the hell have you done with her, you–?"

A voice pushed through the haze roaring in his eardrums, calm but firm and urgent. "Please calm down, sir. I understand you're upset. I want to help you, sir. Please calm down."

Eric heard himself trail off, as if he were witnessing a distant argument draw to an unexpected standstill. The woman's voice burred with a cool timbre and the hint of an Asian accent he couldn't place. She said, "Thank you, sir. Now to whom am I speaking?"

Eric wasn't ready to give ground. "Who am I speaking to?"

"My name is Chun, sir. You've called the Cooper Gardens Animal Control Centre. Do you have a concern about a dog?"

He caught himself stamping like he was working the kick-bass pedal in a heavy metal band. The tips of his fingers tingled. He loosened his grip on the phone.

Feigning calm until his nerves steadied, he explained about Hayley. He described her in detail, down to her favourite food, which was chicken mince, and her favourite toy, a clown doll made of rope and leather. He felt ridiculous. It was right there on her sleeping mat by the back door.

"I'm very sorry, Mister Ullman. We don't have a dog fitting Hayley's description with us at the moment."

Eric asked for the depot's address. With only the slightest pause, Chun gave it to him. Eric wrote it down and hung up.

The phone chimed immediately. "Craig? You won't believe-"

"Is there something wrong with you?"

"Craig, love, I've had a really difficult morning-"

"Shut up. I've been calling for twenty minutes." Craig's voice had a down-low pitch that sometimes meant he was horny but more often signalled anger.

"Eric, I have a project board meeting in six minutes. Dealing with your shit is messing up my preparation."

"Craig, what are you calling about?"

"The school, Eric. They called me on my office phone. A number which I presume you gave to them."

"I gave your name as an emergency contact in case-"

"I worked that out for myself, thanks. Get my name off the list, Eric. I don't want to be disturbed at work by a school principal who thinks I'm a free babysitter."

Eric's teeth crushed back and forth. "What did they call about?"

"Matthew started a fight and hurt a kid. The principal wants to talk to you about suspension."

"Matthew started a fight?"

In the same tone he used to discipline incompetent interns, Craig said, "You need to sort this out, Eric. Take charge for once, okay? Straighten Matthew out."

#

"Is everything all right with your domestic situation, Mister Ullman?"

Eric cocked his head. His attention had wandered when he caught a glimpse of movement through the window. It was just a cat haring across the school courtyard.

"I'm sorry, Anne – my what situation?"

He shuffled in his chair, returning Principal Lynch's cold frown with an apologetic nod. Beside him, Matthew let out a small hiss like a leaking bike valve.

"Are you and your partner providing Matthew with a stable home environment, Mister Ullman?"

"What? I'm here to talk about Mattie."

Anne Lynch wrote something in tiny angular letters on a form. "That's precisely what we're talking about, Mister Ullman. Matthew has been exhibiting markedly abnormal behaviour. In my experience, when a child demonstrates temperamental changes of this sort, it's invariably associated with something they've witnessed or experienced at home."

Eric felt a scratching sensation crawl down his back. "Matthew is upset because the family dog is missing. We're all upset about Hayley."

"Matthew told me about the dog, Mister Ullman." The principal looked down at her form, took more notes and filled boxes with cross-marks. "Matthew's teacher told me this has been going on for weeks."

"Matthew's environment is very supportive." He pressed hands to knees to stop his legs shaking. "He has everything he needs at home."

She adjusted her glasses with a fingertip to each hinge. "I understand he has not had access to his mother in some time."

Matthew stared at the floor, his ears turning bright scarlet.

Eric said, "She's missed her last couple of visiting weekends. It's nothing, okay? Just ordinary mix-ups."

The principal leaned across her desk, a storm building across the equator of her face. "Mister Ullman, I don't think there's anything ordinary about this. Matthew bit another student in front of several witnesses. I'm afraid he is suspended from school for one week."

"You can't do that."

"The suspension is mandatory and immediate. I'm also recommending you meet with a community service case worker."

Matthew snarled. Eric rose out of his chair to protest but the words weren't there.

"Mister Ullman, your home life is not my concern. Matthew's welfare is. I urge you to consider, are you are really setting a good example for him? Or are you just doing what you want to do?"

Eric blinked, willing strength back into his knees. "I don't want any more counsellors around Matthew, Principal Lynch."

"I strongly suggest you see this one, Mister Ullman. If there is any repeat of his aberrant behaviour when Matthew returns, you will be looking for a new school."

"Oh," said Eric.

#

All five calls went through to Craig's assistant, who told him the same thing each time: Mister Morrow was in a meeting, Mister Morrow could not be disturbed, Mister Morrow would be in touch as soon as he was available. The assistant declined to take another message.

Eric bumped his head against the plastic window, loud enough to startle attention from the bus's other passengers for an awkward moment.

Matthew hunched down on the bench ahead of him and did not turn. His earphones emitted the faint whine of hammering drums and tortured guitars. He hadn't said a word since they'd walked out of the school gates. Eric's suggestion they take a bus to visit the animal centre was met with cold indifference. Matthew didn't ask why he picked a shelter on the other side of town. Eric didn't mention the video.

The Cooper Gardens Animal Control Centre was a squalid quadrangle of grey-washed brick buildings surrounded by high hurricane fences. Its pungency was apparent from the street, a cloying cocktail of faeces, urine, meat products, and industrial disinfectants hopelessly inadequate for the task of masking it all. The hours of business were spelled out on a peeling aluminium sign screwed to the front.

The reception area was no more impressive: an unattended counter with a bell; a soft drink vending machine with long cracks kicked into its front panels; a framed motivational poster of a dog catching a Frisbee across year upon year. Half a dozen people formed up around a large dog smiling cheese in a staff photo dated two years ago. The phone half-hidden by the counter was made of battered beige plastic, at least twenty years out of warranty.

Matthew smacked the service bell and then dropped into a plastic chair without a glance in Eric's direction.

A woman emerged through a doorway to the back office. Her golden-tawny face, spattered with dark freckles, wore a cheerful half-smile. She was barely taller than Matthew, but stylish glasses and a business-casual look put her well out of her teens. In a tone falling just short of bright confidence she asked, "Eric Ullman?"

"How did you know?"

"It didn't sound like you would take my word for it when we spoke. I expected you even earlier."

Eric hated people making assumptions about him. "I came as soon as I could."

Chun shrugged. "Also, nobody else has called all day, so who else would you be? Who is this with you?"

"My son, Matthew," said Eric. "It's his dog Hayley who's gone missing."

Matthew yanked the headphones from his ears. "Have you seen her?"

Her smile was warm and sympathetic. "I told your father she's not here. Would you like to come and look?"

Matthew nodded, lips pursed to conceal his disappointment.

The back office was a collection of filing cabinets facing off against a computer workstation and a metal-topped examination bench. "The kennels are through here."

Chun led them into a warehouse fitted out with several rows of stacked animal cages. An exercise yard visible through high windows would not have covered half a football field. It was mottled with holes and a few indomitable hunks of grass.

The smell was worse than the outside air had hinted. Their presence provoked were a few desultory woofs of acknowledgment.

Eric guessed the capacity of the centre at over one hundred dogs. "Most of these cages are empty."

"Normally we are over capacity. The patrol vans haven't brought in any strays all week. That's why I was so sure about your dog. It has been very quiet."

Matthew paused in front of a cage containing a sleeping bundle of frizzy chocolate-and-milk hair. A handwritten sign on the cage read "Stray. Age eighteen weeks. Breed indeterminate. No chip."

"What happens if nobody comes to collect them?"

"I am afraid that every unclaimed dog in this row will be destroyed in the next few days."

"Mattie, that means they will be given–"

"An injection to make them die. I know." He turned from them, fists in his eyes as if to push the tears back in.

Eric tried to put his hands on his son's shoulders but they were rebuffed with a violent shrug. "Mattie, it's okay. That hasn't happened to Hayley. Right, Chun?"

Chun put an arm around Matthew, speaking in a soft voice. "Only animals with no collars or microchips end up here. If your dog was brought into any pet rescue centre, they would read her chip and contact you."

Matthew rocked on his heels, rubbing his eyes agitatedly. "Did we get Hayley chipped, Dad?"

Eric paled. He tried to think back to the day he'd brought her home. She'd been a bargain; fifty bucks to an old school friend who'd needed to get rid of a litter. She'd been wormed and vaccinated already so he took her straight away. And hadn't Mattie been overjoyed, rolling around the floor with the bouncing, yapping bundle of puppy?

He couldn't understand how he'd gone from that to arguing with Gemma. In the end, when she'd run out of steam, she'd made him take full responsibility for the dog. He couldn't remember if she'd made him take Hayley to a vet to get a microchip.

Chun led Matthew back to the reception area. Eric followed as far as the back room and waited by the examination table. Chun bought Matthew a soft drink from the machine.

When he was settled, Chun said to Eric, "Why did you bring him here? I told you we didn't have your dog. Can't you see how upset he is?"

Eric's whole torso felt constricted. He held his phone up to her eye line; gooseflesh made the hairs on the back of his hand rise like hackles. "Why did you send me the video?"

Her eyes widened. Cracks showed in her straight-backed confidence. "What video?"

Never taking his eyes from hers, Eric replayed the call. She glanced up as if suddenly aware she was alone with him. Then movement in the video caught her attention. Eric watched her eyes grow wider, then narrow.

"What was that?" he demanded as soon as the clip froze. "You reacted to something."

Chun's freckles burned dark as the colour fled her face.

"Tell me," he said. "Tell me!"

"Mammoth. The dog's name is Mammoth." Chun took the phone from Eric's fingers, stabbing its face with both thumbs to replay the final moments. "Because of his fur, you know? And his size."

"How do you know him? Is he yours?" Eric was brutally aware he was bigger and stronger than this girl. If she didn't want to tell him, he could make her do it. Warmth flooded into his hands.

Chun flinched and pushed the phone back at him. She put a speckle-painted fingernail between her teeth and bit down, her eyes darting fearfully through him. Past him.

"A man used to work here. Kevin Parkhouse. He worked here for many years before I was hired. Mammoth is Kevin's dog."

Eric grabbed her shoulders as if he could shake answers out of her. She felt rubbery, limbless beneath his grip. "Parkhouse? Is he the sick bastard who made this? Does he have my dog?"

"Don't."

He pushed her back, steering her toward the wall. Over her shoulder he saw Matthew spring up from his seat, shocked. Eric winced but didn't relax his grip.

"I said don't."

Chun rolled her head around and closed her jaws over his forearm. She grabbed the forefinger and thumb of his other hand and turned them in opposite directions. The hard sole of her boot raked down his shin.

Pain flared everywhere at once. Eric's eyes bulged as Chun's mouth released its grip with a tearing noise. The agony spread to his pinned wrist as she forced him to collapse to his knees.

He sprawled onto the floor, coughing bile onto dull white tiles spattered with old stains. "Sorry. I'm sorry. I didn't mean to–".

As he lay there staring, she retreated toward the office.

"Last year I caught Parkhouse taking death-listed animals home. Instead of destroying them properly, he fed them live to Mammoth." She spoke from the safety of the office door with the flat distance of a radio newsreader reporting the gold price. "He lost his job. He shot himself in his living room last Christmas. The dog wasn't there. I haven't seen it. I never want to see it again."

"Wait," said Eric, trying to rise. "I said I was sorry. I just–"

"I'm closing now. You and your son have to leave. If you don't go now, I'll call the police."

#

Matthew waited until Eric sat down, then wordlessly chose a seat at the front of the bus. Eric called Craig, over and over, pumping the redial button with the metronomic rhythm of a poker machine addict. As soon as the message began "You have reached the phone of–" he cut the call and tried again.

He could barely close his fingers. Chun might have cracked the bones.

One stop from home, he snapped out of his trance to see Matthew through the window, walking alongside the curb with tears streaming down his face.

Eric mashed the button to stop the bus and jumped out of his seat, pushing and jostling his way to the front. The driver braked hard and everyone fell forward except Eric, who let the momentum propel him the rest of the way. Before the driver could protest, Eric just said, "Door." Eric was off the bus before the doors finished hissing open.

He looked back down the street. His son was nowhere to be seen. No answer came when he called Matthew's name.

He broke into a quick walk that became a fast jog and then a breathless sprint back to the previous stop. Beneath a street lamp just beginning to outdo the dying sun's luminescence, he frantically turned and called out. . The only sign of life was a man back down at his bus stop, whose face was obscured by the camera he held up. When Eric called, "Hey, did you see a kid running around here?" the man took a silent step toward him. Eric didn't have time to backtrack.

This was an old, established neighbourhood with tall trees and dense gardens behind high fences. Everywhere he turned were yards concealed behind brick walls, shrub thickets and sculpted hedges. Matthew could be hiding anywhere. In the fading light, Eric knew he stood no chance of spotting him if he decided not to be seen.

He yelled Matthew's name up one street and down a couple of side lanes. A few house lights flicked on and front curtains twitched in response.

In a few minutes, he found himself back on the main street. The bus stop camera man was gone.

By the time he trudged into his own driveway, Eric was convinced Matthew must already be home, taking some time to himself.

When he saw none of the interior lights turned on, his confidence faded.

Craig's Audi sat in the driveway. Eric groaned, realising he'd lost track of the time. He hadn't even started on dinner yet.

As he circled the car, the motion sensor floodlight above the garage door flashed on.

Blood, candy-cane red in the searing light, pooled around the dark lump sprawled across the concrete step.

Eric's breath caught in his throat. The figure on the ground made a gargling sound and a splash of fresh red bubbled from beneath it. Eric reached down and touched the body on the foot.

The sharp-edged soles of Craig's Italian leather shoes were barely scuffed.

"Craig?"

The ragged sound came again, hoarser this time and more urgent.

"Craig!" Eric shuffled forward, mindless of the gore and rolled the body over.

Craig's eyes were the first thing he noticed, wide and pleading, drowning in confusion. Dirt and blood spattered his pale, plastic face. A dark hole ringed with flaps of wet red skin bored through his throat. Some reflex in the depths of his oesophagus convulsed and disgorged a swell of thick ooze.

Craig made a sound like a rattlesnake blocking a drain. His eyes rolled one way and then another, as if he had tried to fix them on Eric but overshot. Then they fell still.

Something began to rise in Eric's chest, an angry denial like a howl starting in his balls and forcing its way up.

He opened his mouth to release his numb horror, when something moved ahead of him.

A low shape plodded out of the gloom, pausing with its head just inside the ring of light. Hayley. Her blonde muzzle was dark with gore. Her tongue slipped out and lapped blood from shining teeth. She panted heavily.

Matthew emerged from the darkness and fell in beside his dog. He shook all over and his eyes were locked on her face. Neither seemed to notice Eric.

And now, another figure disgorged from the swallowing dark of the yard. A tall, nearly bald man holding a camera phone up to his face. Eric recognised his shape and posture.

"Mattie. Don't move."

Vapour hissed from Hayley's open mouth. Twin stalactites of dark, viscous drool hung from blood-soaked muzzle hair. She looked at him now, and in the vivid glare her unblinking brown eyes conveyed judgment. "Mattie. Hayley's hurt Craig. Just keep still, okay?"

Matthew dug his fingers into the scruff of Hayley's neck and kneaded. Her ruffled hair painted his hand with blood. "Craig was angry, Dad. He yelled at me because you weren't here."

"You saw what happened?" Eric eased himself to his feet. He took a slow, tentative step. Hayley growled once, low and brief, and then again when he tried to complete the step. He froze. She resettled into her sentinel stare.

Taking a low slow breath, he said, "Did Craig hit you?"

Matthew's mouth was a flat line. "He was going to. Hayley stopped him."

Eric stood over his lover's cooling corpse and wondered what he felt. Anger? Grief? Terror? Nothing seemed to fit. Craig's eyes were wide open to the grey night sky. In their emptiness they looked right through him.

The man with the camera stepped fully into the light. Under the floodlit glare his sparse comb-over was plastered to a chalky scalp by mottled crusts of dried blood. A small hole ringed with delicate bruises on his left temple was out of balance with the empty cavity that extended from above his right ear down to his jaw. Fragments of teeth hung more from habit than muscle.

Matthew considered the pale man as if noticing him for the first time. "He followed Hayley here. His name is Kevin."

Eric's thoughts slowed, simplified.

"Mattie, just walk toward the front door, okay?"

Matthew shook his head. "I'm going with Hayley, Dad."

"Going? Going where?" Eric's hand throbbed. An eerie calm settled on him. Matthew's words were like a story that was losing his attention.

"She's won her place in the pack, Dad. I will too."

Eric opened his mouth, unsure what to ask.

The pale man stopped recording him and click-clicked a finger against his phone's screen. Eric caught a glimpse of grey eyes looking in different directions. Then his phone rang.

"Answer it," said Parkhouse. In the clear air, his voice had the same hollow menace as it had in the messages. Its scratchy faintness hissed like a recording coming through someone else's headphones. "Answer it. Stay out of the way. Answer it."

Eric did as he was told.

An image opened on the screen of a room in disarray. Small furnishings – chair, shelves, a metal table - were scattered around a white room dotted with red. Eric's eyes struggled to adjust to the fuzzy focus. It took a moment to recognise the back room of the animal shelter. Over the edge of a beige cabinet that had spilled its contents across the floor like viscera hung a slender, heavy boot below smart business slacks. The leg above the knee was obscured by fallen shelving.

Eric's shin throbbed as he recalled the boots.

"Mattie-"

"You should go inside, Dad. You don't have to be here for this."

The soft padding of paws on gravel surrounded him. He felt the hulking hound behind him before he saw it, as if the air was trying to get clear of it. Mammoth dropped to its haunches beside Eric, indifferent to his existence. Eric choked away an absurd impulse to scratch the thick brown curls between its ears.

The man pointed the camera at him, eager to catch the moment.

Matthew hugged his dog like a proud parent. "Hayley made the kill, but the top dog eats first."

"Mattie!"

Mammoth's ears flicked up at his exclamation. Hayley hunched and bared mottled fangs. Low canine growls came from all around.

Mattie hunched forward. His unbroken voice, incapable of growling, hummed with innocent joy. Hayley's tail thumped against his legs.

Mammoth rumbled. Pale Parkhouse obediently shuffled closer, his camera locked on Eric's face.

Eric turned a circle, slow and careful, every eye on him until he faced Mammoth. Dogs crept into the light, their bodies low, ears flat, and tails down. They formed a ring like onlookers at a schoolyard punch-up. He felt Mattie and Hayley behind him, urgent and eager. His eyes were locked on Mammoth; he didn't look back.

He hunched down and placed his gouged palm against Craig's cheek. It was already turning cold. The fingers of his other hand folded around his phone until it was part of his fist.

"These are mine," he said to the pack alpha. He bared his teeth, hungry, white, and ready. "If you want what's mine, you have to take it from me."

I like using horror techniques in the service of other genres, but I rarely write supernatural horror in and of itself. Probably because I don't like openly exploring the things that really scare me. The horror in this story for me is how easily the relationships that matter to us can slip away if they're neglected rather than nurtured. The smallest shift in our personal priorities, the most minor upheavals in our economy of attentiveness, could be all it takes to lose everything. And the real horror is that it's never just one infraction, but a series of choices becoming habits, and sometimes the mistakes aren't visible except in retrospect, when it's too late.

For the record, I'm not scared of dogs, but I really do not want to be eaten by one.

THE MIRROR WITCH AND
THE *WORMWOOD MIRANDA*

Kimiko Shimizu's birthday sleepover was the best because we got to stay up all night and be space pirates. I don't mean playing pretend. That's for little kids. I mean we summoned the mirror witch who took us to the *Wormwood Miranda*.

You know how to do it, right? Richelle told me you and Carmen Lodge got the mirror witch to give Mr Blunt the PE teacher a rash and that's why he had to take term three off and go to Thailand for treatment.

No? Well, that's what Richelle said but whatever.

So okay, after pizzas, Nina makes everyone lemon, lime and bitters with extra bitters and Kimmy gives each of us a mirror with lines scratched on the rim. We all stand in front of her big mirror, which she says her grandmother said she could have when she died, but her grandmother's in the Hyacinth Park rest home so I don't even know. Anyway, we all angle these hand mirrors until they're reflecting each other and then on the big mirror the scratches line up to make an arrow shape.

And we have to say this, like, spell or chant, I don't know, three times through, which went:

Mistress monstrous, can you hear us?
These reflections call you near us.
With your heart as dark as pitch
You must grant us just one wish
We are fierce so you should fear us
Mistress monstrous, can you hear us?
Come to us, you mirror witch!

D'you notice how much it sounds like "Martian Rover" by Ophelia Vernon? Yeah, we sang it the last couple of times. Have you heard Priya sing? She's really good. Like she could audition for The Voice. Like I don't think they'd let her get through cause she's just a kid, but she's really good.

The mirror witch looks like Charlize Theron but old. That's what I thought anyway. Priya says she looks like her viola teacher's girlfriend, except that she was a redhead. Kimmy says the witch looks like her grandmother looks in old photos from when she was at university in Prague. Richelle said the witch didn't look like anything but she heard a voice like a big cat roaring except that she understood it like real words.

Kimmy brings out this offering bowl and Richelle says "Do we have to cut ourselves and drip blood in?" and then we all go quiet because, well you know, maybe? But Kimmy fills the bowl up with jelly beans from the party stash. They don't have lollies where the witch is from, hey?

The witch drags us all through the mirror into her world and Nina almost vomits because she overdid it on the bitters. We fall through this void of shimmering dust and weeping stars and really it's a bit too high-gloss for me. But then we end up on the deck of this old sailing ship in the middle of space.

I don't know how we could breathe. Mirror stuff, who cares? The mirror witch took off before we could ask. I saw she'd swiped a bottle from Kimmy's Dad's liquor cabinet so maybe they don't have booze in the mirror place either?

So the ship is haunted by this ghost of the old captain, who's this cranky old nanna called Misery Janks. She staggers around the deck complaining about how the *Wormwood Miranda* hasn't had a crew for four hundred years. Priya's just soft and she gets all weepy and says we'll be her crew and bring her back to her home port so she can lay to rest and whatever? None of us know sweet FA about sailing or anything except for Richelle's uncle takes her surf kayaking down the coast sometimes, but we go along with it. I hear old time sailors were drunk all the time so how hard could it be?

But Nanna-Captain Janks doesn't want her bones buried in her old garden or whatever, so she says let's go raiding and pillaging. I suppose that's pretty antisocial now I think about it but we were all sugared up so we said yes.

We set course for the nearest star, where we find this world full of chanting lizards, crystal mountains and warring tribes of mantis-people. And for ten and a bit years we sack their treasures and scatter their bones, looting and plundering everything that's not nailed down. We take whatever and whoever we please and drive Nanna-Captain Janks' enemies back to their nests out behind the cold stars. We grow to womanhood. Hard, merry cutthroats, every damn one of us. Proud, straight-backed killers, thirsty for mantis-blood. It tastes a bit like red cordial.

And one day the *Wormwood Miranda*, riding low and slow with the looted riches of another war-queen who thought she could outsmart us, is coming back to her home port, which is this awesome floating palace orbiting a planet swirling with purple and orange lightning-clouds, when the mirror witch returns. She's not too steady on her feet, so we think she must have just finished knocking off the bottle of scotch by herself. Then she says it's time to go home.

We all say goodbye to Nanna-Captain Janks, who isn't happy to see us go but has to admit we were the best crew she's ever had. She even has a sneaky cry when she thinks we can't see her. Then the mirror witch brings us back through to Kimmy's place just as the sun comes up.

Back to being the children we've almost forgotten we ever were, in a dull and lifeless world we no longer recognise. The days here taste of sawdust and sunburn, and life is a weary trudge towards an inglorious grave. I ache to return to the stars.

Anyway, that's why I didn't do my homework last weekend.

Do you know what trigonometry is?

Can I copy your answers?

This story of a kind of Neverland for teenage girls kicked around in my mind for a couple of years, pretending it was an idea for a weird novel. For some reason I believed it, right up until the moment I realised that I'd never had a single other idea that built on the central image of pirate teenagers on a worn-out ghost ship crossing swords with bug-people.

As soon as this book comes out, I'll probably come up with the plot for a trilogy of novels about Kimiko and her friends tearing up the mirror place.

MNEMO'S MEMORY

With a sweep of sealskin-clad fingers, Captain Hollioak brushed icicles from his brow. They drifted down to the snowdrift gathering about his deck boots. Some swirled overboard to join the creaking Antarctic pack ice far below. Overhead the canvas thrummed with the cutting wind, ribs rippling across its surface and shed flurries of ice particles.

Two figures emerged from the murk. Clanking footfalls marked their unsteady progress.

"Lady Gracemere, I must once again protest at your footwear. Your every excursion ravages the decking. Mr Thackeray is beside himself."

He withheld the carpenter's precise words.

Lady Elizabeth Gracemere's pale features were hidden behind both tinted eyepieces and a sturdy woollen scarf, which concealed any possible remorse. She hitched the hem of her skirt, revealing rigid boots bound by metal bands to a contraption of gleaming rivets and shark tooth-shaped spurs. Her companion's feet, or rather the extremities of its unbending legs, were similarly attired. "And I assure you, Captain Hollioak, that I have no intention of being swept into the aether to suffer the indignity of a long and fatal fall."

Hollioak bristled. "Your safety is assured, my lady. I have never lost a passenger overboard and by God's leave I never shall. Even this clanking factotum of yours need fear no harm."

His reflection in the automaton's amethyst faceplate was uneasy and distorted. The monochrome paintwork on its brass body bore a superficial resemblance to butler's attire, but its unnatural stillness prevented any sense of humanity. Next to Lady Gracemere, it was a cold, haunted thing. Never more so than when it spoke in a hollow echo of that warm, familiar baritone. "No fear, Hollioak. Complete faith, I assure you."

"I beg you to recall, madam, my request that it not speak in my presence." Hollioak hoped her Ladyship would interpret his stiff bearing as formal deference. He could not bear to hear his dead friend's voice emerge from the machine.

The steam butler was testament to her mechanical genius. But its uncanny assumption of Lord John Gracemere's verbal habits and, worse, its unsettling familiarity with his widow, hinted at a darker spiritual malaise on her part. The hissing steamwork facsimile of her late husband, replicating his voice and so many of his mannerisms as its limited articulation allowed, was as disturbing as it was grotesque.

Lady Gracemere touched a gloved hand to the automaton's shoulder. "I recall your request, Captain. I presumed the petition was on behalf of your crew. I little imagined you dismayed by the march of science."

"By no means, Madam. It is a remarkable work of engineering. All the more remarkable given that you -"

"Are a woman, Captain?" Her arch reply was more chilling than the bitterest crosswinds.

"Are a widow in mourning, my Lady." Hollioak grimaced, certain he had given offense.

Lady Gracemere peered past him into the gloom ahead. "How long until we reach our destination, Captain?"

"We will be within sight of Mount Erebus in no more than three hours, by my reckoning."

Lady Gracemere nodded, evidently confident in his aeronautical skill, if nothing else. Hollioak was by no means satisfied to let the matter rest, however. Risking what good standing remained to his credit, he said, "Once again I urge you to take some Time to contemplate terminating our present venture. You could be certain of my wholehearted support."

"I hope I am not wrong to be certain of your support in any event, Captain Hollioak. Please don't suppose me ignorant of your discomfort. It was uncivil of me to discharge your obligation to his Lordship on such grim business. But I mean to avenge my husband. To do so I must hold you to your oath. Do I have cause for fear on that score?"

Hollioak deflated in the face of her crystalline determination. "Indeed not, Madam. The *Bishop of Sarum* is at your disposal."

"Then I pray you will make no further attempts to dissuade me. Please summon me when we approach Doctor Winter's stronghold."

#

Elizabeth could not sleep. Captain Hollioak's protest had stirred unsettling memories. It was over a year since the telegram informing her to arrange a funeral with no casket.

Her work on Mnemo had already begun before the fall of the *Marquess of Salisbury*. While society gossiped about airships in flames and the eligibility of widows, she withdrew to her laboratory. From that moment on she wore workshop coveralls more often than her mourning wardrobe.

Making the most of a dull ring of gas candle-tubes, she tinkered with the bundles of steel cables articulating Mnemo's four-fingered hands. The work demanded concentration but her thoughts kept drifting to the impossible position in which she had placed Captain Hollioak. She pressure him to disregard his orders and ferry her to certain doom. Smoked goggles had not hidden the anguish of uncertainty in his dark eyes. She sympathised. A man like Edward Hollioak, a commander of fighting men, could not afford the appearance of indecision.

She shook her head. "I require a distraction. Mnemo, replay Recording 15."

A moment of crackling hissed from Mnemo's speaking grill.

Then John's voice, one of the few precious mementos remaining of the man she had loved, filled the small cabin. "...His Majesty's interests in the Southern Hemisphere, Elizabeth. The conflict between the Tsar and the Emperor will spill out of control at any moment. The world cannot remain at peace for much longer."

Though she had never shared his interest in political affairs, she smiled to recall his fire. He had burned with passion that day, stalking about her lab while she calibrated her recording equipment for the first time. It did not last. Obsessed with preventing the horrors of revolution from gaining a foothold in England, his simple devotion to King and Country took a dark turn. Within a few months John was embroiled in the affairs of Doctor Winter.

"Madam, has the recording made you sad again?"

She swallowed and brushed her eyes dry. "How should I feel, Mnemo? The recording is all I have left of John before the madness of this Winter business."

"You know it's not that simple," replied the automaton. "Why do you keep the truth from Hollioak?"

The words sparked an unexpected ache in Elizabeth's chest. For an aching moment, she could not say whether it was inspired by her husband's voice or the Captain's. She crushed the sensation, reshaping it into renewed resolve. "The truth would distract Captain Hollioak from his duty," she said. "I cannot allow it. Besides, you are incorrect."

"In what way?"

"There is nothing simpler than revenge."

#

Elizabeth's small cabin, piled high with trunks of equipment, a modest wardrobe and a variety of sensitive instruments, had no windows. A subtle shift in the drone of the dozen Haight-Trommler engines suggested the airship was slowing. She confirmed it with a glance at the flicking hands of her pocket seismograph before she slipped it into a coat pocket. She fitted the last harness in place. Compact belts hung with tools. Pouches bulged with replacement parts. She slotted weapons into oiled sheathes and slick holsters. She slipped on the heavy arctic coat John once wore on a Greenland expedition. Her miniature machine shop was concealed beneath fur trimmed leather and brass sealing-rings.

Were *The Bishop of Sarum* not approaching Mount Erebus under cover of dense snow clouds, she imagined the view from the foredeck would be magnificent. Elizabeth promised herself to return in some future summer to take in the sight of its glowing crater, its billowing steam vents and its stalagmite-shaped ice spires.

It was not wicked arrogance to anticipate the future, was it? Just harmless self-deception.

"What do you think, Mnemo?"

"Your preparations are exemplary, Madam. His Lordship couldn't have done better."

"We will know soon enough."

"I must inform you that there are two men listening at your door."

At this declaration, a blistering sailor's oath preceded two pistol-wielding brutes through the cabin door. Elizabeth permitted herself a faint smile before turning to receive them with an expression of rankled perplexion. "Gentlemen, whatever can be the meaning of this intrusion?"

The sailors were Hibb and Adkins, Yorkshiremen of hulking stature and surly disposition. More than capable of overpowering a slight woman in heavy dress should she give them cause. They might even best Mnemo. Fortunately there was no need to test either proposition.

"You are to accompany us, Lady Gracemere."

"Captain's orders," added the second, failing to conceal a knowing smirk beneath a mat of iced beard.

"Delightful. Lead on. Do make room for my assistant there, if you please."

Hibb stood his ground in the doorway. "Just you, your Ladyship. Your engine-man there ain't summoned."

"Of course, how silly of me." Elizabeth raised her hands before Mnemo's face lenses and twisted her wrists like a Turkish dancer. "Stay here Mnemo."

"Very good, Madam." The echo of John's amused twinkle almost made Elizabeth smile again.

They led her through cargo holds and cramped corridors made almost impassable by her many layers. Elizabeth feigned ignorance of their destination.

She had committed the ship's layout to memory. The brig was situated a full deck below the Captain's cabin and officer's wardroom. She could be led there unseen by any more than a handful of idle airmen.

She felt a pang of regret on Captain Hollioak's behalf. She predicted Doctor Winter's advanced knowledge of her expedition. She had accounted for treachery in her own plans; she had not shared her suspicions with the Captain. Captain Hollioak would be aghast to learn Winter's coin had bought the loyalty of some among his crew. Elizabeth took no pride in concealing her intelligence from him.

The crewmen, ignorant of her information, kept up their commendable performance of escorting her to Hollioak. She pretended not to see their worried glances and shifty responses to unexpected sounds. To their evident relief – and Elizabeth's – they reached their destination uninterrupted.

"Captain's waiting inside," said Adkins. He took firm command of Elizabeth's elbow and steered her through the door into the gloom beyond. For form's sake she exclaimed "Captain Hollioak? I cannot see you." The two airmen laughed. Adkins ended their brief acquaintance with an indecent shove to her behind. She yelped in outrage as the door slammed. The point of a carpenter's spike punched through the door frame.

When the airmen's rough laughter faded, Elizabeth tested the door with a shoulder. It was stuck fast. She was sealed in.

She smiled and set to work.

#

Hollioak announced himself with an emphatic cough at Lady Gracemere's cabin door. "We've crossed the Ross Island coast, Madam. We must assume ourselves within range of Winter's artillery."

A bell was calling the hands to their stations. Under ordinary circumstances Hollioak would be in the helmcastle with Commander Dempsey preparing for battle. These circumstances were anything but. It rankled that Lady Gracemere had yet to divulge the final details of her plan.

"Madam, the hour is upon us."

She was not present. The spacious cabin was stacked with engineering paraphernalia. There was nowhere she could be concealed. The factotum stood in her place. Curling his lip, Hollioak asked, "Where is Lady Gracemere?"

Mnemo hissed and emitted a barrage of quiet pops like distant cannon fire. "Edward Hollioak," it said. "Unaccompanied. Message two."

Hollioak scowled. "I beg your pardon! I asked –"

"Lady Elizabeth has been taken prisoner by crewmen in the service of Doctor Winter." Mnemo's interruption stilled Hollioak's indignation. Lady Gracemere kidnapped by mutineers? Hot blood swelled his chest like an inflating balloon.

"Damn you, why didn't you say so at once?" The automaton's complacence was all the more infuriating for sounding like Lord Gracemere. In life the man would have leaped straight into action. "Why didn't you do anything?"

Unruffled, Mnemo said, "Lady Elizabeth's instructions were precise: to wait twenty minutes or until your arrival. Eighteen minutes and twelve seconds elapsed."

"Her life may be in danger!"

"Lady Elizabeth expects her detention is a precursor to an attempt to take control of your vessel, Captain, before you can turn your guns on Doctor Winter's facility."

"What? Who are these mutineers?"

"My information is incomplete. Crewmen Adkins and Hibbs are certain. Their accomplices may be few or many. You must trust your own instincts."

Mnemo's words hit him like the revelations of a ghost. How many times had John Gracemere told him just that? "Am I supposed to trust you?" he said. "A memory made of brass and mirrors?"

"No, Hollioak," replied Mnemo. "Trust Elizabeth Gracemere. Now please stand aside." He barely had time to comply before the automaton lurched past him, its faceplate flashing.

Hollioak burned to restore his ship to order. Instead, he drew his pistol and followed, his thoughts grim. Trust was all very well but only action accomplished anything.

#

Having located the structural weak point of the floor, Elizabeth set aside her small mallet and held up a chemical lamp. She marked out a circumference with coloured chalk.

She heard a crash of splintering timbers from the forward holds. It was followed by muffled shouts and smacks of pistol fire. Elizabeth stood back from the sealed door. Her confidence that the plan was working did not stop her closing a hand around the dirk sheathed at her back.

Outside, cries became shrieks. Elizabeth spared a small measure of sympathy for any wretch trying to obstruct Mnemo. She had made no provisions for mercy in his instructions.

Mnemo crashed through the wall like a fox with the hunt at its tail. Its flailing arms shredded the timbers, clearing a path for its clumsy legs.

"Lady Gracemere," said Captain Hollioak with a fierce look, collapsing past Mnemo through the destroyed wall. A patch of bruised skin wept blood into his brows. On his stern, thoughtful features the injury was like an oil stain on fresh crinoline. "Are you unharmed? Thank God." He fell to one knee.

The gesture startled her. Then she recognised he was overcome with pain. "Captain Hollioak was struck by Airman McCrea," Mnemo observed.

"Damned turncoat," muttered Hollioak. Then his eyes widened. He said, "Forgive my language, Lady Gracemere. I am unaccustomed to guarding my tongue aboard my own ship."

She smiled at his gallantry. "It's nothing I haven't said myself while struggling with an uncooperative repair." Kneeling as carefully as her restrictive layers allowed, Elizabeth retrieved a small nursing kit from an outer pocket. Holding the Captain's jaw with a steady hand, she turned his wound to the light. She dabbed it with cleaning alcohol. At the sting, Captain Hollioak's eyes snapped open. "Thank you. I believe I am clean enough now."

She held the light closer, not replying. His eyes were flint at the rims, softening to azure bands about the pupils. Elizabeth removed the stained linen from his forehead and, after a moment, her hand from his face.

"Can you stand?" she asked.

"I can accomplish that much." Testing the contours of his head wound with hard, steady fingers, he said, "Lady Gracemere, is it bold of me to speculate that you are unsurprised by this mutiny?"

"Oh. Yes, I rather expected Winter to undermine you." Elizabeth blinked away a sudden pinprick of tears. "I feared if I shared my intelligence with you, you would act to thwart him. All my hopes are pinned on his underestimation of me. Can you forgive my deceit?"

He met this revelation with a raised eyebrow. "On two conditions."

"Which are?"

"The first is that when our business on Ross Island is complete, we compare profane vocabularies. As a sailing man, I collect obscenities the way you must collect compliments."

It was Elizabeth's turn to widen her eyes in mischievous astonishment. "Imminent peril appears to have freed you from the shackles of decorum, Captain."

"I never find it much use on the field of battle, Madam."

"Then you have my wholehearted consent, Captain."

Mnemo made a small mechanical grunt. "Several men approach, Madam. It is likely the mutineers have regrouped."

Captain Hollioak nodded in agreement. "Any loyal man would be at his post."

Elizabeth's mind raced. "We must hurry. Tell me, Captain, have we arrived at our destination?"

"If we have not deviated from the original flight plan, then we are holding steady off the north-western slope."

"Good enough." Elizabeth opened a panel in Mnemo's torso. Inside were additional necessities for her plan. The cable she uncoiled to the floor. She freed the breathing tube of her mask and clipped the oxygen tank to her coat.

"Lady Gracemere, without a landing tower you cannot safely disembark. If I could get you to the foredeck we could belay your climbing cable but -"

"We cannot risk further encounters with mutineers." She glanced at the frown of tactical assessment creasing his brow. The spirited bonhomie was gone again, carefully stowed in some secure compartment until the fighting was done. She hoped she would see it again.

"Until I can secure control, you are safest here."

She worked her mask's straps loose. "I have something other than safety in mind. Mnemo?"

The automaton stretched its arms in a cruciform pose, gripping the wall struts until cracks showed beneath its thick digits. Its clawed feet centred on the chalk circle inscribed on the floor. Its legs drew up, receding partway into its abdomen. Lady Elizabeth placed a hand on Captain Hollioak's chest, easing him away from the automaton. Then with an ear-splitting crash Mnemo's legs pistoned out, rupturing the cabin floor.

A yawing grey expanse was exposed through the hole. A blast of Antarctic air rushed in. The sweat on Captain Hollioak's brow, beard and eyelashes froze into a dusting of ice. To Elizabeth's eye, it enhanced his already formidable look of determination. If time were less pressing she would have given the expression deeper consideration. Alas.

"Convey my sincere apologies to Mister Thackeray for the damage, Captain." Elizabeth lashed her rope to the carabiner on

Mnemo's shoulder. Another section she threaded through reinforced slits in her coat to the harness about her waist. "I must take this route alone. The cold outside would kill you in a minute, I'm afraid."

Captain Hollioak's regret was obvious. "I will do what I can to distract Winter."

"Be careful, Captain. Winter did not insinuate traitors in your crew just to capture me. I believe he intends to take your ship. Expect heavy fire and light damage." She smiled ruefully at the gaping perforation at their feet. "Perhaps lighter than I have already inflicted."

She could see the awful suspicion growing in his eyes. Guilt took fresh hold of her. "How do you come to know so much about Doctor Winter?"

"Oh dear." She drew a deep breath. Unavoidable as the moment was, she felt flummoxed and ill-prepared.

"It is because I know him better than anyone else. Because once my heart held nothing for him but passionate regard. Doctor Winter did not kill John Gracemere, Captain. Not in the way the world believes. My husband's obsessions became madness and in his madness he forsook one name for another. He abandoned his name, his title and his country."

Captain Hollioak's jaw tightened. "He abandoned you."

"He did."

"Of all his crimes, that may be his most unforgivable." Captain Hollioak's throat was clenched with submerged emotion.

Once, early in the voyage, when he still hoped to convince her to turn back, he recounted his last sight of the *Marquess of Salisbury*: flames casting long orange streaks across the Severn's black surface; men falling from the sky, screaming and afire; the ship's lift sacs swollen beyond their limits, snapping their restraining nets, splitting rents in its protective airframe and bursting in blinding phosphor glares. At the last its fat hull, slung beneath burning balloons and useless screeching engines, had dropped and burst. Its scattered bones blazed a forest. The fire burned for days and devoured all hope of survivors. She knew he was reliving the same moment now.

"That was your second condition, was it not? To know what I know?"

He closed his eyes and nodded. "I would kill him if he were standing here."

"I know. You are at home in the heat of a raging battle, Captain. I crave method. Precision. One step after another, each piece in its place until the mechanism is flawless."

"That's not my experience of most plans, Lady Gracemere."

So that he could not read her face, she fitted her mask. Her voice sounded hollow through the gentle hiss of oxygen. "I have asked so much of you Captain. I think we must dispense with these awkward formalities. When we meet again, call me Elizabeth."

"Then you must call me Edward."

The wind whipped at his dark hair, flaring it like spray from an angry wave. His eyes were hard with the certainty that they looked upon her for the last time. Perhaps he was fixing this final sight of her in his memory, as Elizabeth was.

"Godspeed, Edward."

She stepped into the hole and vanished into the grey darkness.

#

Edward's anxiety built as he watched the thrumming vibrations in the rope. Its tensile strength was unquestionable. Yet it strained against the anchoring automaton with the force of Elizabeth's descent and the relentless power of the biting wind. It whined with tension and slapped at Mnemo's metal frame.

"Do not be concerned, Captain," said the automaton. Tiny puffs of sawdust escaped as its tightening grip crushed timber. "She is an accomplished climber."

From outside came the sounds of cautious footsteps, whispered conferences and drawn knives. The mutineers were gathering themselves for a renewed assault. Time was short. Edward's curiosity bested his caution. "How much of him is in you?"

"I am nothing of Lord Gracemere. I am a flawless reproduction of a widow's fond memory, Captain Hollioak." Gracemere himself would have been similarly disingenuous.

"Did she even mourn her loss?"

Mnemo's pause suggested an odd reluctance to answer.

"She made me to supplant her grief, Captain. Mnemo is the receptacle into which she poured her sadness and fury and frustration. Any bereaved soul might weep in a favourite garden or whisper secrets to a portrait. I am no different."

Edward said, "You are remarkable." He was unsure who he meant the compliment for.

"I am the product of remarkable hands, Captain."

"So you are."

Edward tucked the pistol into his belt. "If I may, I will use the rope to gain access to the coffers. They will hesitate to pursue me there."

He took hold of the rope, which bit frostily at his palms. He levered himself into the gap between the floor and the lower hull of the *Bishop of Sarum*. As soon as his feet found purchase, he clambered into the musty darkness.

The rope slackened. Elizabeth had reached the ground and cast herself off. He released his breath in a muttered prayer of thanks.

Above, there were shouts of dismay and a shot was fired. Two pounding footsteps from Mnemo's elephantine feet thundered directly overhead.

More shots were fired, and a voice ordered, "Knock it down, boys!"

A rumble of footsteps crossed above, closing on Mnemo. Thumps and curses. One last shot, which ended in a shattering sound.

Mnemo said "Godspeed," as though to nobody in particular.

A moment later the automaton, its arms wrapped about three screaming air sailors, plummeted through the thin scrape of light before Edward's eyes and disappeared into frozen space.

Imprisoning an exclamation of horror behind pursed lips, he began a steady, silent crawl into the heart of his ship.

#

Smoked lenses protected Elizabeth's vision from the blinding effects of the snow glare. They made it difficult to pick details out at a distance. She saw the faint outline of the airship, swathed in cloud, and Mnemo's parachute, grey as a quarryman. When it became obvious what the figures falling away from Mnemo with animalistic cries and thrashing limbs were, she raised a hand to her throat. For months she had known she must harden her heart to the lives her revenge might endanger. No qualms for those who threw their lot in with Winter. As she watched the helpless figures tumble, it was for one soul alone that she feared.

She closed her eyes as the dark shapes crashed to earth, bouncing and breaking upon the frozen scoria. The sound of their impact was thankfully swallowed by the wind. A moment later, the hissing whine of Mnemo's articulating motors broke through the emptiness.

"Mnemo, is Captain Hollioak -?" She could not speak the words.

"Captain Hollioak is still aboard the airship, Madam."

"Thank God. I only hope he - Mnemo, there is a man attached to you."

The air sailor, a young midshipman whose name Elizabeth could not recall, was dead, stuck in place with his arms wrapped about Mnemo's shoulders and back. The deadly chill must have sucked the life from him in an instant, though sheer terror could not be discounted.

"Kindly avert your gaze, Madam," said Mnemo. Elizabeth turned away. The heavy layers of her mask and hood could not protect her a noise like the splitting of a green branch as Mnemo detached his doomed passenger. The crunch of the corpse dropped onto loose stones signalled the grisly business was done.

"We must hurry," she said, looking up the sloping outer wall of the Erebus volcano. It was bare, lifeless rock, broken into flaking scree, steaming black soil and a few obstinate patches of glistening snow resisting the radiant heat. "The cold is unbearable."

Mnemo fell forward onto its hands, absurdly resembling a calisthenics enthusiast. Its powerful fingers punched into the loose rock. Curved metal prongs emerged from its feet like dull talons.

"Clip on, Madam."

Elizabeth fixed a short cable between herself and Mnemo.

"Begin." At her instruction, Mnemo detached a hand and reached up. One leg elongated while the other dug in. The cable went taut as Mnemo pulled itself upslope. Upon its next movement, Elizabeth was dragged two steps forward. She leaned away at a comfortable angle and walked behind Mnemo, letting it drag her toward the summit.

Their destination was a crenelated wall built along the rim of the volcano's caldera A bulky artillery emplacement jutted from it. At their current rate of ascent, it was no more than eight or nine minutes away.

Elizabeth turned her face skyward, seeking the airship in the gloom.

"Mnemo, did Edw- did Captain Hollioak say anything about me?"

"He complimented your engineering skills, madam."

"Humph. As well he might."

But then, why should Edward have shared his thoughts with the hollow reconstruction of a dead man? She knew well enough that he recoiled from Mnemo.

Still, she hoped that he might understand. Perhaps one day he might even find it possible to forgive her shameless manipulations. She pictured him twenty years on, a deep-lined face surrounding sharp grey eyes, hair of distinguished silver, recounting this day at some London club. She imagined him speaking of her, not unkindly and with perhaps a dash of the daring to pepper the tale.

Elizabeth smiled beneath her mask as her clockwork butler dragged her up the face of an active volcano to confront a killer.

#

Edward made slow progress in the stifling confines of the coffers. The space was cramped and the angles awkward, not intended for protracted periods of habitation. The thin radium glow of his pocket watch provided just enough light to make out the carpenter's scratches on the hull timbers, by which he was able to navigate his way fore and aloft.

With his freedom of movement constrained, his thoughts took flight. His best efforts of will were not enough to keep them from Elizabeth. What sort of man was he, to have stood silent as she threw herself overboard and into deadly peril? And yet such confidence shone from her eyes, like chips of emerald. What course did he have but to make way in the face of such determination? Certainly she was bound on a dangerous path but he could scarcely guarantee her safety aboard The *Bishop of Sarum*, not while it remained in the hands of turncoats. Better that she see to her own duties and he to his.

The memory of her eyes carried him through the veins of his ship, until at last he arrived beneath its heart.

"I say again, Ensign, you are relieved. Stand down from the helm or I will seize it by force."

The dense planks of the bridge decking muffled the voices from above. Edward recognised the speaker with a sinking heart. Commander Dempsey had served under him for six years. What inducement to mutiny had Winter offered? Little less than the *Bishop* herself, he suspected.

Edward eased himself around the armoured casing of the gear assembly, which sat beneath the helmcastle and conveyed its directions to the *Bishop*'s array of engines, ailerons and propellors. An inspection hatch beyond opened onto the bridge's aft deck.

He took a breath to steady his aching extremities, drew his service revolver and shoved the hatch open.

Edward pressed the muzzle of his pistol against the back of Dempsey's head, just below the brim of his bicorne hat. "Stand down, sir," he said, "or you shall despoil Ensign Farmer's uniform with your brains."

Dempsey stiffened. His sword clattered to the floor. His pistol followed a moment later. Beyond him, the helmsman stood pale and shaking, backed up against the helmcastle: a brass wall decorated with dials, grills and the dozen mahogany wheels that determined the Bishop's orientation and altitudes.

"Captain Hollioak." Dempsey's first word was tinged with bitterness, the second dripped venom. "How did you get free?"

"Perhaps you underestimate my resources, Commander."

"I could have ordered your death."

"I almost wish you had done so," said Edward. "It will give me no pleasure to see you on the gallows for this day's work."

Dempsey scoffed. "You speak like you're not already in Winter's grasp, Hollioak. You may have the bridge, but my men have the run of the ship."

Ensign Farmer found his voice. "He may be right sir. I've heard shots from all over."

"They'll surrender on your order, Dempsey. If not then I-"

The floor shifted violently beneath them.

Edward's air legs bent to compensate. Stiffness from the cold climb seized his right knee. He collapsed.

Dempsey's foot lashed out and caught Edward beneath the chin. Blinding pain overwhelmed him. A scuffle of movement ended with Farmer's groan.

Dempsey's head dipped low as he snatched up his sword. Edward raised his pistol and fired it.

Dempsey fell back, clutching at his shoulder. Edward squinted along his sights. Dempsey looked down the wavering barrel and cursed again. He threw himself bodily through the door to the foredeck. Edward's shot chopped a hole in the timbers where Dempsey's head had been.

Edward flung himself against the door and threw its bolts, breathing hard. "Ensign, are you harmed?"

The shaky junior officer rubbed at his jaw and gave Edward a cautious shake. "Rattled, sir. In one piece, thanks to you."

"I've bought us no more than a minute, I'm afraid. Dempsey's men will regroup in moments. What's our position?"

"We're circling about a mile out from a stone fortress built on the lip of a volcano crater, sir. Cloud cover's thick and light's poor. Forward watch observed some artillery mountings and a docking tower a while back. No ground response yet."

"No doubt they await a signal from the mutineers," said Edward. "We'll come about and launch an attack from the south. Sound the –"

Another shudder rippled through the deck. The anchor-guys and the rigging sang out a humming tune. They shared the sailors' instinctive horror of damage to the great silk-and-canvas bags that held them aloft.

"Sabotage," Edward said.

His eyes raced over the flicking monitoring instruments until he found one inactive. "Number five intake vent. Clogged it with oakum, I'll warrant."

"They're mad! If it catches alight –"

"They're gambling we'll set down immediately." Edward made a snap decision. "Is the docking tower in sight? Then align on it and full ahead, all able engines."

"Aye, sir, and I pray for loyal ears to hear me. But where are you going?"

Edward reloaded his pistol and claimed Farmer's sword. "To take back my vessel."

#

For all Elizabeth's attention to the tiniest details, the reality of enacting her plans was maddening. Every step seemed to throw up some bothersome wrinkle, like the portcullis grate separating this steam vent from the stronghold's interior. It had not been equal to Mnemo's strength but these small impediments were a growing concern.

"Was that not rather loud, Mnemo?"

"Quite deafening, Madam, I'm sorry to say."

It occurred to her that Edward's battle experience would have been useful in this infiltration. The military mind was always having to compensate for the unexpected. A pity she hadn't factored him into this final phase. It was most unfair, selfish even, to wish him by her side. But there it was.

A harsh mechanical voice like a grindstone sharpening gears shrieked in the darkness. "Remain where you are, if you please." Elizabeth froze, dismayed at the sight of the guard automaton. Her particular focus was the point of the sabre emerging from the bulbous stump at its wrist.

"Ah! What a - crude innovation. I hardly think the intimidating effect outweighs the loss of digital utility." In the echoing service tunnel, her voice lacked the intended note of cool dismissal.

"I don't think intimidation is the sword's primary purpose, Madam." At the sound of Mnemo's voice, the automaton swivelled its head, as if noticing Mnemo for the first time. "May I?"

"Yes, thank you, Mnemo. Please take care." The sword tip was level with her eye.

Mnemo trundled forward. The automaton's violet faceplate flashed in warning. It said "Remain where you are if -"

Mnemo's faceplate split and opened like a warehouse door, spilling a burst of colours. Fuchsia and heliotrope lights played over the guard's head for a fraction of a moment. A sharp smell of scorched oil and an almost inaudible crystalline crack reached Elizabeth. The sword arm quivered and began to straighten with a whining sound. Its point wobbled and drove forward.

Elizabeth squealed and fell backwards. She dropped into an undignified position. The blade passed overhead, close enough to have impaled a hat. Fortunately she possessed no such item. The automaton's arm was drawing back for a second strike but before it could launch its attack, it froze. Elizabeth counted twenty hammering heartbeats; it remained still.

"Excellent work, Mnemo."

"With respect, Madam, the credit is all yours." A new click beat rhythmically from somewhere inside it. Elizabeth pictured the elegant mechanism within, now busy with activity. She rose with fresh vigour.

"Let us call it a shared triumph." Once, she had said such things to John Gracemere. "Come now. Time is short."

\#

To Edward's surprise, the deck was clear of mutineers. His ephemeral relief was swept away by one upward glance. Various figures clambered among the rigging and spars along the armoured underside of the airframe, locked in combat. The Antarctic winds whipped and howled, drowning out all but the sharpest sword clashes and pistol reports.

A dishevelled lieutenant emerged from below decks and snapped a sharp salute. "Captain Hollioak! Cabins and crew quarters are secure, sir! We've rounded most of the blighters up."

"Good work, Brooke," said Edward, as other loyalists formed up behind him. "Get some men aloft to secure the aft engines and a fire crew for the port input vents. And a marksman to remove those rogues bothering my riggers, if you please!"

Trusting his men to attend their duties, Edward resumed his scan of the airframe. Ah! There, toward the nose battens – Dempsey and two ordinary seamen, clambering hand over hand up the forward spars. "Brooke, do you see?"

"Aye sir," growled Brooke. "Making for the forward lift sacs, I'll be bound."

"If they put them out of commission, we'll have no choice but to set down." Edward hauled himself up onto the nearest spar, which slanted upward from the foredeck to the underside of the airframe's nose. "With me, Brooke!"

"Aye, sir! For the *Bishop of Sarum*!" Two marines joined the cheer and the assault.

The climb was brutal work; Edward's body already ached with his exertions, the wind ripped at his grip, and he could not afford the delay of a safety tether.

Below, Erebus's crater was a wide mouth waiting to swallow any man who lost his hold. The steam rising from the gaping hole in its summit twisted and writhed as it met the winds sweeping up the mountain's slopes. Snow met the pluming updraft and coalesced into ice crystals that cut like razors.

Sprawled around the crater's rim was Winter's stronghold, a black stone edifice of jutting towers and squat bunkers built into the mountain. A work of heroic engineering and brutal functionality. Like its owner, thought Edward as he climbed. Elizabeth must be within its walls by now. The alternative did not bear consideration.

"Commander Dempsey's sent a greeting party, Captain."

Edward felt the thrum of approaching climbers in the ropes and timbers under his hands before he spied them, clambering concealed along the spar's underside.

"See you give them a warm reception, Mister Brooke. I'll deal with Dempsey."

With that, he steadied his nerves and scuttled off the main spar along a crossbeam. Eight terrifying balance-steps carried him across space to the side of the airframe. He grabbed a handful of rigging and pulled himself against its rigid surface. Uncomfortable off-key notes burred the airframe's normal baritone vibration; more than a few engines were damaged.

Gritting his teeth, ignoring the sounds of battle joined in his wake, he resumed his climb toward the nose.

#

The subjugation of Doctor Winter's automata proceeded very much to Elizabeth's satisfaction. They had encountered a number of his mechanical servitors, each individually distinct from the original design with some offensive customisation such as whirling blades and repeating carbines. In no case had their master elected to protect their crystallometric tabulators. Mnemo's fluorescent outbursts handily overwhelmed each in turns. Paralysed motor functions prevented further physical threats. In short order, the automaton's standing instructions erased themselves. New commands took their place.

Surrounded by an entourage of Mnemo and his oblivious knights-automatic, Elizabeth ascended toward the fortress's upper levels. Her quarry would be found close to the action, though not likely anywhere personal peril might arise.

"Hold steady in Winter's name!" Elizabeth flung herself to the floor immediately this time; the German accent marked the speaker as human.

"No! Get back!" A shot ricocheted off metal plating then stonework. Servo motors whined, metal arms snatched out. The hapless guard was pinned in a moment, his firearm crimped into scrap by crushing metal digits.

The guard wore the silver-grey livery of Doctor Winter; his bulbous breathing apparatus was distinctly German in manufacture. Removing this revealed a young man with a worker's brow and a monkish haircut.

"Shall I order him despatched, Madam? He could raise the alarm."

"Certainly not, Mnemo. We will avoid needless savagery, if you please."

"In that case, Madam, I believe we will find suitable prison facilities on the next level up." Mnemo's dominating exchange of light flashes had furnished it with a detailed plan of the fortress.

They marched the silent prisoner up to a wing dominated by a greenhouse the size of a manor house. It teemed with fruit trees and vegetable gardens in raised beds and was topped with a sparkling crystal roof.

As Mnemo subjugated the crew of automaton grounds-keepers and set them to guarding the prisoner, Elizabeth's attention was wrested by the remarkable sight above.

The *Bishop of Sarum* hovered some distance overhead, turning in abnormally tight circles and emitting great gouts of smoke from several locations.

"Mnemo, they are aflame!"

Mnemo's neck did not articulate; it leaned backward like a foreign dancer to take in the scene. "The fire is limited to two engines at present."

"What if it should spread to the interior of the airframe?"

"The gasbags will deflate with catastrophic results, Madam."

Elizabeth swore so vehemently even Winter's guardsman blanched. "Right," she said. "I'd better do something about that. Pray leave some guards for our prisoners and continue with the plan, Mnemo."

"As you say, Madam. What will you do?"

"You'll see. Kindly furnish me with directions to the pumping station."

#

Dempsey was waiting for him. The axe he had used to chop away the aluminium sheeting of the airframe's nose hung loose from one hand. He stood in the verge he'd cut open as the wind howled past him into the airframe's interior and drummed on the inflated balloons netted within.

"That's close enough, Hollioak," he called. The wind all but muted the words but their desperate fury rang true. "Don't force my hand."

"This is insane, Dempsey." Edward ceased his approach. He could traverse the small distance between them in a few movements. Dempsey could strike his head off in less time. "You'll kill yourself along with the rest of us."

"Order the *Bishop* to land and surrender yourself Captain."

"You know I will not."

"Put her down or burn in the sky!"

Edward's heart ached. "You stood beside me when the *Marquess* went down. You saw the same carnage I did. How can you entertain such madness?"

"It's your choice, Hollioak." Dempsey unhooked a glaring kerosene lantern from his harness and made as if to throw it inside the airframe, where dozens of bound balloons gave the *Bishop* her lift. "Do you think your men want to die for your honour?"

Edward ignored the images roaring up from his memories. Clinging to the netting to steady himself, he drew Farmer's pistol. "Better that than hand them to a monster."

Dempsey took cover through the rent in the airframe nose. As Edward clambered up to circle to the top of the rent, he caught a glimpse of flaring light. The lantern had surely burst. His suspicions were confirmed as the glare grew brighter.

Once above the missing panels, he could see clearly down into the cavity within the nose. Dempsey was below, nursing his bloody shoulder at the border of a spreading pool of flaming kerosene. The smoky flames licked up the side of one bulging lift balloon.

Edward grabbed a dangling rope and swung out from the frame. His momentum carried him down and through the rent at a frightening speed. His deck boots collided with Dempsey's face. Both men fell and scrambled to stand, weapons in hand.

"Well now, Captain," said Dempsey. "I didn't think you'd give me the satisfaction."

As the flames began to take hold, he dashed forward with his axe.

#

Bundles of hissing pipes affixed throughout by sturdy brackets to stone ceilings served a clear purpose: to regulate the temperature of the fortress into a habitable compromise between the Antarctic freeze and the volcanic melt. Elizabeth deduced the existence of a pumping facility. Mnemo confirmed it.

What she found was unexpected. A cathedral-scale room that was part bedchamber, part business den and a greater part lunatic trick of architectural engineering. It overlooked a rocky vent roiling with lava. What appeared to be a fine stratum of pearlescent glass separated the room from sputtering lumps of molten rock. The radiant heat suffusing the room restored some of the sensation sapped from her extremities. A great assemblage of riveted pipes sprang from a two-storey brass instrument panel like a giant's dishevelled pipe organ. At the feet of mirrored spiral staircases stood a four-poster bed of notably plush appointment.

"He sleeps by the boiler," Elizabeth muttered to herself as she made for the control room's upper storey. "Quite peculiar."

The dense window gave an unobstructed view not only of the roiling magma just below, but also the *Bishop of Sarum* above. Its distress was obvious. Smoke poured from numerous locations. One starboard engine was fully aflame, and the conflagration had spread to the support spars below and the canvas-wrapped skin of the airframe. Frayed netting and loose cables dangled and trailed smoke.

"Hold fast, Edward," she declared, refusing to give strength to a lurking fear for his safety. "Help is at hand."

She needed scarcely a moment to take in the control functions before her hands set to work of their own accord. She kept an eye on a bank of twitching pressure gauges as she diverted flows and bypassed safety valves. Needles bounced into red. Dials showed reservoirs bulging past their limits. She traced pipe layouts, searching for – ah, there it was!

"Out, out, brief candle!" she said, and threw a switch.

Beyond the crystal wall, a pressure hatch swung open and all at once released the fortress's water supply. A great jet of water burst forth and fanned out.

The relentless spray fell directly onto the molten magma of Mount Erebus's crater.

#

The butt of Dempsey's axe swept up into Edward's chin. His head snapped back. He stumbled.

A gas balloon arrested his fall. Pain flared on his back and neck; the bag was well alight.

He brought his sword up just in time to deflect Dempsey's swing. The axe bit deep into the gas bag beside Edward's face. With a huffing sound, the bag split and began to deflate.

Dempsey twisted his axe to dislodge it from the collapsing bag. Edward lurched forward. He butted his forehead against the scarlet patch at Dempsey's shoulder. The traitor gasped in pain.

Both men tumbled over, sprawling on the gantry that circled the airframe's interior. Edward slid and found himself hanging head and shoulders out over empty space.

The deck of the *Bishop of Sarum* bustled below as fire crews scurried about. Beyond, the icy white of Ross Island surrounded the glowing orange of the Erebus crater.

"Got you!" Dempsey kicked his ribs, hard. His hands closed around Edward's wrist and twisted the sword from his grip. His vision went white.

"I'll spare you the flames, Hollioak. It's the sky road home for you!" His dragged Edward forward by his coat collar.

Edward barely heard him. All at once he realised his vision was clear. The crater below billowed with steam.

His airman's instincts took over. He rolled against Dempsey's legs, throwing his balance off. As Dempsey shed his grip to steady himself, Edward rolled away from him. Dempsey lurched forward in pursuit but Edward's flight was fuelled by reflexive alarm.

"Get to cover, you fool!" Heedless of Dempsey's snarled response, Edward propelled himself desperately across the gantry and threw himself bodily into the bundled ruins of the deflated balloon sac. Its canvas skin enveloped him as he fell through it.

As it gave way, Edward caught a final glimpse of Dempsey's silhouette as a wall of steam blasted over him and billowed in to fill the airframe cavity.

Cocooned inside the bag, Edward crashed to the airframe floor. He lost consciousness to the sound of Dempsey's screams.

#

When Winter's guards came for her – the human guards, of course – Elizabeth offered no resistance. The *Bishop of Sarum* had vanished into the steam plume, but she had done all she could to extinguish its flame. The rest would be up to Edward and whatever men he still commanded.

German soldiers with grim countenances escorted her outside through a courtyard, open to the sky and slick with volcanic steam frozen into ashen ice.

The stone beneath her boots was warm. More: a grumbling vibration from somewhere below. It could have been Erebus maintaining its discontent over its drenching. Elizabeth thought not. She could read the mood and health of engines as easily as a blueprint.

A factory.

She had a good idea what Winter was building down there.

They passed through heavy steel doors that lifted with the turn of great cogs. Inside was a miniature railyard every bit as busy as Waterloo Station. Legions of automata loaded and unloaded cars, stacking barrels, massive crates and disassembled munitions. Some of the mechanical labour force duplicated Mnemo's design. Most appeared little more sophisticated than basic geometric shapes on wheels with skeletal limbs ending in pincers.

Elizabeth and her escorts wound a path through the bustle to a flat freight car. They rode on rails through a short tunnel that terminated at another cog-driven door.

It was a parlour; oak and walnut furnishing and fixtures, book cases that stretched to the ceilings and a tasteful selection of Turkish rugs and wall hangings. It incongruously resembled the same room in her own home, to the minute detail.

The soldiers steered Elizabeth into a comfortable armchair and withdrew to the tunnels. Across a small table bearing a silver tea service sat the man whose works had brought her here.

"Doctor Winter, is it?" she said with a heavy voice, as he stood to receive her with a deep nod of his balding head and an appraising look in his hazel eyes.

"I hardly think we need stand on ceremony, my dear," replied Doctor Winter, baring his teeth in a charmless rictus. "We have been married far too long for that. Do call me John."

#

Nobody aboard the *Bishop of Sarum* saw Dempsey fall, but every man-jack of them was attuned to the perils of airborne life. They heard his death-cries well enough; his followers broke at his defeat. Edward's ship was back in the hands of his loyalists before he was back on deck.

Brooke reported the damage; all fires extinguished and two engines out of service. Edward nodded and promoted the startled officer to Acting Commander. "May I bestow both my congratulations, sir, and your first commission? The *Bishop* is yours. I shall lead the landing party."

The *Bishop of Sarum* circled about and descended, its ruptured airframe rumbling against the volcano's turbid air.

The ground observers detected something amiss in the approach. Alarms rang to signal the mutineers' failure.

The *Bishop*'s gun crews directed their barrages against the artillery emplacements, the observation turrets, the walls themselves. Smoke filled what little clear air surrounded the battered stronghold.

The stronghold returned fire, too late.

Thunder cracked across the reinforced lower hull. The *Bishop* shrugged away the ill-disciplined barrage.

Edward leaned close to the marine at his side. "Hold the docking tower until we have secured the ship, Sergeant." An elongated spire loomed out of the murk, rushing at them at an unnerving rate. A team of sailors armed with nets were positioned around the *Bishop*'s exposed docking platform, with Edward and the marines occupying the centre. As the tower swept by, the closest netsman cast off. His heavy cable netting fell across barbed extrusions on the tower's surface, catching and tightening instantly.

Every man aboard the platform heaved forward. If not for the lines each had fixed to the platform and clipped to his wide leather belt, they would have pitched over the side.

Edward unclipped his safety line with unconscious ease and swept forward onto the jutting stone walkway of the docking tower. The marines swarmed past him, rifles raised, while sailors bounced about attaching mooring ropes to the tower.

Winter's guards waited for them at the other side. A troop of German Imperial riflemen, accompanied by two clanking automatons with dull staring red lenses. They were tall steel brutes with crude rivets, bubbled seams and merciless clawed hands. To Edward's eye they lacked Mnemo's elegant aesthetics but the overlapping plates and grooved, studded limbs reflected a shared design ancestry.

"Steady yourselves, gentlemen. Direct your fire to the crystal panels atop the head. We may confuse their senses." Edward aimed his pistol and let out a long breath.

"For England!" cried the *Bishop*'s men.

#

"You haven't touched your tea," said Doctor Winter. "Do you imagine that I have poisoned it?"

"Not at all," replied Elizabeth, studying him. His watchful eyes were stained dark with calculation. Frostbite and hard labour had roughened his once-slender fingertips. "Grief has quite altered my palate. I find I can no longer bear bitterness."

"That's quite a change." He sipped his tea. Elizabeth doubted his sentimentality.

"You speak too lightly of transformations. What am I to make of an Englishman skulking at the bottom of the world in a stone fortress of German manufacture, dispatching mechanical soldiers to murder sailors, steal cargoes and scuttle ships."

"You are well informed. How did you find me?"

"I assisted the Air Admiralty to analyse reports of unexplained attacks by air and sea. I pieced them together with clues from the various public pronouncements of Doctor Winter. With sufficient facts to hand, locating this fortress was a simple matter of mathematics."

"And you pressed the admirable Hollioak into your service. I gather you have formed a close alliance."

"Captain Hollioak has conducted himself honourably, little as it may mean to you."

"Well, I cannot claim to be unfairly judged, Lady Gracemere." Winter chuckled over his teacup. "My behaviour has been decidedly scurrilous."

He rose and detached an Admiralty sabre from a hook beneath a striking portrait: Lord and Lady Gracemere on the grounds of their estate in Sussex. Elizabeth recalled standing for the artist for a week of one warm summer, years ago when she had been in love.

"Scurrilous is hardly sufficient. You styled yourself as a pirate king from a comic opera. To what end, may I ask?"

"Why, to put an end to war, of course." Winter struck a duellist's pose, probing with the sabre in a short-thrust advance upon some unseen foe. His smirk brimmed with irony.

Elizabeth held very still. Encouraging his delusions posed severe risks, not least to herself, but she had always been able to coax him into endless pontification. It served her plans to do so now. "Whatever can you mean?"

"Europe is a political cesspit, my beloved. A squabbling nest of greed and spite and petty mistrust. Anarchists. Captains of industry. Communists. Peers of the realm. All as bad as each other. One imagined slight is enough to set them all at each other's throats. Good men like Edward Hollioak, are sent to die in meaningless wars or return, dead-eyed, embittered or missing the best pieces of themselves."

"Your solution is conquest? Or is that the purpose of your German masters?"

His eyes glittered. "Masters? Ridiculous. This alliance is a temporary necessity. Their funds built this facility. In return I made sport of their economic and political enemies. When my armies fall across Europe and lay it prostrate, I assure you they will fare no better. Anyone who resists, I will crush. They can hope only for absolute peace under my protection."

"An oppressor's peace."

"It is the only certain kind," declared Winter. His sword point dipped down to scratch across the floor, metal on stone. "Come now, Elizabeth. You've circled half the globe in pursuit of me, well aware of what you'd find. We both know you've no passion for country gardens and gossiping with vicars. You'll never go back there."

"You're very sure of yourself," said Elizabeth, marvelling at her own historical naivety. How had she had ever mistaken this insufferable arrogance for self-confident charm?

"Of course I am. England has nothing to offer you but Sunday sermons, stultifying boredom and the whispers of dullards."

"You have a counter-proposal, I presume?"

"You saw my factory. In another month it will be operating at full capacity. Fully resourced it can build fifty of my Winterguard every week. In six months I will have an army. One that has no need of wages, nor coats for warmth, nor respite to visit loved ones at the end of the day. They just work until they break. Completely loyal, completely tireless. They are remarkable machines, you know."

"As a matter of fact I do know that."

Winter ignored her. "I will unleash them on a dozen locations in Chile and Peru. They will build more factories and that dozen will make a hundred."

"I see. And then - prostrations, was it?"

"Don't try to deny you're already dreaming up improvements to my assembly lines and production queues. Think what you could do with the resources I can provide. Think what we could accomplish, between your practical talents and my ambition. You were my wife for eleven years, Elizabeth. Resume your place and I will lay the world at your feet. You can hardly expect a better proposal."

"I am not so certain of that," she said, suppressing a distracted smile with some effort. "But I am certain of my grief. I thought you were dead. I loved you and with you gone I fell into a well so deep I expected never to emerge. Only one thing preserved me from despair."

Winter's knuckles whitened around the sabre's hilt. "Do you mean Hollioak? I knew it. You may mark my words, Madam. Your new paramour will regret the day he laid eyes upon you, if there's still a breath in his-"

Shouts from beyond the door interrupted him. Elizabeth let out a long sigh of relief. "Mnemo."

\#

The enemy force advanced. Edward steeled himself to order an attack. The odds were discouraging.

Before the words left his lips, the automata grabbed the nearest soldiers and swung them about like clubs. Germans were swept away like pine needles in a storm. An unlucky few were thrown from the platform to plunge down the icy face of Erebus.

The rest fell back in disarray and beat a howling retreat down the docking platform stairs.

One of the automata trudged away in pursuit. The other discarded the limp corpse it carried and stomped toward Edward's astonished company. "Captain Hollioak," it said in John Gracemere's static-washed voice. "I have a message for you."

Edward signalled his men to port arms, unsure which emotion had taken the greater hold of him; relief at avoiding another battle or horror at the means of their deliverance.

"Recite it, if you please."

Under his breath, Edward whispered heartfelt thanks to Elizabeth.

#

The doors flew open. Winter's automata marched in, forming up in parade ranks to either side of Doctor Winter's supper table. The German guardsmen were nowhere to be seen.

"What is the meaning of this intrusion?" Winter's voice was mild but Elizabeth did not mistake the menace beneath it. She knew the tone well.

An automaton spoke. "The prisoner from the *Bishop of Sarum*, Doctor Winter. You requested they be brought before you."

"Hmm. Well, let's see them." The ranks parted slightly to make room for another pair of Winterguard, carrying a battered and weary Edward Hollioak between them. His coat was missing and his uniform was matted with blood. He locked eyes with Winter. His mouth fell open.

Elizabeth rose, speaking quickly before either man could state his mind. "Captain Hollioak, may I present Doctor Winter, with whom you are regrettably acquainted?"

The furious dismay twisting Edward's features tore at her heart. Could she have spared him this?

"John Gracemere," Edward managed at last. "I didn't want to believe it."

Winter beamed. "You should have trusted your instincts, Hollioak. May I congratulate you on how far your sense of righteousness has carried you? Half a world in pursuit of groundless vengeance, enduring mutiny and sabotage, hunting a killer who never was. I fear this moment must be a disappointment."

Edward rushed at Winter but an automaton arm snapped up and blocked his advance. The tip of Winter's sword twitched but did not rise. "I see your brash temper remains intact," he scoffed.

"Captain, you are injured. Are you badly hurt? Edward!"

Edward broke his gaze from Winter and turned to Elizabeth. His face was bruised and spattered with dark droplets, but his eyes were thoroughly clear. "I'll manage," he said at last. "I'm sorry. This must be dreadful for you."

Winter bristled. "It's you who should feel-"

"Oh, shush." Elizabeth placed her palm against Edward's cheek, her fingers resting on the pulse behind his jaw. "Edward, please, there's nothing for you to apologise for. I wish I had never dragged you into this."

"If you had left me behind I would be the sadder for it." He winced as he raised his injured arm to touch her hand.

"Well, well, it seems I have been succeeded in your affections, Elizabeth." Winter extended his sword's point to touch Edward's throat. "How fortunate are the dead not to know how our loved ones remember us."

Elizabeth felt the world go still. She had worked hard for this confrontation, certain that it meant death for one or the other of them. She had not counted on having something to lose. "Your reputation as John Gracemere has survived intact. The world remembers you fondly, even if I cannot."

Winter said, "At the risk of appearing ungrateful, I don't care a fig for my reputation. Guards, take Lady Elizabeth away. I would prefer not to spill blood in her – Guards?"

His Winterguards made no response.

"Infernal devices!" He banged the sword against the nearest faceplate.

A metal hand grabbed the blade. The automaton twisted it from Winter's grip. The metal made a screeching sound as it was crimped into a V-shape.

In the same moment the Winterguards released their hold on Edward. He stood, shaking but unbowed.

"You always overestimated your abilities," said Elizabeth. She tapped her tea cup against the dome-head of one of the Winterguards. "You destroyed the *Marquess* to cover the theft of the blueprints for my Mnemonic Man, didn't you? You thought you could turn my inventions into war machines? Well, I suppose you were right. But you never really understood what you stole."

Winter clutched at his arm, pale with pain. "What are you talking about?"

"My designs for sapient machines model the complexity of a human personality using repeated diffraction of light waves in a crystalline matrix. As such their instructions are susceptible to subversion through coded bursts of light. It was a design flaw that I was yet to eliminate. Fortunately."

Edward gasped. "You intended to be captured all along?"

"I'm sorry I didn't tell you." She pointed the teacup accusingly at Winter. "I could not risk someone in your crew conveying my plans to him. Better to appear as a distraught widow hell-bent on bloody revenge."

"No!" From beneath his chair Doctor Winter produced a short wand wrapped about with copper cable; the cable snaked across the floor to an enormous toggle switch on the wall.

He slapped the wand against the side of the closest Winterguard. Both flashed a startling violet. Elizabeth and Edward clapped their hands to their eyes at the overpowering glare.

The Winterguard fell to the floor, whining and sparking. "I commanded them once, I can do it again. I won't be stopped so easily." As they blinked furiously to regain their sight, Winter turned and made for the door to the factory.

"As a matter of fact, John Gracemere, you will."

Mnemo blocked the doorway, interposing itself between Winter and liberty. More automata closed in behind him, blocking Elizabeth's view.

"Remove yourself, wretch!" Winter raised the charged wand again and lunged with a duellist's athleticism.

One of the Winterguards behind him crunched a metal foot on the trailing cable. It too flared bright and blurted a metallic groan. Jets of oily steam blasted from popped rivets. It toppled and lay still, smoking no less vigorously than Erebus itself.

Winter shook the inert wand and coughed in disgust.

Mnemo said, "Sir, I must ask you to cease this indefensible conduct. I find it most unbecoming."

"*You* find it -? How dare you!" Shaking in a fury, Winter produced a pistol from beneath his lounging jacket. "No machine stands in judgment of me!"

"Really, now, John –"

Winter swept about to direct the pistol at Edward. He cocked the firing hammer. To Elizabeth, he declared "I will not bear this final insult, wife! Bid your cuckolding dog farewell."

Mnemo's digits wrapped about Winter's hand and closed, crushing the pistol's trigger guard around his fingers. Winter howled in agony. He tried to yank his fingers free but they were fixed fast in their mangled cage.

In a moment the pain overwhelmed him. The strength drained from his legs. He collapsed.

Mnemo said, "I'm sorry I had to do that, John."

The Winterguard beside Winter bent forward. It wrapped its arms about Doctor Winter as delicately as a father claiming his firstborn and bore him up. It said, "You left us no choice, I fear."

More Winterguards surrounded Winter, who moaned softly and clutched his ruined hand. The automata raised their arms and interlocked them. Winter was set upon the impromptu stretcher.

"Traitor," they chorused. "Murderer. Confess your crimes. Submit to judgment."

Winter looked from one impassive faceplate to another, as though recognising old acquaintances for the first time. "They – they all sound like me," he exclaimed, faint with wonder. Perhaps it was shock.

"You never understood what you stole from me," Elizabeth said sadly.

"Come now, sir," Mnemo said. "You are in need of medical attention. With your permission, Madam?"

"Take all the time you need, Mnemo. The New Zealand Aeronautic Corps will arrive within a few hours to take him into custody."

Edward shook his head. "You left nothing whatever to chance, did you?"

Elizabeth favoured him with a searching look. "I was as thorough as possible. One must always contend with unknown variables."

As the phalanx of Winterguard bore him from the room, Winter called, "Elizabeth! Hollioak! Forgive me. Let me return home with you."

"For my part, sir," said Edward, "you may rot for your deeds. But the decision is not mine."

He held out a hand. Banishing the last vestiges of doubt, Elizabeth rested her palm upon it.

"I have secured a guarantee that you will escape the gallows, sir," she said, suddenly free of the urge to look upon Doctor Winter. "As for the rest of it, John Gracemere is dead, and I find myself quite reconciled to widowhood."

Mnemo said, "Very good, Madam. Good day to you, Hollioak."

Edward nodded. "And to you, Mnemo."

Mnemo's Winterguard bore the protesting traitor away and Mnemo followed.

"Tell me something, I pray. When you were thinking of everything, did you plan for success?" Edward's grin was somewhere between amusement and admiration. Elizabeth found it quite infectious.

"In all honesty, I never expected to live this long. I thought he'd shoot me in the head. My plans did not depend on my survival, provided he stole Mnemo as well." Elizabeth couldn't account for the heat in her cheeks. "My good health leaves me at a loose end."

"You have considerable holdings in Sussex, as I recall."

"I shan't return to England."

"I rather thought that might be the case."

Edward inspected the hand laid across his as though fascinated. Elizabeth's breath caught. Finally he seemed to come to a decision. He raised her hand and brushed his lips across her knuckles. It was a touch as soft and warm as a summer breeze.

"Must you leave?" she breathed.

The corners of his eyes crinkled. "The *Bishop of Sarum* is extensively damaged," he observed. "The repairs will be a devilish business."

"As it happens, I have recently assumed control of a fully-equipped manufactory with a mechanical workforce of limitless capacity." Her heart beat in time with the hammers of industry echoing through the fortress. "Repairs are a trifling matter. Can I persuade you to consider some modifications?"

"Modifications?"

"Oh yes, I have a number of ideas. Detailed schematics too, if my cabin remains intact. Tell me, Edward, what do you think of the notion of extra-atmospheric travel?"

"Do you propose to sail to the moon?"

For one long, dreadful moment she thought his wide eyes were searching hers for signs of madness.

Then he leaned in and pressed his lips to hers. She sighed, wrapped her arms about him and pulled herself close.

"I think," he said, some while later, "I can't imagine anything beyond your reach, Lady Gracemere."

"I hope not, Captain Hollioak."

This short story collection would not exist except for this story.

'Mnemo's Memory' was originally published in an anthology called The Worlds of Science Fiction Fantasy and Horror Volume 2. When I originally submitted it, the editor liked the story but felt it could be stronger: the original climax sidelined one of the main characters, and another sacrificed themselves to save the day. The editor asked me for a new, more heroic ending. I liked the idea and obliged, rewriting most of the story in order to set up the new climax. What came out was the version you've just read – faster-paced, more adventurous and with bigger explosions than the original.

Unfortunately, that's not the version that appeared in the anthology. Imagine my horror, on opening my contributor's copy of The Worlds of... to discover the original draft of the story. The version with the downer ending and *cough* several typos.

Mistakes happen. I wasn't too upset about it. "Whatever happened, happened," as they used to say on Lost every other episode. Besides, at that stage of my career I considered any publication credit better than nothing.

But I was disappointed, because dammit, I was proud of the new and improved incarnation of the story. I wanted to show it off, and there was little hope of selling reprint rights to an 11,000 word story originally published in an low-visibility micro-press anthology.

My original plan was to put the story up for free on my website, once the publication rights reverted to me, along with a few other stories I couldn't do anything else with. Of course it would be the superior edit (or "The Unexpurgated Edition", as I like to think of it). It was the obvious solution, though it felt unsatisfying. The thought that Mnemo and company deserved better nagged at me

The idea to collect my published and various stray stories occurred to me early in 2017. Once the notion occurred, I couldn't shake it. Once I stumbled across the beautiful cover art in a designer's catalogue, I was sunk. I had to have it, and once I had cover art, I needed a book to put it on. So I taught myself how to publish a book.

(I don't really have projects. I have impulses which I retroactively convince myself were a great idea).

*'Mnemo's Memory' was originally published in **The Worlds of Science Fiction Fantasy and Horror Volume 2** (Altair Australian, January 2017), edited by Robert N. Stephenson.*

THANK YOU FOR READING

To stay up to date on my upcoming projects and get more free fiction, sign up for my newsletter, which comes out every six weeks or so:

https://davidversace.com/newsletter/

If you've enjoyed this collection, I would really appreciate it if you would give it a rating and a review on your platform of choice. Reviews and word of mouth recommendations are the life blood of modern publishing, and the only reliable way for most readers to find out about new authors.

You can also drop me a line at author@davidversace.com or find me on Facebook under **davidversaceauthor**.

Cheers!

ACKNOWLEDGEMENTS

I've been "going to be a writer" since I was about nine years old. For more than thirty years, through high school, university and a (long) public service career, I've always been about to make a start on my writing career. A few times, I even wrote some things.

The truth is, I would never have started taking storytelling seriously if not for a handful of people who inspired me to take concrete steps rather than think about the destination.

In particular, I want to thank Andrea K Höst, my high school friend and the author of The Touchstone Trilogy and The Trifold Age novels, who convinced me that self-publishing was a real thing; and Stuart Barrow, whose encouragement and good cheer kept me going through my first (wildly terrible but technically successful) attempt at National Novel Writing Month in 2003. Without their examples I would still be an aspiring writer.

I have the astonishing good fortune to have the Canberra Speculative Fiction Guild (CSFG) as my local writers' group. The generosity with which its members share information, build skills and encourage each other is second to none. Most of the stories in this collection walked the gauntlet of the CSFG short story critiquing group and emerged all the stronger for the ordeal. Thanks to all my CSFG comrades-in-arms, but especially the critters who have weighed in on my work over the past few years:

Mitchell Akhurst, Chris Andrews, Phill Berrie, Craig Cormick, David Dufty, Kristy Evangelista, Elizabeth Fitzgerald, Kim Gaal, Donna Hansen, Rik Lagarto, Chris Large, Oliver Lewis, Juliette Morley, Nicole Murphy, Tim Napper, Linh Nguyen, Ian McHugh, Shauna O'Meara, Simon Petrie, Gillian Polack, Rob Porteous, Mike Richards, Tim Roberts, Leife Shallcross, Cat Sheely, Val Toh, Kaaron Warren, and Angus Yeates, amongst many others. These people are my crew, and I owe them big time.

To all the editors who had a hand in making these stories better: Simon Petrie and Rob Porteous (again), Jennifer Brozek, Dan Rabarts and Lee Murray, Dirk Strasser, and Robert N Stephenson.

To the friends, too many to name, who indulged my terrible scribblings over the years, notably the ones who had to suffer through over-complicated roleplaying game plots during my frustrated novelist phase.

To my best friend in the world, Evan Dean, with whom I hope someday to collaborate on a work surpassing in greatness our song 'Karmic Moose'.

And finally to Fiona, Connor and Bella, without whom none of this would matter.

ABOUT THE AUTHOR

David Versace writes fantasy and science fiction in Canberra, Australia, where he is a member of the Canberra Speculative Fiction Guild. His work appears in the anthologies *Next* and *A Hand of Knaves* (CSFG Publishing) and *At the Edge* (Paper Road Press). His short story "The Lighthouse at Cape Defeat" was a Best Fantasy Short Story finalist in the 2016 Aurealis Awards, where he has since been a finalist on two more occasions.

He is a voracious consumer of speculative fiction, comics, wine, and television drama. He is a bass guitarist of unremarkable quality. He would love to show you pictures of his dog but those are exclusive to his newsletter and social media feeds. You should subscribe for the cute dog pictures, if nothing else.

His heartfelt dream is to stop drifting aimlessly through the Australia Public Service, where he has worked for over 20 years. Until the dream becomes reality, he remains focused on corporate governance, risk management and business continuity, the sexy invisible lifeblood of well-regulated government.

He lives with his wife Fiona and their two children. They tolerate his enthusiasms with patient good humour.

David is online at **www.davidversace.com** where you read over 100 flash fiction stories and get a free ecopy of this short story collection.

www.ingramcontent.com/pod-product-compliance
Lightning Source LLC
Chambersburg PA
CBHW071917130726
47909CB00014B/2053